T0248094

KITTENTITS

KITTENTITS

★ ★ ★ ★ ★ ★ ★

HOLLY WILSON

GILLIAN FLYNN BOOKS
A zando IMPRINT
NEW YORK

zando

Gillian Flynn Books is an imprint of Zando.
zandoprojects.com

First Edition: May 2024

Text design by Aubrey Khan, Neuwirth & Associates, Inc.
Cover design by Eli Mock

Library of Congress Control Number: 2023948982

978-1-63893-108-9 (Hardcover)
978-1-63893-109-6 (ebook)

10 9 8 7 6 5 4 3 2 1
Manufactured in the United States of America

FOR THEO

KITTENTITS

1

AFTER THE FIRE

ONE

It's Labor Day the day Jeanie comes. I'm ten years old and homeschooled by Evelyn. It's Calumet City, 1992, three months before the World's Fair in Chicago. In three months I'll necromance the dead live on WGN, but today I wear side-striped shorts, dorky and tight, the kind kids who go to school wear at gym time to play kickball.

The day Jeanie comes old fat Evelyn comes in, says No sass talk today, Molly, this is what you're wearing. Meaning these side-striped shorts, this puff-painted shirt she puff-painted. Spongy letters floating across my nips saying Welcome, Welcome. Yellow puff bees buzzing around the letters, my nips. All this for Jeanie, the first Resident Friend since the fire, our first Resident Correctional Friend ever at the fire-rotted, nun-haunted House of Friends: a Semi-Cooperative Living Community of Peace Faith(s) in Action.

I'd like to barf oceans on this shirt. I'd like to make some whiny kid put it on then barf on it while Jeanie watched and the whiny kid cried. That's how you welcome someone the day she gets out of prison. That's how you make her feel at home in her new halfway house where for eighteen months the state of Illinois requires her to live.

You remember what to do? Dad asks me.

He means for Outreach, but my brain's still on Jeanie, what she might look like, what prison features she might have: acid burns, stab scars, a filed tooth for biting. Stripes of pale finger skin where brass knuckles once lived. Maybe fingers missing or maybe even no fingers. Maybe just one finger to curl Come here.

To Dad real snotty I go Yeah, do you?

Because how could I forget? We do Outreach each Wednesday, rain sleet snow.

Dad was blind until ten months ago when he hit his head in the fire. Two people died, Evelyn's forty-year-old son Bruce and Sister Regina, but Dad got back his vision when a flaming ceiling beam banged his head. Boom just like that and he saw 20/20. I'm not allowed to use the oven now and for weeks after Evelyn wept like crazy. She stopped rolling her hair and let the garden go to shit. But Dad calls the fire the Miracle of Fiery Complexity. If you ask him today why inside he still wears sunglasses, why he still walks into walls and asks to touch people's faces when they speak, he'll look at you a long time super super quiet then whisper Miracle of Fiery Complexity super super quiet and then if also super quiet you say Says who? he'll say The Lord normal volume and that's all you get.

Outreach is we go door-to-door to the poor people in the apartment squares. If a kid answers the door I say Hey, is your mom home? Then when she comes Dad starts in about Organic Community Gardening and Evelyn passes her pamphlets around. Usually the mom will let you in for politeness, but careful, careful! Her feet are not feet, they are two life rafts sinking, two clumps of teeny kids barnacling up two cankly masts. Watch—always the bottom clinger gets foot-flicked to the yard where bits of flushed toilet paper seep through the ground swamp, turdy whitecaps on a fish-pissy lake. Then the kid says Shit Mama and the mom says Shut your mouth Rodney but what I'm saying is about organic community gardening they give no shit.

Still, I do my job, which is hand the poor kids their House of Friends organic community garden treat: a Dixie cup of chocolate pudding with smashed Oreos for dirt and gummy worms for worms. It's like the ground, I say. With worms, I go. Like a garden, I say, and Ooh, they go, ooh, stick in their fingers all at once.

On the walk back Dad says he thinks we got some joiners and Evelyn says Definitely those twin girls for sure.

But those girls weren't even twins, they were just sisters. One had bigger eyes and a mouth shaped like a shovel while the other had half-bit Chiclets for teeth. It's like Dad and Evelyn, jeez. Like Oh my god, Dad and Evelyn. Sometimes you guys are so fucking dumb.

Dad still holds Evelyn's arm when we go down the sidewalk the same way he did when he couldn't see. The effect's like he's a tard like Evelyn's Bruce was and since I've got no time for tards I walk ten feet ahead. I jingle dimes in my pocket like whistling a song. We should be having ice cream, we should be stopping for pizza, I'm thinking. We should be home waiting for Jeanie, but no one alive or dead gives two shits what I think.

No, instead after Outreach we do what we always do, we go to the graveyard to visit old dead Mom and new burnt-up Bruce. We don't bother with Sister Regina, her ghost's at home haunting us. Dad and Evelyn don't see her, but I sure as hell do.

Dad stands over Mom's grave sunglassed and gloomy, gives her the weekly update like he has the 468 weeks since she died. More rain, he says. Labor Day barbecue, he goes.

New Correctional Friend, I say, tugging his shirt to remind him.

New Resident Friend, he says, waving me away.

This is how it is when he's busy grieving, always correcting then shooing me away. Evelyn says he just doesn't want me seeing him crying, but I think he wants to hog my dead mom whatever effing way. Like last week when the drive-thru lady slipped a 2 Live Crew tape in my Happy Meal and I borrowed his headphones when we got home first thing. I was walking around listening to 2 Live Crew all super fucking happy and he saw me for once happy and yanked the headphones away. He was like Never ever touch these! These belonged to your mom! These are not yours! Get out, go away! Then he starts inspecting up close the orange foam ear things and I'm all God, what the hell? What are you even doing? and all super sad face he goes Little wads of Her earwax used to be stuck in these and I said That's so gross, that's effing disgusting and he said It's what I've got, now go away.

But it's not. It's not all he had. He still had the swim floaties Mom blew up when I was a baby that when we found them after the fire were still filled with her air. I asked if I could have them and Dad started crying and said No you cannot, now go upstairs.

So I climbed to the top step and sat there, hidden, watched him press a floatie valve against his cheek for five minutes while he closed his crying trash eyes and let out Her air.

Which wasn't fair. Her breath was mine too.

Evelyn must have agreed because that night after dinner when I went up to my room I found the second floatie on my bed, still inflated. The note next to it said What breathes lives or some similar gibbershit, so I sat on my bed and did the same thing Dad did, aimed my mom's breath all over my face, let it hit my eyes and mouth, let it fan my bangs out until the floatie went flat, no more air.

Dumbshit me, I'd thought maybe this would let my mom's ghost out. Her ghost's been hiding since the day she died, nine years. I thought whatever particles left of her from her puffs into the floatie might expand and take ghost shape and that she'd phantomize in front of me slowly. If it were me and not Dad who let out the air.

But nothing phantomized. Her ghost is nowhere.

But Evelyn, Evelyn's so nice she weeds strangers' graves. She waves me over now to Bruce's lumpy mound where she's sitting. Bruce as far as I know is not a ghost either, because I don't fucking know, I don't know what the rules are. Maybe the rule is moms and tards don't get them.

Time for my quizlet on Jesus as Peacemaker Evelyn says. After three wrongs she lets me go so I go. I run grave to grave bouncing my heels in the grass, wonder with each one is it a body still or is it bones yet, think what monster hell I might do here with Jeanie. You bring the experience, I'll bring the shovel, I'll say, then in my head practice all the ways to say it.

At home Dad heads to the basement where his puppets and puppet stage are, the sooty floor covered in pipe cleaners and spooled felt. Puppet shows are his job now, but when I was a baby it was adult novelty cakes: boob cakes, penis cakes, your pink frosted vag. Now his art is about the Miracle of Vision, how beautiful the world is, all its colors, he says. His puppets are Petey, a grumpy boy who doesn't appreciate God's creation, and Delores, a boring girl puppet with pretty brown curls. Her thing's to teach Petey to see beauty in everything in shows he puts on for Vacation Bible Schools and Christian school assemblies. If you ask me the best part it's not the puppet show, it's the finish, how Dad folds the whole thing up with the puppets still inside the stage then stuffs the stage into a giant suitcase he had some guy make special. All this and a dashboard full of sunglasses Dad hauls around in Evelyn's white Econoline Tuesdays.

Ten months ago when Dad hit his head in the fire was 425 weeks after the last thing he saw with his eyes. I was a drooly dumbshit baby back then, but ten months ago in the fire he hit his head on a beam that was on fire and the first thing he saw in the wild blaze was me, ten years old and my hair in flames. Later he said what a shock it was seeing me, how different I was, that in his head all this time he thought he'd been seeing the real me, a girl with pretty brown ringlets and skin clear like a fish, a girl with pink pretty lips and eyes not too close together. But this is not what I look like at all.

He said this while drinking Evelyn's black coffee so when he said it his face was pinched and bitter.

Well I guess you thought wrong, I said, like who cares, whatever, and he said he still couldn't believe the me in his head wasn't true.

And I was like Motherfucker, you'd better believe it. I was like Eff you, Dad, my hair is red!

Then he said he'd imagined everyone like warm floating animals when really we were more like walking cacti with thick arms and legs, heads covered in splinters and nasty juices inside. And this is why now we are Quakers, he'd said then went upstairs to his room where he likes to sit in the dark.

Before we were Quakers we were Christian Scientists. Before we were Christian Scientists I don't remember. Before my dead mom who I don't remember was dead, the three of us were nothing which I'm guessing was awesome.

One time before the fire when Dad was still blind he thought when I came down the basement stairs I was Randy the mute plumber. He said Randy, it's one of those days I'd kill for some blow.

That plus the three-ring binder of X-rated cake photos under his bed is how I know we haven't always been holy rollers.

TWO

Jeanie comes at noon via dirt bike. She vrooms up to House of Friends all crazy-haired, no helmet, parks off behind the carport like someone might steal her bike if they saw it. She's wearing cut-offs, a Candlemass T-shirt, and dirty ripped Keds, tattoos going up and down all ten fingers. At supper she won't eat the fake meat tacos Evelyn made special and flips her shit when Dad tells her we're semi-vegetarian here. Fuck this shit, she says and curses loud all the way up to her room where now she's scratching up the walls and crying in quick little rips.

I sit Indian-style outside her door, slide plastic-wrapped cheese under it she snatches up with her tattooed fingers, five striking snakes coiled from knuckle to tip, hissing tongues like hangnails, the most badass ones ever. Twice Sister Regina's clutchy ghost floats by but I don't look up or try to shoo her. I don't even smell the smoke that follows where she floats, right now Jeanie's the most supernatural thing to me ever.

I slide her three more slices and then run out. No more cheese, I say, my mouth at the gap between the door and the floor, say it loud because I don't want her to think there's more cheese I'm not giving her.

I squoosh myself down harder to peek in the room, see her dirty Keds faced away like she's looking out the window. Junk from her duffel bag's dumped all over, metal-tined hair picks and packs of cigarettes. Straight razors and toilet paper and tubes of thick-bubbled hair gel every color. It's all so awesome I decide to stay here until she comes out. I could wait here forever, I could live off my scabs, I'd count Sister Regina's ghost float by fifty times or a thousand to see her.

I sit here one hour, thoughts of Jeanie trampolining through my brain, griming my fingernails up with knee scab bits, when finally the door opens and Jeanie comes out grinning, her dark hair teased in greasy backward waves. She's got spit crust on her chin and spill stains on her shirt, it's like everything about her is giving you the finger.

Hey, little sister, I'll race you wherever, she says.

This is the first time she speaks to me.

This is the first thing she says to me ever.

I don't even have a sister, all I've got's Dad and Evelyn. Sometimes my dipshit friend Sweetie who lives across town. My mom's long dead and my inner-city pen pal won't write back to me, so mother-duh, of course, I'm like To the carport, fuckers! Let's go!

And just like that Jeanie takes off down the new stairs, flies out the kitchen door, and cuts through Evelyn's onions, the mud kicking up under her cool ratty Keds. Thank effing god I've got on my L.A. Gear Heatwaves. In L.A. Gear Heatwaves a girl can go anywhere.

She disappears behind Evelyn's van where it's super dark and spooky, where feral cats and raccoons live in the brambles wild. Where a torn-up bird nest is stuck high in one corner where the slow-rotting wood pile meets the roof's slanted tin. In the brambles under the nest the feral cats hang out with their mouths open, they're waiting for the baby birds to fall to feast on like Thanksgiving. Like the cats are the white people and the raccoons are the Indians. Or vice versa if you want, who the hell cares, all I know is sometimes I watch them.

Come here! she shouts. Come here! Jeanie goes. She's behind the wood pile waiting.

I run up to tag her but she's standing still, arms crossed fierce and bitchy in front of her. Long scratches run up and down her legs like cats were just clawing up her.

She grins again at me ear to ear, says Bet you haven't seen this before, then pulls up her stonewashed cut-offs on the inside side where it's clear she's got on no undies. She digs in her lady pelt until she gets hold of a string then says Tug on it, I fucking dare you.

And I do, I fucking tug on it, I do! Because goddamn it, I'm no pussy.

Suck on that, she says laughing while I toss the bloody wad into the onion bed then she runs back to the house doing this funny horse whinny. I'm on her heels so fast, my heart banging hard, her badass blood mixed with the scabs under my fingernails. I've never been so happy.

We skid into the community living room where here's Evelyn sitting. She's watching her show and piling paper plates by size, her face this sad potato. Like Oh gosh, oh crud, all these paper plates. All these piles, all these sizes.

Nine others lived here before the fire, seven not counting Evelyn's grown-up son Bruce and Sister Regina. Afterward all seven fled to Wichita and Tulsa, Indian-named places with tornadoes, not lakes. For ten months now it's been only me, Dad, and Evelyn. We go up and down the new stairs like nothing happened, but we still see the flames and we still smell the smoke. The basement's still sooty and part of the roof's still caved in. Plus Sister Regina's ghost is hard to ignore. Dad who does not see her tries humoring me, says just hug her and maybe she'll float away happy. I say that's easy for you to say when all day you're in the basement cutting face parts out of felt. And Evelyn.

If she's not dorking around the community garden she's in the community living room watching her stories. And if she's not watching her stories she's humming "This Little Light of Mine" while piling paper plates.

But now, since today, Jeanie.

What I'm trying to say is that before, things were quiet without any ruckus, but now here we two badasses stand before Evelyn high-fiving, me in my wicked Heatwaves and Jeanie in her Keds, Jeanie with her twitching finger snakes.

You can tell that's what Evelyn's thinking too until she sees the mud on the floor, the mud on our shoes, when then her face is all like What of my onions!

But before Evelyn can say anything, Jeanie busts out a burst of Oh Shits: Oh shit, oh fuck, oh shit, she says. I'm fucking late for Debra.

Debra is Jeanie's parole officer. Her P.O. is what she says.

I need your keys, Jeanie goes to Evelyn, meaning the keys to the Econoline Evelyn wears on a chain around her neck. I need them right now, she says, jabbing her hand out like Give Them.

Evelyn's a dipshit but she's no dummy, she sees Jeanie's finger tattoos wriggling and hands her the keys. And right here, how I admire Jeanie's gusto. This is how you get the keys to the van when you need the van keys.

And then I say, because this whole time I've been not speaking, I say: The rule is, Jeanie, no un-Quaker person living at House of Friends can all the sudden ask to drive Evelyn's van and get to.

Here Jeanie gives me the most awesome snarl ever and I flip her off with both hands and I can't stop giggling.

Now that Jeanie's here I have someone to explain things to and can get a break from the normal stuff I do, which is: all day picking knee scabs and watching Bozo on WGN. Hiding in closets from Sister Regina's ghost. Writing letters to my pen pal Demarcus who's only once written me back. His name is Demarcus and he lives in Bronzeville, Chicago. Evelyn signed me up for him first thing when Dad and me moved in.

When I'm really bored I might hang out with golden-haired Sweetie who is half Black but somehow golden-haired like her white lesbo mom Leslie. Sweetie only wants to do gymnastics when I don't know how. All she wants to talk about is her Black lesbo mom Helen's mouth cancer while doing dumb tumbles on her fancy mat.

Compared to Jeanie, Sweetie's just some kid. Jeanie's a woman who was probably never a kid. Watch her twirl the van keys all the way to the carport. Watch her trot like a gun dog toward a shot-down bird. She's still got mud splatters on her calves left over from her dirt bike, dark constellations I could pilot from if I ever got lost.

Halfway to the van she stops and turns all the sudden, drops down to me fast, gets up close in my face.

One day we'll fly my octopus kite, she says to me whispering. You can watch me ride dirt bikes with my old guards, Rusty and Jerome. We'll drink Dr Pepper and vodka and we'll be killers, she whispers, her tongue flicking super soft on my ear when she speaks. It's warm and wet and it doesn't bother me to feel it. Already this is the way between her and me.

Now she stands straight, looks at House of Friends behind me, then in her normal voice says One day we'll do a hot air balloon. We'll throw whatever we want over its edges, she tells me. Spiders and kittens, steak knives, she says.

Then boom just like that she's in the Econoline pulling out of the carport. She backs over the curb and peels away.

Now it's just me alone in the brambles and the quiet so I kick rocks against the wood pile to wake up the sleeping cats. I grab one to throw and see I've still got Jeanie's blood on my fingers. In the sky now all the clouds are pistol-shaped, fat.

THREE

THIS IS HOW I LEARNED WHAT'S WHAT. How to be a little girl in the world and be seen and heard. To live a life of glory that dignifies your suffering. It's all about talking, it's about how you speak. If you want to be badass and powerful you have to know the right way to speak. I wasn't born knowing and neither were you. I had to learn and it wasn't gradual, it was all the sudden. A lightning strike, a thunderclap, a slap on the cheek.

Some people learn younger, but I was seven when it happened. It was on my first-ever visit to JFK Memorial Library at Cal City CC. Dad was still blind then and big into books on tape, so by the arm I led him to the Audio Corner then left to thwack my hands down the rows of videotapes. It was a slow library day, it was graffiti clean-up day, Goth Roger the media librarian sanding off what people pocket-knife on wooden desks. I didn't know him yet plus he's fucking weird, teased black hair and shirts with frilly wrists, laces going up the sides of his pants. So I dived around the corner when I saw him, walked down the wall of windows and hid under the farthest desk. Dad would be done soon but I wasn't ready, I wanted to be alone longer with my thoughts in the library.

I remember the boring brown shoes of a woman walking by on my left. Otherwise it's an empty moment, a bucket of nothing, but it's always this moment I enter the memory at: turning to see the woman in her brown Rockports shuffling and then turning again to look straight up at the underside of the desk. Some words are carved, some are black Sharpie. They're terrible and beautiful and when I read them the lighting hits:

Jizzcock, Shitmagnet, Shitbag, Bitchtits.

Fucktard, Asstard, Dumbass Bitch.

Tamra is a whore. Tamra is a cunt. Tamra is a retard.
I heart Tamra's tits.

We are something, we are nothing. Time isn't real.
The self is a trick.

I read it ten times but after once a switch flips. Electricity floods my wires, something turns on. For the first time ever there's something to transmit. Numbers have color, I can taste vowels, it's like the words reached out and grabbed me and they said sit the fuck down.

I wish I could explain better. There's an inside and an outside to it, what it was and how it felt, but no way getting you to my side, I don't know how. But I will tell you this. The alphabetic power of that moment transformed me. It was a baptism, an inauguration, a legit holy gift. So when next Dad's calling, when he's cane-tapping my way, I crawl out from under the desk and I stand up and say:

Motherfucker, be quiet, this is a library! Asstard, you're always such an Asstard Bitch! for the first time I say.

Is such language mean? Does it cause suffering? Maybe, who knows, I don't fucking care. My tongue had been freed and my words were heartfelt. Heartfelt because that's where I fucking felt them, burning.

But Dad did not like it! His face was so red. Because I hate red faces I've toned things down since then, but in that moment, imagine it: this sad blind man mad at me, his sour sunglassed face super Elmo-fucking-red.

He waits for his face to stop pulsating then says Whoever guards his mouth preserves his life. He who opens wide his lips comes to ruin. Proverbs 13:3, he says.

Bullshit, I say and he says Molly, the vileness out of your mouth defiles you, and I say Nuh-uh, sir, you've got it wrong. I am my false self no more to no one. I reject compliance, I reject worry. I worry no more, now I am the worry.

You better set a guard over that mouth! he says. Better watch the door of those lips! But I'm like Fuck that shit, I'll talk how I want. These words are awesome and speaking them transforms me. I am a window and their divine light shines through me.

That's enough, Dad says and then like from a dream Goth Roger appears.

Dear patrons, good evening, the library is about to close, he says. Might you come back tomorrow and shout your Bible things then? he goes.

Dad reaches in his backpack and hands him a Free Spaghetti Dinner flier because House of Friends was Cal City king of free spaghetti dinners before the fire.

I've got Cemetery Club that night, but thank you, Goth Roger says.

Maybe some other time then, goes Dad.

I hope so, Goth Roger says. Some night when I'm free.

I say The first step toward freedom is to believe in freedom, and when I say it I feel the words under the desk pulsing alive in me.

I say I am a colossus, and these words exalt me. I say Fuckers, from now on you better listen to me!

FOUR

I'm embarrassed to let Jeanie see my room but also I want her to see my room so bad. I kick stuff around to make it more like things dumped from a duffle bag then go downstairs to pump Evelyn for info on Jeanie. For example how old she is and why she was in prison. Can she take me to the mall later and in December to the World's Fair.

Evelyn's in no mood for questions, she's got seed catalogs to go through, taco meat to reheat. All she tells me is Jeanie's twenty-four or maybe twenty-three and that I'm never ever to get in a car she's driving.

Finally hours later Jeanie gets home from Debra's. I look her up and down like I know all about you, but this is just a trick, I know almost nothing.

At supper in the kitchen we're eating taco burgers when I ask Jeanie if she wants to see my room but she says nothing, she must not hear me. She's staring down at her plate, scraping her fake meat off her bun like fake meat and buns are poison together.

Evelyn asks about Debra, is all up her butt about what day would be good for having Debra to supper. Again I say Hey Jeanie, do you want to see my room or what? But there's no time for her to answer as here Dad takes off his sunglasses and drops them all dramatic on the table.

Jeanie, did you ever as a child hunt for Easter eggs? he says then blinks his eyes crazy under the dim light of the kitchen. Like the kitchen light is the light of God, like it's already enough of heaven to blind him.

What kind of question is that? Jeanie says and here, oh fuck! Dad moves his hand like he's going to touch her.

Jeanie, we are the Easter eggs God has hidden, he says. Not made of plastic, but of flesh and blood. Like Easter eggs we come in a variety of colors, he goes, and also like Easter eggs something precious fills each one of us up. Jeanie, what do you think that is? he says. What is the thing filling each one of us up?

Dicks and chocolate, Jeanie says and Dad says It's not chocolate or jelly beans nor M&M candies, and here Jeanie just stares at him all black eyeliner eyes, all hard hungry eyes like a raccoon atop your garbage.

So Dad turns to me all like You, what's the answer.

Peace and God's love, I say and then, to Jeanie: Jeanie, hey Jeanie, wanna come see my room?

And finally she says Yeah okay, whatever, show me.

Alright! I say, first I have to get it ready!

I run full speed up the stairs, fake taco beef jiggling in my belly, then knock open my door and see the room like I'm Jeanie, how everything I own is all sad dumbass kid shit: my bed under the window, its low sunken mattress, the bedposts stickered up and down with glitter roller skate stickers. And fuck, the Hawaiian Garfield sleeping bag I use as my blanket, Garfield and Odie in coconut bras. It's like Molly, you fucktard, that was never once funny.

All over the floor is crap I'm too old for, old toys from the days of little me. All stuff Evelyn saved from the fire that I never wanted back: my stuffed bat Oro and my busted Lite-Brite. My Funshine Bear Care Bear missing its eyes and feet. The one cool thing is my *Back to the Future Part II* sunglasses where the frames are asymmetrical triangles, hot pink and black. Evelyn doesn't like them but I think they're awesome, plus they're from my one time shoplifting, September 23, 1989.

I put on the sunglasses and holler downstairs to Jeanie, Jeanie, you can come see my room now! I say.

I hide behind the door waiting to jump out to surprise her, but she doesn't come, I have to go back to the hallway and yell down the stairs again.

Jeanie, come on, I'm ready! I say.

After a few minutes I hear her coming, her saying What do you want? What is it? but the whole time I'm hiding behind the door laughing then throwing the door open loud and wide.

Surprise! I shout. It's fucking me! I say and all she says is This room better be mothereffing something.

Her arms are folded and there's a dish towel on her shoulder and she walks in the room like it's always been hers. Like

La tee da, all this shit's my shit. La tee da, what's this girl-tard doing here.

Close the door, she says then she opens my window, pulls a gold-tipped cigarette from the back pocket of her jeans. After the fire Evelyn posted No Smoking signs everywhere, but I don't mention it. I don't want her thinking I'm a tattletale the first day she's here.

She lies back on my bed and lights her cigarette, puffs giant smoke rings out my window, then heaves a big sigh. What I do is go around to my things and hold each up to show her and when it's something stupid I say I shoplifted it from K-Mart on a dare.

She says Yeah, that happens, then looks away. Thin sheets of smoke steam out her mouth without her even opening it, squares of flattened fog I try to breathe in.

There's a moment of nice empty quiet between us and part of me wants to start telling secrets now. Like sometimes at night I have a dream I'm a tour guide at Universal Studios in Florida. I wear a name tag and khaki shorts and stand at the front of a tram. In the dream the tram moves full speed while I tell the same awesome joke over and over but instead of a microphone my voice is amplified by a storming sky overhead.

But maybe it's too early for secrets. Instead like I just thought of it I say Jeanie, oh my god! Jeanie! Has anyone told you the real story of House of Friends? I bounce sideways back and forth in excitement, *Back to the Future* sunglasses perched on top of my head.

What do you mean, the real story? Jeanie asks me, leaning over to tap her cigarette on the windowsill. Then she's elbow-punching my pillow like she's been doing it for years, like on the floor my stuffed bat Oro's her own personal one, like this is where every night she has tram-guiding nightmares.

But the truth is that when I imagine all my stuff belonging to her it makes my stuff seem better. I like seeing her lying on top of Hawaiian Garfield on my bed.

Really? I say. You've never heard the story of House of Friends? Because I thought for sure they told it in prisons.

She shakes her head no slow like Go on, tell me, so I tell her the story exactly how these neighborhood kids told me the day three years ago Dad and I first moved in. It begins with me almost whispering going: Okay, so did you know this place wasn't always House of Friends? Did you know it used to be a Ronald McDonald House? I say.

Jeanie shakes her head no like Yeah, keep going.

And do you know what a Ronald McDonald house even is? I say then tell her it's a house for kids who have leukemia, a house where they live eating free fries and McNuggets until they're dead.

Here Jeanie's eyes widen into giant circles, like Jesus effing Christ, I never fucking knew.

Yeah, and this one particular leukemia boy slept in the room Evelyn gave *you*, I say. Little Boy O'Reilly. That was his name. One night he choked on his cheeseburger and died in your bed.

Jeanie flicks more ash on my windowsill and says No way, Kittentits, I don't believe you.

He did! I say. In your bed! I tell her. And that's not even all! I say.

I tell her how the neighborhood kids told me after he died how all the other Ronald McDonald kids started dying one right after the other. Like flies, the kids said. Like a curse, I say. In really gross ways too, I tell her. One girl's eyes popped out and one boy ate his own foot and another girl boiled from the inside out and her skin fell off her bones like cooked chicken.

I tell her after the final kid died the McDonald doctors fled and the house sat empty for seven years. Then gangs moved in from Chicago and started using it as their headquarters.

Tomorrow I'll take you around and show you where they knifed gang signs behind the doors, I say.

I can't wait, Jeanie says, leaning back on my pillow.

Yeah, I know, but remember the curse? I say. Because after a while the gang members started dying too. They started knifing people in their own gang for no reason at all then they'd carve sick satanic shit all over the dead bodies. Then the gang leaders freaked and abandoned the place exactly how the Ronald McDonald doctors did, I go. That's when the Quakers bought it, this was like six years ago. That's when Evelyn came with her retarded son Bruce and a bunch of other Quakers. Plus Sister Regina. She wasn't a Quaker, she was a nun, I go. Then three years ago me and Dad. Then there was the fire and now there's you. Now you're here too, Jeanie.

I ask has she seen Sister Regina's ghost yet to see if she sees ghosts or not, but her eyes are closing, I think she's asleep.

So have any of you died? Any dead Quakers? she says, her eyes shut but I guess not sleeping. She listens this way while I tell her about the fire.

Bruce the tard died, I say then tell her about him, the exact spot where he was on God's spectrum of retardedness, about his clubby fingers and the deafness I know he faked. How his hair stayed wet for hours after it stopped raining and how Saturday mornings he liked watching me stuff Big League Chew in my cheeks. I tell her about Sister Regina and how her ghost floats through walls to hug you, how if you don't let her hug you her ghost smoke will turn cloudy and then she'll scream this long piercing scream.

What about you? Jeanie says, her eyes open now. She sits up and taps my chest with the butt of her smoke. Are you gonna die? she says. Do you have a disease?

No, I don't know, I say, because I'm not sure whether dying's the badass or the dumb thing. Maybe, I say.

Sometimes I cough, I go. Sometimes when I run my heart bangs hard.

Here Jeanie's cigarette droops out of her mouth like she forgot to suck it.

I'm not staying here long enough to die anyway, I say. When I'm sixteen I'm moving out. By out I mean Florida, and if not Florida, just Chicago. If not trams and sunshine then I want cold winds blasting between skyscrapers to swallow. But I guess Dad and Evelyn will probably die here, I say.

Jeanie throws her cigarette out the window. You don't have to worry about me, Crotchtard, she says. No way I'm dying here, I've got a plan.

Yeah, me neither, I say, I've got one too.

Well you wouldn't know it to look at you, she says.

Later that night when I'm going to sleep I hear Jeanie through the vents tell Evelyn she'll be gone a few hours, that she's got some sick friend she has to see. This sends Evelyn all atwitter, all like Oh no and Oh my and Here take the Econoline. She can't tell like I can that Jeanie's lying, that probably Jeanie's dirt bike brothers are throwing her a party, what any good brother does for a sister just out of prison.

I've got coconut bra Garfield unzipped on top of me, I'm sucking the zipper to think new ideas. Like how cool to cut a hole in the back of my closet into the room that was Sister Regina's and then to cut a hole in the back of her closet into the room Evelyn gave Jeanie. Each night I could crawl to her and she'd be there waiting, she'd be watching the clock all ready to go, she'd be like Shit, Molly, I thought you weren't coming!

Then she'd loan me whatever clothes I wanted, shirts with no shoulders and jeans with ripped knees. She'd back-comb my hair, spray it into a wild rebel puff, then we'd sneak downstairs with me riding her shoulders. And should Sister Regina see us and float near to hug me? Jeanie who sees her will hiss like a ghost killer. She'll hiss then yell Hi-yah! then knife her away.

We'll ride her dirt bike out of town to the highway, to the roadhouses where the best-lit ditches are. Then Jeanie will do ditch wheelies while a crowd cheers around us, fat beery guys with beards rubber-banded and their eyeshadowed girlfriends who for tops wear bras.

Then here's the big part where Jeanie gets off her bike and

points at me. Little sister, this one's all yours, she says. She cones her hands around her mouth like a cheerleader yelling, What my little sister can do on a bike will make you guys scream! she says.

She winks at me and I get on her bike and rev it, start down the ditch doing at first easy tricks. But each time when it's time for the hard one I get stuck and can't imagine it. I don't have enough in my brain about dirt bike tricks. So I stop and rewind the whole thing all the way back to the beginning, me cutting through my closet to sneak into hers. I pause on the part where she helps me get ready, this time have her talk more about makeup and shit. About my eyes and my cheekbones, how they go with which earrings. Hoops or feathers, skulls or bones.

Even this gets old, so next I pretend to be dead in a coffin, pull Garfield up high and cross my arms over my chest. Eyes closed tight, I imagine away all my layers, all my hair and skin and muscle gone until I'm nothing but bones. I go up and down my skeleton to check all my pieces, back and forth, back and forth, because I know all the bones. I do it over and over until the checking turns to feeling each bone until my jawbone, which is where I start thinking: Molly, there's no skin on you, no lips or nose or eyes on you, there's only a girl skull left on you, a jaw, a hinge, a hole. No noise comes out where it used to come out noisy and now you are completely quiet, bone air bone.

The next thing I know is I'm waking up and it's morning, fresh boogers and golden crusties plugging up my nose and eyes. Night spit pools in my cheek pockets like the dankiest fish water, blossoming the canker sores that birthed there in the night.

But ha! Look at me! I'm still lying like a dead girl, my hands still chest-folded and my jaw hung ajar. I yawn and fart and then boom, I'm a fucking miracle! My old skin grows back, I sprout my old hair. My eyes pop back into their sockets fat and juicy, ready to see what the day shoves their way.

Which, the first thing is: Sister Regina. Somehow she got in my room during the night. Her ghost arms are outstretched and her ghost fingers see-through and wriggling. Her nun sneakers pedal toward me like she thinks she can still run.

There's nothing to do but ball up tight and close my eyes and wait for it, wait for it. There's nowhere to hide, here she comes.

FIVE

Demarcus Nassius
5135 South Federal Street, Apt K16
Chicago, IL
September 14, 1992

Dear Demarcus,

Sometimes from here I can see a big thunder cloud over your part of the city and I think G-damn, hope you've got an umbrella, Demarcus. But probably you don't, you are so poor. No way you sleep in a race car bed. Probably you sleep on lawn chair cushions on the floor. For the record I do not sleep in a race car bed either, but a boy down my street does. His house is only somewhat nicer than my house, Demarcus, so at the end of the day we are the same (me and that boy). Hey, I notice you have not written me back in forever. But look at me writing you when I am so busy, jeez!

So guess what, I have a new babysitter, her name is Jeanie. I had a babysitter one time before but her name was Kimberly. Kimberly was not okay, she dropped acid at her cousin's house before coming over and for the rest of what should have been our time together she stayed in the bathroom hallucinating she was the letter *R*. But Jeanie is awesome! She's got plans and tattoos, is just out of prison.

We're best friends now and guess what, I'm pretty sure twelve years ago when she was twelve she killed her stepdad with an ice pick and guess what, that is only two years older than me. She hasn't told me the story yet or said anything about it but Demarcus, sometimes with best friends you just know.

Demarcus, maybe you don't write back because maybe you're afraid to. Like maybe you're afraid of itty-bitty white girl me. Not surprising! I've gotten that vibe from others before. Maybe it's because I'm homeschooled or maybe it's because my mom's dead but sometimes I wonder if it's because in my last letter I told you about my mom's graveyard, remember? How I put a handful of her private grave dirt in my pocket to microscope for later to see were there weird things in her dirt (by the way there were)? Well maybe you want to ask me questions about having a dead mom or what was in the dirt, which you should, Demarcus, one day your mom will have her dirt (you think you're special but guess what you're not) but you don't because you think it will freak me out/make me cry and that's why you never effing ever write.

But Demarcus, I don't cry and by that I mean never. Eff you, Demarcus, get ready to be wrong because watch me right now tell the whole story of Her, my mom. Watch me shed not one effing tear once ever.

My dead mom: Sharon Louise Sibly, RIP. 1961–1983. Who she was, how she died, who killed her, et cetera.

Who she was: the best fucking drama major Cal City Community College has ever seen. She would have made it to Hollywood and she would have been Geena Davis when she got there which means last year she would have been Thelma in *Thelma & Louise*. Instead she met my dad and got knocked up with baby me and had to give up her dreams and drop out of Cal City CC. She quit school and got a job making gold stars at the sticker factory but then she died so now guess who never gets any.

But wait, how did she die and who killed her? you're asking.

Bob Reynolds, a random drunk driver guy. I bet when you think drunk driver you think just some dumbass drunk guy killing someone the regular way, like my mom Sharon Sibly on her way to Sonic for chili dogs then Bam! Bad Guy Bob Reynolds crosses into her lane doing ninety.

But Demarcus, guess what, my mom was drunk too!

Drunk Bob and drunk Mom were going down the road opposite directions, drunk Mom at the wheel of Dad's Pinto and Dad (dipshit now, dipshit then) asleep on the passenger side, neither one of them buckled in. Then here comes drunk Bob Reynolds swerving in his big white 1-800-Plumber van but Demarcus, let's be honest, some might say it was really my mom who drunk-drivered him because later on the coroner said in fact that she was the drunker one.

Does it even matter, Demarcus?

I vote No it does not. Everyone is on their own path, Demarcus. That's what Jeanie the Stepdad Killer says. The main thing is Bob smashed into Mom (or Mom smashed into Bob, ha ha!) and next they both died alone in the road there together. The crash woke up Dad and blinded him permanently and when I think about his part I always imagine it this way: his one bloody hand feeling around for my mom, him grabbing at his trashed car crash eyes with the bloody other.

But ohmygod where was I, was I okay? I know you're thinking.

Well thanks for your concern but who the fuck knows? I was just some dumb fucking baby then. Probably I was in my highchair eating my baby slop while my caretaker Kimberly was on the bathroom floor writhing. Probably I was drooling at the dust specks afloat in the air. The point is wherever I was, Demarcus, it was my path to be there. Just like it was my mom's path to work in a sticker factory for eleven fucking months before dying.

Anyway, Sharon L. Sibly had a psychological death wish says Bob's wife Elsie in the long letter she writes us each year Christmastime. When we write her back—we always write the people who write to us back, Demarcus—we say Merry Christmas Elsie, sorry about Bob, but you ma'am are a coffee pot calling us black as everyone knows that that car crash was mutual.

Demarcus, I said when *we* write her back, but that was a lie. Dad does the writing while I stand nearby and shout things.

Well holy shit, Demarcus, look.

Any drips on this paper? Any tearstains? Voila, I told you so, et cetera, et cetera. Write me back and remember: your mom's going to die too. Maybe in a long time, maybe soon, but definitely someday. Definitely not never.

Yours sincerely,
Molly

SIX

TWO WEEKS AFTER JEANIE COMES the rest of her stuff shows up from self-storage. I'm not there when it happens, I'm at JFK Memorial Library, the community college library at Cal City CC. I'm watching a VHS tape of Anton Chekhov's *The Seagull*, the 1980 Cal City Presents! version which stars my dead mom as Nina, this Russian girl who wants to be an actress so fucking bad, wants it more than anything.

It's the only recording there is of my mom, and unless one day her ghost finally finds me, the only her that speaks and moves I'll ever see. Sometimes when I feel gloomy I come here to watch it. Goth Roger the media librarian still works here and he's the one who checks it out to me, unlocks the door to the tiny study room where inside on this rolling cart's the library TV. The VCR's built in and there's a chair and study table, a READ poster with Bo Jackson reading *The Old Man and the Sea*.

I wait for Goth Roger to turn it all on, for his black lace fingers to push all the buttons the right way. Before handing the remote over Goth Roger usually has something weird to say. Like today he puts his arms out all Jesusy and Zen, says Young initiates in the ancient mystery cults suffered year-long trials of preparation. I consecrate this sacred space to Molly's preparation either until the gods oppose it or until twelve fifteen.

It's like Goth Roger, jeez. He's so fucking weird but also he's super nice to me. One time when I came out of the study room for some reason he thought I'd been crying. Dearest, your little black heart is wounded, he'd said. Then he offered to make a copy of the tape for me.

I said that no, I didn't want one, but that I had a question. What the fuck is *The Seagull* even about? I said.

How the heaviest things happen offstage, he told me. In your own life, Molly, who has witnessed your suffering? What suffering of others do you actually see?

It's all a bunch of fancy Russians talking in a fancy vacation house, I'd said, but today I just nod because I don't know anything about mystery cults, plus I can't do my thing until he goes away.

When he goes away I push play and lip-sync my mom's lines as she says them. Body-sync her, too, every head tilt, every hand wave. Most times I do this I start feeling better by intermission or if I don't it's the opposite, I feel way sadder but in a good way. Like watching my dead mom alive playing this olden-time alive dead lady sucks out the harsh gloom stuck through the gray steak parts of my body. One time, fuck, I even started crying. It was like: Molly, witness harshness. Like, You need to witness this, Molly.

Today I get to the part where the Arkadina lady claps for Nina, is all Bravo, Bravo, you are such a good actress! Then Nina says It's the dream of my life which will never come true.

When my mom delivers that line she looks off wistful in the distance which means I look off wistful in the distance too.

WHEN I GET HOME Jeanie's stuff is on the porch plus also the mail's waiting. There's a brochure for the World's Fair plus the electricity bill. I grab the World's Fair brochure and run up and down the hall yelling, screaming World of Worlds, Future of Futures! while Jeanie back and forth hauls her shit up the stairs. Mostly it's trash bags filled with dirt bike gear and jean jackets, though she's also got a plastic sack of broken starfish and doom metal tees: Jucifer and Goatlord, Witchfinder General.

The last thing she brings in is a padlocked black box. She stops me bouncing in the hall to say Never fucking touch this.

She takes the black box upstairs and I'm waving the brochure right behind her, It's the world's biggest international exhibition ever, I say.

She says what I said but with her voice high and whiny and I say Ha ha, you're so effing funny!

She says I smell like finger gag, like her cellmate Cumguzzler Tina from Cincinnati, like a hot mug of whipped turds on a windy day.

Inside her room I try showing her the brochure again, point to the foldout map of a hundred carnival rides and fourteen shooting galleries. Already my tongue's tasting corn dogs and funnel cakes. Already the map's spiral avenues are tattooed circuits on my brain.

That's Autotopia and here's Arcadium, I tell her. Here's Night Town and here's the World and the Sea. The World and the Sea's in the very center, it's where each different country has a pavilion. All the pavilions circle the Sea of International Waters, a giant man-made lake where a glass elevator goes down. At the bottom you're let out inside the all-glass Submarine Palace where on New Year's Eve they're doing a live Corpse Reanimation there! They're going to bring a dead silent movie star back to life, she's called the Sleeping Silent Princess and she's got her own Submarine Palace ride called Return of the Sleeping Silent Princess: The Crystal Cathedral Experience where at the end you get to see her lying in state in her crystal coffin like it's the day she died!

I point all these things out, but Jeanie doesn't look where I'm pointing. I say I bet the Submarine Palace has to be pressurized, but Jeanie's busy in her closet putting her black box away.

A glass palace underwater. I can't stop thinking about it. I can already see it, humming blue and green. Trilly flutes and harps playing for badass me and Jeanie, us walking and laughing under silver underwater archways. Our skin aquarium-lit while golden light shines out our eyes like lasers—

Did you hear what I said? Jeanie shouts, one of her fingersnakes aimed at me hissward. She says Touch this box and you're fucking dead.

I nod like Yeah okay I heard you, but she grabs my arm hard and says Crotchface, what did I say?

I don't say anything because I've already forgotten. I'm two places at once, my thoughts churning pictures only: Ferris wheels and roller coasters and golden thrones and Jeanie. Midway prizes, roller coasters, corpse reanimations, her.

SEVEN

I ASK JEANIE WHAT PRISON'S LIKE. We're behind the apartment squares fliering the wipers of poor people's beaters with Evelyn's Organic Community Garden fliers.

She says nothing, just puffs her smoke then flicks it, heel-grinds it three times with the heel of each Ked.

By now I've seen her do this a dozen times but everything else about her stays a mystery. I spy on her all day long, tiptoe everywhere she goes behind her. She's awrying my thoughts to where I can't sleep, she's a dirty-Kedded question mark haunting my dreams nightly. I've tried everything, I've asked her every question, I've been like, Jeanie, tell me about you when you were a girl like me, what things you did, etc. I've said Hey Jeanie, where's your family at? Where are you from even?

I was never a girl like you, she said. She said it while unwadding her black T-shirts from the dryer while I practiced walking through Sister Regina without shutting my eyes. I have no relations, she said, I was born in jail, got dropped off there by the Stork of Corrections. Then she changed the subject, called me Jagoff, twisted my nips. Pretended to mistake my underwear for Evelyn's.

I don't know, though, something's different today. She keeps pausing lots to look at the sky overhead, stretched so soft and smooth and rat-bellied. It's like something's going to happen soon, a strike of lightning, a boom of thunder. Like something very doom metal is coming.

C'mon, Jeanie, what was prison like? I say and finally she says Be more specific. So I ask how the food was and she says Not bad so I ask what her favorite was and she says Fish Fillet with baby carrots.

I ask about Cumguzzler Tina from Cincinnati, whether they watched each other change plus how they went to the bathroom.

You're a nosy little fucker, she says but then says No. She says they had a system.

I ask her to show me later and then I go for it, ask her the most important question.

Jeanie, are you a killer? I say. Is that why you went to prison?

Eyes back to the rat shadows, Jeanie looks off in the distance.

I tried, Kittentits, but someone fucked it up, she says. She says Never trust someone else to kill your sister.

Five stories up a guy shouts down at us. We better not fucking touch his fucking Taurus, he says. I give him the finger like Up your big butt then grab Jeanie by the arm and beg her Tell me all of it.

Not much to say except I wanted her dead, she says. So I took Mama's final disability check and paid my boyfriend Mangus to kill her. Sadly before it could happen the police discovered the plan. That's all, not much of a story really.

You wanted your sister dead, I say and Jeanie says I still fucking do.

How old were you when you tried to kill her, I say and she says Seventeen. And it was murder-for-hire, not murder, she says.

So you entered prison a juvenile and left a woman, I say.

Absofuckinglutlely, she goes. And you better believe it's a good thing too. Now that I'm out I'll need to watch out for her.

You think she's going to come after you? You think she'll come looking for you at House of Friends? I say, inwardly fucking freaking.

I don't know, Jeanie goes. She's a crazy fucking bitch, so yeah, I think so. Probably. Wait, have you seen my scar? she asks me.

What scar? I say, which is bullshit, I've seen it. Last week she got back from the dirt bike track after riding all day long in the rain. She came in the kitchen to ring out her soaked shirt bottom, pulled it up to squeeze over the sink. For a moment her shirt lifted and that's when I saw it: a wide strip of pink gristle from the tip of her armpit ending somewhere below the waist of her jeans.

I say No, I never saw it, thinking maybe she'll show me, maybe I'll get to touch it, but she says Liar, I saw you look at it the other day.

She snaps a wiper off the closest Taurus, scratches Satan Girls Rule on the hood with the tip of its blade.

Me and my sister were born Siamese twins, she says, then two-handed like it's a sword presents me the wiper.

Jeanie's not even my real name, she goes, and just like that she's grinning this jack-o'-lantern grin, her face lit up all wet-toothed, wolfy.

We dump the rest of Evelyn's fliers and go to Kwik Trip to buy Slim Jims, Smarties, and Pepsi. My brain revs the whole time at the thought of Siamese Jeanies, but when I ask about it Jeanie says Shut the fuck up, enough with your fucking questions today.

Then she says Kittentits, show me where the junkyard is and this one time I'll let you come with me.

The junkyard's down a long gravel road that starts behind First Pentecost and Family Dollar. First you have to cut through their parking lots to walk under their trees to climb the haunted drainage ditch where the day we moved into House of Friends two Puerto Rican girls got cult murdered. After three pawn shops and a Taco Bell you'll see the junkyard's twelve giant metal heaps, junkbirds above each one flying.

You can't just walk in, there's a fence and a scare dog. Normally you climb the fence and for the dog you throw Slim Jims, but tonight the dog's gone and Jeanie says Fuck fences. She says it while digging through her cool jean purse then boom she pulls out this monster pair of pliers.

Cool pliers, I say while she begins snipping metal.

These are not pliers, these are bolt cutters, she says. This is a high-leverage heavy-duty twelve-inch. Never fucking touch her, her name is Donna, she says.

We crawl through the hole then she says Now thank Donna, so I look at Donna, her black steel jaws, and say Thank you so much for helping us, Donna.

Jeanie smiles, gives Donna a kiss.

EIGHT

Jeanie picks the farthest row of smashed cars to walk down, checks each car's trunk to see if it lifts. I follow behind her eating Slim Jims and chugging Pepsi, angle the bottle against the moonlight to swirl my backwash spit. At first Jeanie's quiet, checking car trunks and counting barrels, pointing inside the scrap piles where she wants me to crawl. Then when she's yawning I find an awesome rear-ended Corsica and call the driver's seat so I can fake-steer the wheel. Inside the car I say Let me know when you want a Slim Jim and she says Fuck Slim Jims, I want Smarties, give them here. She crunches half a roll in the back of her mouth loud then without me having to ask starts telling me things.

She says: Imagine for nine years being affixed to a crazy person. Imagine being sewn ass to pit, your butt cheeks aligned at an exact forty-five degree angle.

So I close my eyes and imagine it: a mirror-me sewn into me, our brains and bodies telepathic. Her blood my blood, identical muscles strung on identical bones.

Does she look exactly like you? I ask her. Are you guys telepathic?

But Jeanie's not listening, she's staring out the cracked windshield all misty, her eyes super foggy like the fog in a crystal ball.

She says: Until I was nine all my dreams had knives in them. Butcher knives and Bowie knives. Surgical cleavers too.

I go to steal some Smarties but she slaps my hand away.

I dream of knives sometimes too, I say.

What you really want is a motored saw, she says, motioning me to give her some of my Pepsi, her finger-snakes jabbing for the bottle in the dark.

When you're Siamese how do you even walk down stairs? I ask her and she's all What stairs? I'm from Kansas. Everything's flat.

She drinks the rest of my Pepsi then lights another smoke. She says We didn't live in a house like you do. I was raised in a wax museum. My mama was proprietress and sculptor.

Oh my god I love wax museums so bad, I say. And I know it's true even though I've never been to one.

Wild West Waxworks and Autograph Gallery of Dodge City, she says and I nod my head hard, like Oh yeah, that one.

Jeanie slow-puffs her smoke, leans on the headrest like to nap, so I fold my hands behind my head and sit back like she does.

Start at the beginning, I say. With you being born.

But Jeanie says she wasn't born, that her and her Siamese sister had to be knifed out of their mother. After they cut us out Mama hollered for hours, she says. She thought we were monsters sent by Satan.

That crazy bitch, I say and then Jeanie turns fast and slaps me.

Little Shit better watch her mouth about my mother, she says. Mombie and I were monsters and we're monsters still.

My cheek's burning hot, her slap stings like a mother, but all I can think now is Mombie, Mombie. The sound of who Jeanie's real sister is.

She leans back in her seat again and says how awesome was her mother, how when they were still babies she kicked out their drunk dad, how she skimped and saved to pay for their leg straightening and every six months new back braces. She raised ticket prices at the wax museum, sculpted new cowboys and Indians. She put highway signs every four miles between El Dorado and Lamar. She gave deep discounts for buses and even when the Chamber of Commerce cunts said she couldn't, she got Wild West Waxworks certified Triple A three stars.

Everything she did was for us, Jeanie says. Our one and only defender. Like say Mombie and me when we're little, she says (she faces me now, she passes me her smoke), say we're at Dairy Queen eating ice cream sandwiches and some Dodge City dickwick calls us freakwads and makes fun of our hair.

You tell that dickwad to shut the fuck up, I say, then suck in on the cigarette and choke on it.

Dumbshit, we're little girls, we're five years old, she says. We don't know how to say shut the fuck up yet. No, the dickwick calls us freakwads and Mama stands up and lights into this Bible speech she'd already got memorized.

She smiles like remembering and grabs back her smoke.

My mama in the middle of Dodge City's DQ, she says. My mama's head bobbing up and down making this bumblefuck back the fuck up! First she made him apologize to both of us together and then to each one of us individually. Then just guess, guess what she does?

She kicked him in the balls super hard, I say. She lit his sorry ass on fire!

Fuck no, she says. Fuck no, Kittentits. That was not my mama's style. She told him God is love and gave him a two-for-one to the Waxworks.

That's so effing Christlike, I say. Then what?

The guy left and she got on her knees and stuck her face right between our two freaked-out ones, she says. Then she starts hugging us and touching us and whispering Bible shit in our ears.

What Bible shit? I whisper, because I know all of it.

Jeanie sucks a long time on her cigarette before saying it: If the world hates you, know that it hated me first. If you belonged to the world, it would—

Love you as its own, I say. But you do not belong to the world, I have chosen you out of the world and that is why the world hates you, I say. John fucking 15, verse 18–19, I say.

Jeanie nods and stubs her smoke on the dash of the Corsica, and for a while we both stare out the windshield at the pretty junkyard moon.

Mama got too worked up about religious shit, Jeanie says finally and I say that the Dairy Queen guy was just jealous because of how cool it is to be Siamese.

Lighting up again Jeanie says One time Mama found these two white poodle skirts. She cut and restitched them then had us pose in the Autograph Gallery. She said we looked like a postcard and wanted to take our picture to tape to the cash register, but right when the flash fired I jackknifed behind Mombie hard.

That's so badass, can I have a cigarette? I ask her.

All my life I ruined Mama's pictures, Jeanie goes.

Yeah, but all your life Mombie ruined your life, I tell her and she says Little Sister, you do not even know.

Then she unloads on me everything about Mombie, how in front of their mom what a Miss Priss Showbiz she was, always checking and double-checking for any secret talent: opera, ventriloquism, tap dancing, twirling guns. When Mombie wanted to be a mime she painted her face white and stopped talking. When she wanted to try the harp she stole from the register and bought a used Paraguayan one.

Here I think of my mom and Nina from *The Seagull*, the both of them. How their dream was acting and it never came true. I wonder what one day my failed dream might be. I wonder what it's like being in a talent show, your mom in the audience clapping for you.

Kittentits, snap out of it, are you even listening? Jeanie asks me.

Fuck yeah, I say. Paraguayan harp, I go.

Yeah, so the harp and the miming and all the other bullshit, but then each night in our room she'd go crazy, Jeanie says.

She'd pull and squirm and pinch me up and down. She'd tell me as soon as I was asleep she was going to light my face on fire and then, when we were eight, we snuck into *Blue Sunshine*, she says.

Kittentits, have you ever seen *Blue Sunshine*? she asks me and I say Yeah, I'm pretty sure. I think so, maybe.

You'd remember, she goes. It's about killer hippies who go crazy after they lose all their hair.

Oh yeah that one, I definitely saw it, I tell her and she says Yeah I thought it sucked but it struck something deep in Mombie. We're home after the movie and I'm on the toilet pissing—

Here I interrupt to say But wait, where was Mombie?

Where she always was, Dumbshit, on my left, Jeanie says. She's squatting in the space between the toilet and the tub and she's all *Blue Sunshine* this and *Blue Sunshine* that, going on and on about how we'd be these famous actresses. And I'm like Bitch, fuck no, I don't want to be an actress and then she says if not for me being the one thing that made her special she'd bite my eyes out of their sockets then rip my beating heart out of my chest. She says our mama's a fool with failed artistic vision and that all we need to get started was to run away somewhere to rehearse. She's like Let's go now, let's start right now. Any circus, any town. I mean it, she says.

And what did you say, I ask her. Because I'm dying to know.

I wiped my ass and we stood and I said Fuck you to hell, Mombie. No way am I joining a circus, I said. I am not a sick circus freak like you.

Fuck no! I say.

So Mombie snaps hard to the right and she starts spitting and clawing, then she's got something pink in her hand. It's like Holy fuck, it's Mama's razor! Jeanie says.

She was trying to slice out your eyes? I say, and Jeanie says No, she was trying to shave our heads. She thought she could make us look like the *Blue Sunshine* killers using only Mama's Lady Bic, she says.

And that's when you tried to kill her, I say.

No, that's years later, shut the fuck up, Jeanie says. No, I punched her in the face and yelled for Mama and I told Mama right then that I wanted the knife.

Here Jeanie stretches and takes a long drag, puffs three perfect smoke rings like three perfect nooses.

And that was the last time she said no to the knife, Jeanie says.

My mom's dead, I say.

So is mine, Jeanie goes.

Then there's a long long silence and I say Jeanie, hey Jeanie. Jeanie, I say, tell me again which side Mombie was on? Then I think Molly, you dumbshit, it's the side she's got the scar on, the left side, her sister side, the space you're sitting in now.

But Jeanie doesn't hear me, her eyes are closed and now she's snoring, so I lift her cigarette careful from where it's held between two tattooed snakes.

I suck on it hard and try to hold my coughs in, try to fill the space like Mombie would, in my mind grow to Jeanie's height. I look at her sleeping face and imagine wanting to set it on fire. Imagine her waking up wanting me burned off like a tick.

NINE

Demarcus Nassius
5135 South Federal Street, Apt K16
Chicago, IL
September 25, 1992

Dear Demarcus,

Hi how are you, excited about the Fair? Probably there's a day they let poor kids in free. If there is you should go and maybe I'll see you there because probably I'll already be there that day with Jeanie. Otherwise, Demarcus, save your money. Give it to your mom to buy food, shelter, clothes. Myself, I haven't decided yet but I'll go probably. If only to shut Jeanie up about it, God!

Speaking of Jeanie, we've got plans for later, but first let me tell you what Jeanie's life path is. Jeanie is a Destroyer, a kind of Mankind Terrifyer, a person born to shock and frighten and then disappear. Yesterday when she hung out with me she told me the story of her Spiritual Discovery/Recovery, how she was twelve when it happened, two years older than me. She was in the middle of killing her cousin Terry's parakeets she was supposed to be pet-sitting, their squawking hurt her head, plus they had bird cancer bad so she was putting them out of their misery. One by one she's throwing them against the wall of the trailer when her mom gets home from the gas station with groceries and sees: blood and feathers all over their trailer, half-dead birds twitching on the floor of their trailer, Jeanie's arm froze in mid-throw in the air of the trailer, her used-to-be blue eyes now bright flashing green.

So her mom takes in this spectacle, this horrible vision, Jeanie's bird revenge so animal-wild, so awesome and unholy. And for the very first time she's horrified to look at Jeanie. But also for the first time she's seeing her daughter demonstrate excellence in what she's doing.

This was the moment my awakening began, Jeanie told me. She said Free will's bullshit, that acorns grow into acorn trees. That if from birth you're planted with AutoZone Assistant Manager energy then that is the exact thing the Universe demands you be. When I said No way, that I didn't believe it, she knocked me down and called me Thundercunt and said Thundercunt, this is why the Universe sent me.

She says we're best friends now and that I don't need to worry. She'll keep me fixed on my path. She'll help me and terrify me. And Demarcus, when she knocked me down I didn't cry, I'm no pussy. I looked up at my new best friend and I said Thank you, Jeanie.

But Demarcus, I have two secrets I haven't told her yet. I'll tell you right now but you must promise to write me back. The first secret is: Dad and Evelyn think how the fire started is some big mystery, but the truth is it was Bruce. Bruce left his hot plate on in the attic. The hot plate from his toy metallurgy lab. Metallurgy's the behavior of compounds and metal alloys, Demarcus.

So the night of the fire everyone's sleeping, me and Bruce and Liesel, Evelyn and Dad and the others. I'm asleep and I know nothing, I don't know Jeanie yet. I don't know what it's like to have a dad not blind yet. So I'm asleep in bed dreaming whatever unknowing dumb shit when suddenly Evelyn's screaming and smoke's curling under my door. When I open the door there are dog-sized flames barking down the walls. Ripping straight lines across the ceiling. I'm last down the stairs before they collapse, Demarcus, and by that time everyone's outside except Bruce and Sister Regina.

Demarcus, imagine it! House of Friends a giant fiery flame, falling roof shingles impaling all the squirrels and stray cats, people from the apartment squares hotfooting over to watch it. The fire chief said it was a miracle I survived, Demarcus, which brings me to secret number two.

One time a long time ago I choked on a nacho, and one time before that I swallowed a packet of silica gel. Neither of those times did I die, Demarcus.

What I'm trying to say is: I am fucking eternal.

You could shoot me six times and I wouldn't bleed. The bullet holes right away would grow back together. I'd have six little scabs the shape of an 8, and what is an 8? It's infinity, Demarcus. An 8 is a snake swallowing itself, Demarcus, and therefore the exact right thing to symbolize me.

Before the fire and the nacho I wanted to always touch things, Demarcus, like if I saw Evelyn's pink scalp through her hair I'd want to stick my fingers in. If I'd known Jeanie then I would have touched her shirts in the armpits constantly, plus also certain metal things made me want to lick them: pay phone cords, leg braces, notebook spirals, tire rims.

But now that I've defeated death twice I don't need to taste or touch things. Because why the fuck bother? I'm not going anywhere. I'm not going to die, let these things come touch me! I'll let them lick my hand, who gives a shit, whatever. I'll let them think: This is what it tastes like to not be an animal, plant, or thing. This is the taste of something perpetual and always. God maybe. Like if beams of God-light had been shot through space-time into me.

Oh shit, Demarcus! I have to go because remember Jeanie? The sun's down now and she's waiting on me. She says sleeping boys in race car beds are top-shelf to terrify, that this time with my help she can lift the bed.

Write soon,
Molly

TEN

Three o'clock.

I'm on the porch waiting for the mail to get here because it's my job every day to bring it in. It's always junk: Evelyn's seed catalogs and Dad's puppet part orders, chicken strip dinner discounts from Dairy Queen. Once a year at Christmastime Bob Reynold's wife's letter, but nothing ever ever for Jeanie or me. Yesterday I threw it all straight in the trash but today I sit here all optimistic.

No one's home now except me and Sister Regina. Dad's doing a puppet show at the apartment square nursing home and Evelyn's at K-Mart buying birdseed and rakes. On the white board for Jeanie it says Debra 3:30, but she left hours ago in dirt biking gloves and knee-padded jeans.

The sun hangs orange in the sky above me, streaks the air like dirty cheeseballs dragged down your face. It's so windy I don't fuck with the lighter I find in Jeanie's jean jacket, though tempting. But also if she didn't want me wearing her jacket and fucking with her lighter she should have put it away. I've been staring at the sky waiting for the mail guy for hours. Now I'm on the porch floor gargling my spit and scissoring my legs.

Finally he's close, his boots clomping the porch of the squatter house next door, so I run into the yard, arms out to meet him, but as usual he ignores me like I'm some dumbfuck kid.

I wait until he's done delivering then give his backside the finger, grab down the mail and flip first through the bills: the gas bill, the water bill, a sale on Michelin tires. A brochure from Camp Quiet Pond I wad in my hand. A preapproved Visa for our old Resident Friend Liesel, and then, at the very back: a small white envelope addressed in red pen.

At first I blur my eyes to keep from seeing who it goes to, let hope hatch like a hundred hungry ducklings in my gut. But it's not for me. It's not Demarcus. It's a letter for Jeanie. Thick loopy handwriting, no return address.

The stamp's a World's Fair stamp of a double-decker Ferris wheel. I look at it up close while I run my thumbs along the envelope back. And I swear I'm not thinking Rip this letter open right now, Molly, but watch my fingers, see what they do?

Inside is a single sheet of paper. Hello Sister is all it says in ink that smells like licorice perfume.

IN THE KITCHEN I FOLD Jeanie's letter and put it in my pocket. I hold on to Liesel's Visa offer because I like to keep credit card things. On the table's my lunch cereal plus the Cacti of Arizona word find Evelyn told me to finish, but Mombie's letter's got me so excited that instead I fill out Liesel's Visa card thing. Filling out forms like these is what I do sometimes, the tiny squares to write in so calming and blank.

Resident Friend Liesel was here before the fire, a snub-nosed woman who wore braided wicker hats. Her thing was teaching poor kids sign language and Navajo, so of course all the poor kids hated her bad. They made fun of her pants, how she called them slacks, how she patched the knees with smiley face patches she made them call Aponi and Karack.

I try to hear her weird warbly voice in my head again but only catch the shadow of it, her saying Give me those about some scissors I'd snatched. The words toss and ping lighter than they had in real life, not five accordions falling down a slide anymore, but one accordion rolling soft and gently.

Does any of this matter?

Hell no, it does not. Liesel's long gone, her lungs a little blacker. She's off teaching Navajo to the poor kids of somewhere else and I'm here in the kitchen filling out this form for her Visa. It's not hard, I either know the answers already or can guess them no problem. Occupation: Missionary. Salary: $95,000. Cashback Bonus: hell yeah, motherfuckers, most definitely. Payment Protection Plan: of course not, that crap's for dummies.

These are not lies, they're soft soothing truths I like writing.

The one thing I don't know is Liesel's SSN, so I pretend I'm a detective and that Liesel calls me crying. She tells me she lost her social security card in the fire, begs and begs pretty please to help her find it. At first I say No, I've got this circus murder I'm solving, but she begs and pleads until I say Okay whatever, I guess.

The first place to search is Jeanie's room. I look in her drawers and under her bed, in her floor-piled pants and jackets. I look in her closet and see the black box there and almost go to touch it.

On my way downstairs Sister Regina's ghost floats behind me. Stay back! I tell her. I'm on business! I say. Then something psychic in me says look in the basement, look under the fire tarp where Dad's rolled bolts of felt sit furred in ash, where Evelyn's grandma's ear trumpets lay velvet-cradled in swan-hollowed cases, where shoeboxes of melty Polaroids are rubber-banded and stacked, all those old pictures stuck together forever: young versions of the Resident Friends eating apples under giant dorky oak trees, them last-placing in sack races on Christian college grass.

Under the fire tarp I find the things Liesel didn't take with her, an old Vermont driver's license, a framed master's degree. A five-by-seven photo of a starving kid named Erasto, a Save the Children boy Liesel used to shame the mouthiest poor kids and sometimes me.

There's a box of paperwork with her Resident Application. Under Describe your Faith Mission she wrote To empower marginalized youth through language (Navajo and Sign). Under Domestic Skills she wrote Most/Many and under Emergency Contact(s), None. Her social security number's written above all her medical conditions and allergies, and I'm sorry to see it because it means the mystery just died. All the other stuff under the fire tarp can't be clues now: Bruce's metal leg braces and size 14 basketball shoes, his charred Fisher-Price play kitchen with the oven door missing.

Bruce who started the fire last November. Bruce who turned on a hot plate in the attic and left it on.

Upstairs I finish the credit card application. I lick the prepaid envelope and raise the mailbox flag. I sit on the sidewalk to wait for Jeanie, the sunsetting sky now pink and floaty, clouds like white people's asses hanging low over a toilet-rimmed land. It's like the under-fluff of flamingo butts sinking down on top of me, butt feathers tickling my cheeks like cotton candy while next door teens light tiny fires in cans. The combo effect of all this together is everything seems right in the world for once, a humming feeling like nothing's been bad or wrong ever. Like how right now Jeanie's dirt biking under the same sky I'm under, she's killing bitchin' hills under these same tufts of pink. It's like us being under the same smoky blanket, our knees touching while we dream the same dream together, our eyelids twitching in synchronized beats.

ELEVEN

It's Jeanie home first, not Dad or Evelyn. Here comes her dirt bike spitting and growling, weaving between the lowriders cruising our street. When she gets to House of Friends she jumps the curb onto the sidewalk, shouts Stay back from my wheels! and calls me Crotchtard Dickface.

To almost everything Jeanie says now my answer is laughing. Crotchtard, ha! I go, because she's so fucking funny. It's like Jeanie, god, you're too fucking funny.

She turns into the driveway and unsaddles under the carport, thwangs her bangs to one side, and undoes her fingerless gloves. Through the porthole of her shirt's pit rip I spot the top of where her scar is. It's all I can do not to reach out and poke my finger in.

Instead I roll up and down on the balls of my feet, try to thwang my bangs too the same time as I'm talking. Guess what guess what guess what, I say. Guess who you got a letter from!

Huh? Jeanie says. She's flicking sweaty grit out the back of her hair and not looking.

Your sister Mombie, I say, pulling the letter from my pocket. I tell her I opened it on accident thinking it was for me from Demarcus, but how really it was from her Siamese twin sister she'd tried to kill.

Oh fuck. Oh fuck no, she goes. Here her eyes are like bolts of lightning flashing.

She grabs the letter quick, fists it in her pocket.

Don't ever jack my shit, she says then grabs me by the collar of her jean jacket I'm wearing, jams both her thumbs into the bony divots of my neck.

Don't you ever wear my things and don't you ever say sister. Don't even say her name, she says, whispering spitty and slow.

Before I can say sorry she shoves me to the sidewalk. She spits on one of my Heatwaves, on the tongue right where the orange flames are stitched.

I'm a little dumbshit who doesn't know what to do when spit on. What I do is heave deep at the back of my throat to hawk my own giant loogie onto the flames of my other shoe, my own best snot water matched to hers.

Even so pissed, she can't deny the symmetry. Even tight-knuckled and snarling she can't say my right shoe's not the perfect mirror of my left.

TWELVE

SUMMER'S OVER FOR GOOD, here comes the fall, trees hot-dog red and potato-chip yellow. This is how the end of September goes, each day crashy, windier the next. One day I ask Evelyn where does wind come from and she says the ocean and I say Eff no, I say it blows from the vast flatness of the Great American Plains.

Those are Kansas winds, I say. Smell the wheat and hay. Smell the dried hides of buffalo crotches, sniff the prairie stink of the lonesome range! Then I do the Navajo war dance Liesel was never supposed to teach me, whoop my voice in and out on the palm of my hand.

Jeanie barely speaks to me. Shoving past me up the stairs she might go Move it. Walking by me on the couch maybe Hey, Little Shit. She goes to the dirt bike track most days anyway, and if not to the track then to see Debra, her P.O. And if not to see Debra, to apply for jobs involving cash registers, not coming home until evening then acting funny all night: pulling shut the curtains and closing the blinds, staring at the telephone like it's about to start a fight.

I say not one thing about her Siamese twin sister Mombie and after a few days she begins to relax. Like today for five minutes she staples Evelyn's newsletters with me and even hangs around to watch that pioneer bitch *Dr. Quinn*. She has an appointment with Debra but there's a Fair commercial, the new one, robots in wigs handing out balloons.

World of worlds! I say, copying the announcer. Future of futures! I go, making pit farts with my hand.

When the TV's on why can't you shut the fuck up, she asks me and I say Jeanie, oh my god, you should get a job at the Fair!

She puts on her jean jacket and says the way I'm smiling's creepy. If she doesn't get away from my face she'll die, she says.

Whatever, I go, and turn the TV up to thirty. Dad and Evelyn are outside rototilling, so of course as soon as Jeanie leaves someone calls.

It's the perv again, some weird dude breathing heavy. He's called every day for the last two weeks. God, you're such a perv, I say when I pick up and hear the breathing. Why won't you talk, why are you such a perv-dog? I say.

Like always, the guy says nothing, breathes some more then coughs and hangs up.

My own prank calls are way better, to prove it it's what I do the whole afternoon. When they ask who's calling I normally say Your mother, but today after a few warm-ups I say Who the fuck are you?

Usually they hang up after that but sometimes they bitch at me, like today the old man who calls me Miss Britches, guys like him are the best. He's all like Little Miss Britches! Like Goddamnit Miss Britches! I fought the goddamn war and witnessed the deaths of a thousand good men! Goddamnit, he goes, goddamnit, Miss Britches! I'm goddamned retired now and I want peace in my home!

Then he asks who my mother is so he can see what modern whores look like and here I say Queen Elizabeth! then I say No, Pocahontas! Or sometimes I say Madonna, it all depends on my mood. Usually this is where I start laughing to show how awesome I burned him, but today I don't really feel like it so I just say Okay, nice to talk to you too.

The moment I put the phone back on its cradle it starts ringing right away. Which scares me so much I jump and stub my toe. Fucking oldster star 69'd, I say.

But he didn't, it's not him, it's the pervy breather a second time.

Oh good, it's you, I say, pulling myself up on the kitchen counter, this time listening close to the perv's heavy sighs. The static they ride on's the same noise as a beach shell's and his breaths pull in and out how ocean waves do. I rub my toe and wonder what it's like to dunk a stubbed toe in the ocean, then notice how the perv breathes kind of high for a dude.

THIRTEEN

It's the first of October when Jeanie's finished being pissed at me. It's the first day I'm allowed to talk about Halloween. Today we're having Jeanie's Resident Friend b-day party since her real birthday was in prison before she came. In prison on your birthday all they give you is new shoelaces she told me, so Evelyn bought her a blue sweater and Dad decorated a cake.

Debra her P.O. comes and we have cake and ice cream at Dad's worktable in the basement. Fine by me since Sister Regina's ghost is scared of the basement stairs. She hovers at the top all wispy and moany, but I don't care, I'm all agog that Debra's this short Black lady with Toni Braxton hair.

I can tell Jeanie's embarrassed by the fuss everyone's making. She fakes these big thank-yous, sits on her hands. When she god-blesses Evelyn for taking her in I see right through it. The next time I catch her eye I wink.

Thank you all so much, she's going. Thanks for coming, Debra. This is all just so awesome, I've never felt so at home, she says.

Evelyn tears up and Dad says People can change. Like him, for example, his eyes and his vision. Like even old Evelyn who lost her only child Bruce.

Debra nods, says she's seen it with girls who prioritize. Debra says girls who prioritize would eat their own fingers before breaking parole.

Here Jeanie semi-loses it, makes a face like she's laughing, covers her mouth with her finger snakes while her shoulders hiccup and shake. Is she laughing or is she crying? I don't know but I don't want to piss her off so I look away.

Next Dad gets out his puppets to sing Happy Birthday first as Petey then Delores, then the third time around we all join in. After that we have cake and ice cream in little bowls Debra keeps complimenting then Dad goes up to his bedroom because his eyes need to rest. Evelyn's got some apartment square kids coming so she gets up to go wait for them. I stay right where I am at the card table with Jeanie and Debra as there's nothing but science quizlets for homeschool waiting for me after this.

I rip the tags off Jeanie's new sweater while Debra asks her questions then writes the answers in a little book. Are you looking for a job and are you doing street drugs? she asks her. Are you getting along with the other residents here?

Jeanie's like a robot, she's like Yes No Yes, folds her arms super huffy when next Debra hands her a plastic cup with a lid.

You've got to be fucking kidding, it's my birthday! Jeanie tells her, but Debra's not having it. No it's not, she says.

Jeanie pulls her jeans down, the whole time staring fierce at Debra. She stabs her with her eyes and fills the cup to the brim.

AFTER DEBRA LEAVES Jeanie says Let's go have a real party, so we go to the gas station and it's the most fun I've ever had. She gives me six smokes to puff on and we play six games of *Street Fighter*, she lets me be Ibuki while she plays nasty T. Hawk instead. I kill her two times and she kills me nine and then she goes off to the bathroom leaving her cool jean purse beside me. I look inside and there's Donna the bolt cutters and three blueberry muffins, plus two of Evelyn's nice gardening knives. I dig under the knives and muffins past gritty uncapped ChapSticks, graze my fingertips over the greasy quarters she'd said she ran out of but lied.

She gets back from peeing and hops on top of the gas station's glass counter, swirls the beef jerky in the beef jerky tubs, and taps the lotto case with her feet. Rita the assistant manager says to get off her counter and Jeanie's like Fuck you, Rita, and Rita's like Bitch, eat me.

Hey Rita, you hiring? Jeanie says, getting off the counter. I've got register experience. Lots and lots, she says.

Yeah right, Rita says and then Jeanie tells her all about her mom's wax museum. She worked in the gift shop since she was five, she says.

I went to a wax museum once, Rita tells us. It was Christmas and they had Kenny Rogers and Dolly Parton opening presents under a tree.

How big were her titties? I interrupt to ask her and Rita's like Watermelons! then shows us with her hands.

She's bullshitting you, Jeanie says when Rita can't hear us because now she's on a ladder three aisles over pouring ice in the pop machine. Waxworks are done to scale, Jeanie tells me. No one's tits are that big, she says.

Yeah, no duh, I know that, I whisper. I saw Evelyn's knives in your purse, I say.

I thought I said stay out of my shit, she hisses, ripping a Slim Jim open with only her teeth. Those knives aren't even decent, she says.

What does she even know about knives I ask her and she says she knows fucking plenty. Hey Crotchface, she says, what do you want to do now? What about screwing with the old bitch's garden?

I smile so big, I'm like Let's go, let's go! then next we're walking home through the irrigation ditches behind Family Dollar. I splash my Heatwaves wild in the mud-puddled cement and ask Jeanie personal questions willy-nilly. I ask mostly about her mom's wax museum, like how much were the tickets, whether they ever had Dolly Parton's giant wax titties at Christmas.

No, but we had tons of Christmas lights, she goes. Fifteen thousand red ones strung from Cattle Kate to Sheriff Bridger. We had Custer on his horse dressed as Santa and all his killed Lakota in green pointy hats like elves.

Then suddenly she stops. The last time I was there was a Christmas morning, she says.

We're in the deepest of the ditches and I'm kicking dead toads, but Jeanie doesn't join me, she squats and lights a smoke.

I was eight, she says. Christmas Eve Mama's got this big surprise to get ready, so she sends us off to watch the skaters at the skating rink, something Mombie always loved to do. Then when we get back she blindfolds us and leads us slowly through each wax gallery: the Autopsy of Big Nose George, Yellow Hair Shot by Buffalo Bill, the Mormon Handcart Tragedy. She takes us all the way back to her undisputed masterpiece: Nighttime Falls on Gunfight Saloon.

Gunfight Saloon? I say already amazed by it and Jeanie says Fuck yeah, Gunfight Saloon. So Mama takes our blindfolds off and where normally the Cowardly Onlookers should have been standing there are two brand-new waxes.

Abraham Lincoln and his fat wife arm wrestling! I say. Harriet Tubman and John Brown in swimsuits tonguing!

Jeanie whacks me hard and calls me bitch dingus, says Bitch Dingus, don't be stupid, it was Mombie and me. She'd sculpted us exactly in frilly purple dresses, every mole and eyelash identical except for one important thing.

I ask what thing and Jeanie karate chops the air between us.

She split us, she says. Straight down the middle. She had Mombie sitting at her harp and me standing behind her, a pocket Bible in one hand and the other patting Mombie's arm.

Right here I spot the last ditch toad but Jeanie smashes it.

She wanted us to know how we'd look normal, she says. And you know what? She put me in that fucking dress all pretty and smiling, but somehow still it was really me. It was like: This is how your mama sees you. It's not what you look like but it's what you are.

This gets me wondering about my own dead mom, Sharon Louise Sibly, RIP. What she saw looking at me, her dumbshit baby. How I'd look to her if she saw me today. If I could find her ghost maybe she could tell me so I go to ask Jeanie about ghost hunting but she keeps talking and talking. I see that one of her side teeth is dead and gray.

So me and Mombie are checking out our waxes, she's going. And I'm oohing and aahing and saying Thank you, Mama, thank you, because who cares about the faggy dress or the Bible glued to my hand when now I can pass a real one between me and my bitch sister, when now there's a beautiful giant gap where there's never been? It's like, God, Mombie, god, for once shut the fuck up. Who the fuck cares she put your fingers on the harp wrong?

I tell her if it was me I wouldn't care about my fingers.

Well my bitch cunt sister cared a whole fucking lot, Jeanie says.

She says We're circling our waxes and Mama's being all wishy-washy, like how she fucked up our complexions and that our earlobes are too small. Finally point-blank she asks us do we like it and guess what that bitch cunt fucker Mombie says?

She says she hates it, I say and Jeanie says No. She says No one would go to a movie to see regular girls like these.

Oh my god, that bitch, I want to kill her! I say.

I'd like you to, Jeanie says and lights me a smoke all generous and there's something about the way she says it that makes me want to pinch both my thighs.

So to make up for Mombie I ask Mama if I can keep my wax in our bedroom. I say I love it so much I want it next to me when

I sleep. So Mama gets the dolly and rolls it next to my side of the bed in the storeroom so that lying there at night I could stare at the dark outline of the better me.

Here I shiver even though the sun's beating warm on top of us. When I see how my shirt's sticky with toad juice a wave goes through my gut.

Next Jeanie tells me how her bitch sister had super bad night terrors and how that night they tossed and turned all night long. But I didn't elbow her awake how I usually would, Jeanie tells me. I kept my eyes fixed, held my wax always in my vision. Besides the faggy dress and Bible, I was staring at the future me.

And you were right, I say. Look at you now, I go.

Yeah, just look at me, Jeanie says, half sad, half angry.

I bet having your wax by your bed pissed Mombie off so bad, I tell her, then Jeanie calls me Kittentits and says Kittentits, the next morning she burned the wax museum down.

Next thing I know we're shin deep in Evelyn's onions, we're planning Zombie Whore costumes for Halloween. Jeanie's shoving onions down my shirt and calling me onion tits and I'm calling her dingus tits and laughing until I can barely breathe. I'm like Don't don't don't! laughing and then Dad's outside, twin-awning his hands over his sunglassed eyes.

He goes Girls, hey girls? You know it's free day at the zoo, and I'm like, Please please please Jeanie, let's go Jeanie, take me! Please please please it's free it's free it's free!

FOURTEEN

First we hit the American Prairie, there's wolves and elk and buffalo. I'm a wolf, your dad's an elk, she says. That old fat bitch Evelyn's a buffalo.

What about me, what am I? I ask her.

You're a prairie dog, she says flicking my chin.

We do the Rain Forest, we see the African Veldt, we sno-cone our butts through the Asian Steppes yawning. The more animals we see the more Jeanie gets weird and mystical, all Look how clean and straight everything is. All the zebras with the zebras and the donkeys off on their own.

I say No shit and she thwacks my head. The monkeys with all the other monkeys, she says. All the birds in the same damn cage together.

Yeah they have to, otherwise all the animals would kill each other, I say.

Wow, she goes, you're the smartest Crotchface ever. But look, she says, even the hot-ass zoo studs are kept together, meaning the two teen boys selling ice cream by the elephant house, zittards in sweat-stained money belts and white paper hats. When we walk by them they look at me like I'm a jelly bean to swallow while they look at Jeanie like she's a chili dog to chew.

My legs are tired and Jeanie can't take whining so we stop at the Alfred E. Long Memorial Gazebo so Jeanie can smoke. As soon as she lights up I say Tell me the rest about Mombie. Tell me about Christmas morning when she burned the wax museum down.

I flinch expecting her to hit me but she doesn't, she just sucks her smoke in. She scratches her leg and stretches and then she begins.

That morning before church, she says, Mama's outside warming the Caprice up. Me and Mombie are going through the cowboy gallery and I'm walking fast because we're late and Mama's in a hurry. So I'm dragging her because she's got herself angled behind me and every few seconds there's this strange little sound: chiff, chiff, chiff. And she's doing something with her hands but she's always doing weird shit so you have to understand this all barely registers to me, I'm not at all noticing what's actually happening. Which is her lighting matches and dropping them behind me. I'm in this big hurry trying to get on my stupid coat.

Lit matches, I say. A lit match, I go.

So ten minutes later we're all three in church and it's the part about the manger. The preacher's going on and on about the straw and pigs and the onlooking oxen, how it's totally dark but for the glow of the angel and the holy baby's light. How they're the only sources of light in all the black dark darkness and how each one's glow feeds into the other one's light and how it's this bigger light that lights up the pigs and Mary and the oxen, how everything including us gets bathed in this awesome Christian light.

And we're at that exact part, Jeanie says, when Mombie leans in close to me and whispers. She says Bitch, guess what? I burned down our house.

Here my eyes go big and I ask is that when she tried to kill her?

No, shut the fuck up, she says, that's when I told Mama. We rushed out of the chapel, Mombie going stiff so I had to drag her to the car. By the time we got there the building was engulfed, the Dodge City cattle bitches standing around twitter-twatting. Mombie grinning like it was a picture she'd finished, something she worked so hard on. The next thing I remember is this lady from church taking Mombie and me to K-Mart. She bought us new nightgowns and hair barrettes then dropped us off with Mama at the Motel 6.

Here Jeanie pauses, takes a long drag.

When Mombie fell asleep that night I was up watching the free cable, she says. We'd had Pizza Hut for supper and my fire-starting bitch sister ate too much and fell asleep right away. So I'm in bed watching HBO interview John Travolta about *Saturday Night Fever* when Mama gets out of the shower all quiet and tiptoes all quiet to my side of the bed in her new pink K-Mart robe. She's got two big wet spots on her chest from her hair hanging down and she bends over and puts her hand on my head just like when we were little. Her hair's dripping all over and I don't even care, I'm not even pissed and I don't flinch because before she says anything I somehow know what's coming. Baby, she says to me barely whispering, Baby, she says, you can have your surgery now.

So that's when they split you, I say and Jeanie says Almost.

Mama was smart, she says. She knew what had to be done. Her plan was to move us to the trailer court Cousin Terry managed outside Kansas City, to keep Mombie away from knives and matches until the surgery could be done. We moved out of the Motel 6 on New Year's Day, Jeanie says, and on February 7 I was reborn.

Yeah but what about Mombie? Did she freak out? What did she say? I say.

She screamed a lot and kept threatening to cut off her hands, Jeanie says. The week before surgery she stopped speaking completely. She'd walk wherever I wanted and eat whatever Mama made, but she wouldn't talk, she'd just stare this fiery stare like she was Joan of fucking Arc, Jeanie says.

Joan of Arc can suck it, I say. I'm standing up now doing a little dance, but Jeanie flicks her ashes at me and says Crotchface, shut up, I'm not finished.

So it's the morning of the operation and I'm being nice, she says. I'm packing a bag for both of us because Mombie refuses to pack. I'm putting in comic books and stuff like that in my backpack and Mama's outside loading things up in the Caprice. Then out of nowhere, after seven days of not speaking, Mombie starts emitting this high-pitched wail. Then suddenly she's thrashing and sobbing and ripping my comic books, she's like Please please please don't cut me off of you! Then she grabs the band of cartilage connecting our two torsos like I was going to do the operation myself right then and there.

I say Jeanie, oh my god, did you do it? Did you cut into her?

Crotchtard, don't be a fucking idiot, she says. Anyway, she's all crying and begging and saying Please don't do this and now outside Mama's honking the car so I'm like Listen the fuck up. I say This is for the best because you're fucking crazy and then she goes limp again and won't fucking talk. She refuses to move so I have to drag her out of the trailer and when I finally get her into the Caprice she starts thrashing again, working Mama over, crying and begging Please Mama, please!

It was not unaffecting, she says, taking a long drag of her cigarette.

It's real affecting, I say, wiping grit from my eye. It feels wrong to sit on her left side where I'm sitting. It feels like sitting on someone's grave.

Anyway, Jeanie says, Mama had a big heart and I knew those cries shot straight through to the meat of it. But someone had to get shit started so I told Mama Start the car and I told Mombie Sniff up or die. I rode the whole way to the hospital quiet after that but kept my hands fisted.

I look at her hands and they're in fists now, her finger snakes pulsing white over nip-pink knuckles.

We get to the hospital and there's all these people there, she says. She says it this way like the story's starting to bore her. Nurses taking our blood and Mama signing papers, she says. Mombie doesn't say a single word, staring her weird stare like she's not there anymore. Then we're naked under a paper sheet on a rolling double gurney and then we're in the operating room where the doctors and nurses are busy getting shit ready, unwrapping knives and scissors on shiny metal trays, flicking IV bags with green-gloved fingers. So of course I'm like Who cares how this little bitch next to me behaves when this is a bitch I'm about to be free of forever?

Fuck yeah, I say, but Jeanie just looks sad. She takes a drag then blows the smoke in my face.

So I've got my head on this comfy pillow and I'm feeling pretty good, she says. I'm looking around at the machines, the various-sized scissors. Then they roll the saw in on its own special cart and the next thing I know gas masks are coming down on our faces. Right before the gas hits, Mombie turns to face me. This will always be your fault, my sister says.

Jeanie, I say, stopping the story. Jeanie, this is almost scary, I say.

Jeanie flicks her cigarette, her face like Are you bitchin' or are you a pussy?

Keep going, keep going, I'm no pussy! I tell her. When she said that what did you say?

I don't know, I don't remember, she says. The next thing I remember is waking up after the surgery. For the first time ever the tug of her was gone. She was strapped in a bed eight feet away. She'd been waiting for me to wake up so she could start screaming and spitting so I tell her to shut the fuck up even though I finally knew.

Here Jeanie stops, like that's it, like end of story. She checks something in her pocket and reties her Keds.

Knew what? I say.

That she was right, Jeanie says. That we could never be cut in two hard enough. Which means we could never be cut in two. Anyway, two weeks later we're out of the hospital and the fourth night back at the trailer Mama and her cousin Terry go to bingo. Mama thought the painkillers would keep Mombie asleep, but somehow Mombie figured out Mama's plan.

Oh my god, what was it, what was it, I ask her.

To send Mombie to a stay-away school for young evil bitches while I grew up normal with Mama at home. But Mombie must have known and faked taking her medicine, she says. She must have faked being asleep that entire day, Jeanie goes. Because as soon as the door shut and the Caprice's engine started she was up and looming over where I'm resting on the couch. Even with the drugs it still hurt to move, but it was like somehow Mombie felt no pain. So she's looming over me, one hand raised like to slap me, and very dramatic she says From this day onward you better watch your back. Here Jeanie has her hand up open-palmed like to show me, then brings it down so fast I almost scream.

But instead of slapping me, she says, she punches me hard three times in my staples.

This has to be it, I'm thinking. This has to be where she tries to kill her twin sister, where she's arrested and sent to prison and then to House of Friends.

And then what? I say. What happened then? I ask her.

Then what, then what? Jeanie says in this high whiny way. Then Mombie goes out the trailer and into the night, she says.

She up and leaves? I say.

Dragging her harp case behind her, Jeanie goes.

You didn't fight her back? You didn't try to kill her? I say.

How could I kill her? Jeanie says. She was already gone. She'd packed all her shit in her fucking Paraguayan harp case. Mama was at bingo. I was high on painkillers and sucker-punched bad.

But I thought you tried to kill her is all, I say.

That's way later, she says then calls me Dingus. She tells me to stop jumping ahead.

She says two years later they got a postcard from New York City. It was addressed to the The Betrayers of Terry's Trailer and I Am An Actress Now was all it said. The police said "actress" probably meant pornos. Back then police gave zero shits about white trash girls running away, she says. She says Anyway, by that time I was heavy into doom metal, busy being a single person for the first fucking time in my life.

I'm sucking on the ashed-out smoke she hands me, trying to take this new turn in the story in, when suddenly she says Why don't you go look at the elephants? I need a break from you right now, she says.

I do what she says, I don't want her pissed at me. I trot inside the dark cement building where the elephants live. I read all the plaques for the quizlet I know Evelyn's going to give me, memorize the shape of elephantine trunks and the size of elephantine brains. One's tossing his shit over his shoulder and another one's pissing and I run to find Jeanie in case it's something she wants to see. I bet myself five dollars she'll make her joke about jungle rivers, but she's gone, I can't find her. Not even the ice cream guys are there.

I walk around the zoo for an hour looking then hear noises near the fish fountains. It's Jeanie in the restroom pinning an ice cream guy against a stall. His tongue's out and twirling like a helicopter propeller while the other guy's on his knees sucking Jeanie's black-painted toes. I don't know what happens next because I shut my eyes when they start grinding, but then Jeanie sees me and asks where the hell I've been.

This whole time right here, I say, pointing to the ground, extra lippy.

Fuck off, little girl, the toe-sucker goes.

Jeanie knees him in the mouth, she's like Motherfucker, you better watch it! She's like That's no way to talk to my fucking friend!

Then the guys run off bloody while calling us bitches and I say to Jeanie Hey let's do the gift shop, I've always wanted a key chain with my name.

Fuck no, Jeanie says, you don't even have keys for a key chain.

But when we go by the gift shop its doors open automatically and how's it to know Jeanie said I couldn't go in? How's it going to know opening its doors is like a tug on me? Someone sucked into a tornado has no choice but to go in. If the zoo was the ocean and I was just some guy backfloating then the gift shop's a magic shipwreck where the biggest-titted sirens swim.

God! I say, my voice high and whiny. God! You don't have to pull my arm off! I need my arm! I go.

Jeanie only snarls so I go stiff and let her drag me. In a weird way I like it, it's like she wants to hold my hand. She lets go once to pull a smoke from her pocket and when I ask twice if I can have one she's all You greedy motherfucker, oh my god, no you can't.

So I make my body stiff again, dig my heels in like to draw blood from the sidewalk, and here is when I see it: the hot air balloon.

Tethered to three flame-painted monster trucks in a coned-off section of the parking lot an actual hot air balloon floats gently in the sky. The balloon part's neon yellow and the basket's painted black and the trucks' thumpy roof speakers boom Metallica while a circle of pale white boys slam dance. Next to them a one-armed man sits on a cooler selling tickets.

Let's do it, let's do it, let's do the balloon! I say.

Jeanie says no. She says Her Highness Miss Kittentits spent all her money.

I say Please Jeanie, please please, and then I start to beg her. She says Shut the fuck up, I said I don't have any money.

But you promised, I say, my voice high and cracking. You're a liar, I say, remembering the purse quarters, remembering all the things she said we'd do that first day she came.

But Jeanie's not listening, she forgot where she parked Evelyn's van. She's yanking me across the lot now toward the wrong white Econoline and telling me I have to wear my seat belt when before I never did.

Fine, whatever, I say, because fuck her. Fuck Jeanie. It doesn't even matter because I'm already up in that black basket in my head. I'm already rising over the monster trucks, floating and seeing everything. Seeing all the zoo animals and all the zoo animals seeing me, seeing all the jealous slam-dancing white boys in the parking lot pointing. To the north I see the dirt bike track and to the east House of Friends, Evelyn's butt bent over where we fucked up her onions, scorch marks striping around where the roof caved in.

And then I see Jeanie. Her in the basket beside me, her hair tangling wild from a sudden fierce wind. Her snake fingers slide around in her purse searching for something.

But on the ground in the parking lot, look: the real Jeanie. She's found Evelyn's van the next row over. She's kicking its tires and yelling Stupid fucking van. Then just like in the balloon she's got a hand in her purse fishing, jingling around the quarters in the bottom of the bag. For a moment I think she's caved, that she's grabbing some to give me, but no, she's just digging for the keys to the van.

Crotchflower, she goes, hey Crotchflower. Look at me, why are you crying? Crotchflower, what is it? What, do you need to pee?

FIFTEEN

Demarcus Nassius
5135 South Federal Street, Apt K16
Chicago, IL
October 2, 1992

Dear Demarcus,

Get ready to be jealous D Dawg, yesterday I was up in a hot air balloon! Have you been in one before? Most people haven't so I'll tell you. When you get in there's a fire that blows up a chute, it's hot on your face so the pilot's all like Careful! Because your face could melt off in two seconds easy. Balloon pilots have burn scars all over their faces. But Demarcus, this isn't even the cool thing I've got to tell you, the thing that's cool is: I have Bionic Vision.

So I'm up in the balloon and close my right eye so I'm looking down at everything with my left one only then suddenly all at once I see close up for miles all directions. Like kids playing Wiffle ball at the Wiffle ball park, what's on the shirt each kid's wearing. I can even see them talking and can lip read what they say, like one says Hey is your ghost on second? and the other one says Suck my dick, Faggot!

At first I didn't believe it, Demarcus. I thought: Molly this is crazy! Because no one can see that far with that kind of precision. But the whole time I was in the balloon my eyes worked like this, I swear, so I asked my dad about it and he's like Now you know your secret, I knew this day would come. Molly, you've inherited your dead mom's Bionic Vision.

He tells me I can see what other people can't and that he's always been so proud of me, etc. etc. Then he puts his hand on my shoulder and points to the zoo. Look over there, he says so I close my right eye and zoom in behind Crocodile Station. I see a zookeeper standing over a kiddie pool with a crocodile floating on its back and she's hypnotizing the crocodile with an effing crystal pendulum.

Demarcus, I'm not lying! I saw it all from the balloon. Demarcus, I'm so serious, this is for real.

So I'm up in the balloon telling everyone what I'm seeing and Jeanie's getting bossy, like Look here, now look there. She's like Look right now at the white trash side of Cal City, look at my ex-boyfriend Mangus's dead stepdad's trailer and tell me whether Mangus's dirt bike is there.

And I say Oh, Jeanie, so sorry, I don't see it, it's not there, but Demarcus, I'm a liar because it was totally there! My Bionic Vision was so sharp it cut straight inside the trailer where I saw a skinny white guy boiling hot dogs in faded black undies while running a pick through his long metalhead hair.

So why am I telling you all this? you are probably asking. Demarcus, it's because I have a plan.

Tonight when it's dark I'll look at the moon with my Bionic Vision. I'll search it for oceans then scan each ocean super slow. Then when I find proof of aliens I'll write a letter to U of Chicago and whatever thing I find they'll name after me. And Demarcus, write me back just once and I'll give you a present. The present is when I find a second thing and the scientists ask what to name it, I'll say Name it Demarcus Nassius, name it after my best friend.

This offer is good for one day only, Demarcus. If you're reading this, write this second, don't wait.

Molly

SIXTEEN

Halloween day four o'clock and already Jeanie's plowed through the candy corn. Now she's in the shower and her showers last forever, so I sneak in her room to dress up as a Zombie Whore. I grab the shoebox where she keeps her black eyeliners, smear some under my eyes for death. I draw spiders and centipedes like tattoos on my fingers, do blood drips with her lipstick down my chin. I dig through her shirt box for something slutty like a tube top, double one up then stuff it with maxi pads. To finish I rat my hair crazy high with her hair pick, Bold Hold it in stages how you're supposed to do.

I check the mirror and I look good! I look scary! So scary I hide in her closet and crouch on top of her special black box. My plan's to leap out when she comes back from the shower, I'll jump out yelling Gotcha and oh my god it'll scare out her shit!

For half an hour I'm hunched and crouching, toeing her floor-thrown socks, her stiff-crotched panties, but I don't even care, the whole time I'm spitting giggles through my fists. I'm watching through the door slats when she walks in with one of Evelyn's good towels around her, her wild hair wet and sexy, one butt cheek sticking out the back.

She grabs a smoke from the dresser and I wait for her to light it then I jump out screaming Boo! then wait for her to laugh.

Fuck! she screams, her face as white as Sister Regina's, so I put my arms out straight like a zombie, turn in circles, wait for her to laugh.

But she doesn't.

She looks at me in her tube top then back at the black box in the closet. She sees the tip of her lipstick's all jacked now plus all the eyeliners I dumped uncapped on her bed.

Then all at once I can see what's coming, there's a moment where the switchblades in the dark of her eyes unflick. I turn to run but she's too fast and she grabs me, calls me a mosquito bitch cunt fucker, a fucking mosquito cunt bitch.

Her towel falls off as soon as she hits me, her knuckles connecting hard to my cheek, my neck. Between thumps I see the tattoos I didn't even know about—grinning devils and growling Dobermans up and down her stomach, a snarling octopus on each big tit. They make me think of the octopus kite we haven't flown yet. The Dr Pepper and vodka we've never drunk. The unridden balloon at the zoo.

Now she's got me squeezed into her armpit, my face smooshed hard in the jaggy pink of her scar. It's darker down the middle like it's got a zipper running down it, like her skin's just some bag to hold her bones.

She sees me looking at her scar and hits me again way harder. Never jack my shit! Never ever! she goes.

Then in the doorway shouting Sakes Alive! comes Evelyn.

Sakes alive, sakes alive, sakes alive! she goes. And I don't know, I'm scared, so I bite Jeanie's tit. She yelps and lets go and I dive behind Evelyn. Oh my god, Evelyn, look! I say. She used one of your good towels. Oh my god, Evelyn, look, I go, one of your good blue ones.

Jeanie says nothing, stands there naked, her T-shirts and jeans in piles all around her but her not moving an inch to get dressed. She stands hands-on-hips like a motocross trophy, snarling lips lit pink from the sky out the window, death metal eyes aimed only at me but also stabbing legions somehow. I can't help but look full-on at her tattoos and tits, the red swelling tip of the octopus leg where I bit it, her dark swirl of crotch, the swirling black tufts of it, the coiling spirals springing like soot-curled streets. It's like someone flipped a switch to make light shoot out of it, a spotlight to shine on the good blue towel at her feet. I'm still whimpering and pissed and cowering behind Evelyn, but I'm not immune. Jeanie's a Venus.

Here Dad stumbles in and sees our scene, Jeanie all tattoos and dark-crotched fury. His face crumples in this super sad way, like Another sad thing I have to see with my eyes these days. Like How am I supposed to update your dead mom about this?

He shakes his head and whistles softly. The calf and the lion and the yearling together but somehow no peaceable kingdom, he says.

Which is to make us feel bad, these bullshit dictums. Right as I'm thinking how that's something Jeanie'd say, Jeanie says That's some real heavy Quaker bullshit, Steven.

And I say—I don't know why or what makes me—but I say Hey, that's Isaiah you bitch!

Dad puts his hands up like we're both pointing guns at him. Okay, okay, let's all calm down, he says.

Sister Regina's ghost floats worried in the hallway behind him, sneaks her see-through arms around his waist. He can't see or feel her yet somehow pats her ghost hand anyway then slowly turns down the light switch dimmer, makes drawn-out shushing sounds while the room goes black.

Nothing to see now, no crotch, no tits. I half expect Jeanie's tattoos to burn through the darkness as neon constellations, but they disappear with her, she's a starless night.

Evelyn's the first to speak. I think she was hitting her, she says to Dad quiet.

Well fuck you, Evelyn, Jeanie says and Dad says Well now I don't know, I didn't see.

I think, Evelyn says, this time louder, I saw her hitting her, Steven.

Well we'll see, I don't know. We'll see, says my dad.

Now it's my turn.

Eff you all, I say. You all suck so effing bad!

And whether because it's so dark, I don't know, but I hardly recognize my own voice's thickness. It doesn't feel born in my throat that way.

In my bedroom for forty minutes I cry into my pillow and then when I get up I'm a way better zombie whore. I really look like I just dug myself up. I sniff up my tear snot and go downstairs to the kitchen and it's clear me and Jeanie won't be egging cars tonight. She's definitely still pissed because she drank the last of my Hawaiian Punches, lined up the empty boxes along the counter to be sure I'd see. Now she leans against the screen door tugging her fingerless gloves on, ears tuned for her friends' downshifts and her eyes shut tight.

I make a big show of not caring and walk right by her, slam my way out the kitchen door. The effect's supposed to be Look at me running away, Motherfuckers, when really all I'm doing is going to my friend Sweetie's house.

SEVENTEEN

SWEETIE'S HOUSE IS SUPER NICE, both her lesbo moms are architects. I'm standing on their porch ding-donging their bell. It's shaped like a ladybug and lights up when you push it plus they've got fake spiderwebs on their porch columns and pumpkins all around. It's okay but not scary, mostly sort of nice and friendly, like Welcome Ye Little Children, Happy Halloween.

The last time I was here they said not to come back for six weeks, maybe longer. Not because of me but because Helen's mouth cancer was getting bad. But their porch is decorated which means they're still handing out candy which means maybe Helen's mouth cancer didn't turn out to be that bad.

Sweetie opens the door wearing her dumb silver leotard, her golden ponytail extra bouncy, all scissored ribbon curl. But her face is full of splotches and her eyes are webbed in red like she's been crying. I wonder if today someone beat her up too.

I call her Leotard Retard and say Trick or treat, Motherfucker, then when she says nothing I punch her in the shoulder to be nice.

She says It doesn't look good, Helen's in there dying! and now she really is crying, cupping her eyes in tiny snot-crusted hands.

Hey, I say. Hey, it's okay, Sweetie. I tell myself not to call her lesbo if she moves in for a hug.

I don't have to worry, though, because here comes her unsick mom Leslie. I wiggle my fingers hello like Hey, it's only me. She doesn't smile or wave at me, she's in no mood for zombies, but before she can shoo me away she sees a bunch of kid-sized swamp monsters coming down the dead-end street. One time Leslie told me Call it a cul-de-sac, not a dead-end street.

She sees the swamp monsters and sighs, says Oh Molly, oh Molly, then asks me to stay on their porch to tell trick-or-treaters not to ring. She brings out a bowl of apple-spice mini-bars and when she hands it over I see her see what Jeanie did to me: my busted lip, my knuckle-thumped cheek. Her seeing feels weird, it makes my face hotter, so I say Yeah, okay, no worries, Leslie. Sweetie tries squeezing out the door then to sit with me but Leslie won't let her and yanks her back in. Just before the door closes I see a sliver of hallway, a lady in nurse scrubs standing in the gloomy dim.

After a few minutes Leslie brings out Sweetie's dog Pepsi. Poor thing hasn't been out all day, she says and hands me the leash.

Pepsi's a wiener dog, but a big girl, an old one. She can crap by herself I figure, so when Leslie's back inside I let her run free. I watch from the porch while she sniffs out the best crapping place, think how I've never tried that hard at anything. Even squeezing one out she gives her best effort, her back arched perfect like a rainbow's hump, tarry black dog nuggets instead of gold at the bottom. But her teeth the whole time? Gritted and grinning.

I like Pepsi a lot, she's a really good dog. Even talking to her about nothing she wags her tail. That was such a good poop, you're such a good dog, I tell her. They don't know how lucky they are to have you, I say.

She waddles up the steps and rolls over for petting. With two fingers I trace the pink grid of her belly and chest, its two rows of four nips, wonder if she thinks what I'm doing is pervy. Whenever trick-or-treaters come I throw mini-bars at them, aim at their Batman and Catwoman masks. Because dogs are psychic, I throw hardest at whoever Pepsi barks at. Sometimes I forget to yell Catch. It doesn't matter anyway, rich kids are pussies. They mumble only the most minor cusses back.

A girl dressed as the Little Mermaid is the only one to get huffy. She calls me a mean bitch and sticks out her tongue.

Wow, Princess Crotchface, I'm so freaking scared, I tell her. Then I tell her to get off my sidewalk or else I'll sic my dog. I tell her my dog's got rabies and that each rabie's got a boner, that rabies are giant maggots that have sex with your brain.

Sometimes from the house come sounds like people moving, but the whole time I'm there the front door stays closed. I want so bad to peek inside to see what's happening, but I'm a pussy and stay on the steps with Pepsi to watch rich kids in cool shoes come and go. They've got shoes with heels that flash red when you step down on them and shoes that pop out roller skate wheels when you squeeze the tongues. The coolest thing about my Heatwaves is their flame stitching, but there's no real heat in the orange licks. No real fire because the flames aren't real ones and the bottoms are boring, waffled rubber stuck with dirt-syrup, grit.

I got them right after the fire because the fire melted my old ones. Evelyn picked me up from the hospital and drove us to Foot Locker first thing. Her eyes were busted red and her hair smelled smoky. I was wearing the socks the hospital gives you free.

I went straight to the Heatwaves as soon as I saw them. They were posed for takeoff on a clear plastic ledge. I said These ones, I want these ones! and Evelyn didn't even ask what the price was. When I tried them on she didn't push her thumbs down on my toes. When she wrote out the check she had to ask the guy what day it was and then when he told her she said Thank you, Bruce.

My pen pal Demarcus would go crazy for light-up sneakers. I bet if someone gave him some he'd freak pure joy. How cool if I could buy him some and mail them to Chicago, not say who sent them except on the box write From A Friend. He's no dummy, he'd guess it was me and finally start writing. He'd tell me in a letter how much he loved his new kicks. I wouldn't say a word, it'd be this silent thing between us. This invisible cord keeping us tied.

He appears to me in dreams sometimes, in cool rap clothes

and chain necklaces. He stands by the carport in the brambles at night rapping a slow sorrowful song to make you cry. His shoes are covered in raccoon shit but a golden pick sticks out from his afro, and when he opens his mouth to rap, light pours out. Whenever he moves his hands, light shoots out his fingertips. By the time his rap's over there's light hanging all around.

Pepsi's asleep at my feet now, twitching and dreaming. The trick-or-treaters have dried up and it's getting dark for real. I wonder what right now Demarcus and his brothers and sisters are doing. Whether or not their single mom lets them trick-or-treat. I picture Demarcus as a Frankenstein grabbing candy all over Bronzeville, his brothers and sisters behind him, covered by ghost sheets. Really all I know about him is his mom works freezing french fries, that she sneaks the rejects home in plastic bags. This is what it said in the one letter he sent me, that thawed frozen french fries were his favorite thing to eat.

Suddenly all the lights go out in Sweetie's house, even the porch light above me. I stick my face to the living room window, suction my eyes to the glass. There's a thin strip of light under the door to the hallway bathroom. The door swings open and I half expect to see sick lesbo Helen, her walking around one last time in her expensive chemo wig. Nice mouth cancer Helen who in her electric bed sometimes did my math worksheets for me. Nice mouth cancer Helen who the one time I spent the night let me stay up with her to watch *Night Court*, told me secrets she'd planned to take to the grave: that Sweetie's bio dad was in fact *not* an anonymous donor, that Roz from *Night Court* was way hotter to her than Leslie, that Roz from *Night Court* who she regularly wrote fan letters to was the funniest and most attractive woman she'd ever seen.

But it's not. It's not Helen, it's the nurse I saw earlier. She's pulling on a sweater and grabbing her things. She sees me spying at the window and mouths Go Home, It's Over. She flicks her hands like I'm a booger, like Shoo fly, go away.

THE WALK HOME is two miles of split sidewalk and loose dogs, Mexican guys in lawn chairs eating their night cereal in front of their moms' houses. I hope if they yell at me that this time it might be sexy, not the same old crap about me being too young to walk home alone.

Last time they called me Little Orphan Gringa and asked over and over if I needed a ride home. They got out of their lawn chairs, patted for keys in their pockets, but I kept saying I'm okay, I'm okay, the whole time wishing they'd shout about their dongs instead. Had they shouted something like that I would have cussed back so good at them, I would have called them *pendejos* and earned their respect instead of pity, I would have proven I'm not someone you take pity on.

Tonight they don't even notice me even though I kick rocks into their yards. I ignore them right back and let my mind wander, think about riding the different rides at the Fair. Would it be more fun to ride a Ferris wheel with Jeanie or Demarcus, I wonder. I decide Demarcus then pretend behind me I hear Jeanie's dirt bike growling, imagine her pulling next to me and patting the seat behind her. Her saying over and over Zombie sister, forgive me! while I let her one time gently touch my swollen cheek.

I imagine riding home with my arms wrapped tight around her, her hair smelling like motor oil, her body a stiff board. Each time she revs the bike's engine she curls her finger snakes around the handles, makes the snakes go fat over her knuckles like they're swallowing rats. It's my favorite thing to see, her snakes digesting fat lumps of knuckle, it makes me feel calm and peaceful like I could lie down right here and sleep.

At home Jeanie's bike's gone and everyone else is in bed. Even Sister Regina levitates horizontal down the hall. The only sound is Evelyn mouth-breathing. If Jeanie was home there'd be her secret nighttime White Lion, but she's not so there's nothing so I pull my jeans off to go to sleep. I crawl under Hawaiian Garfield tired but with nice thoughts floating inside me: Demarcus writing me back, Jeanie making up for Halloween. Her taking me to Chicago to pick up Demarcus up in Bronzeville, the three of us going together to the Fair.

Lying here not sleeping plus thinking so hard about the Fair and Chicago, I have the idea that maybe I *am* sleeping, not here but in Chicago, that right now I'm really dreaming I'm lying awake in my House of Friends bed. That when I wake up things will be how they should be: my two best friends and me at the top of a Ferris wheel. Jeanie rocking the seat to wake me, her all Kittentits, goddamn! Who falls asleep on a fucking Ferris wheel? Then Demarcus going She does! Him snapping his fingers at me, him saying Yo girl, yo, we thought you was dead!

How bad I want it surprises me, it's like I can actually feel it. Like in my nose it's the snot or something in my crotch folded deep. It's a real physical thing, not just a thought that's weightless, like if my fingers could talk they'd say Take us and if I refused they'd cut themselves off and leave.

In the middle of the night when I wake up for real something so strange happens you won't believe me. But I'm not lying, this is totally true: for a few minutes I'm not me, I'm Jeanie.

How I know is I see the rain on the sill and think Jesus Christ motherfucker, all fucking ready it's too wet for biking. I think: Motherfucker, is Debra tomorrow or today?

I think Motherfucker, oh my god, don't my big tits ache hard, motherfuck it, I hate this place worse than prison. I hate these hippie assbites so hard except for Kittentits, she's got the signs of badass in her. If not my fake name's not Jeanie and I don't have a giant scar.

I stretch my legs and my legs now are long ones and between them's a crotch carpet of thick curls. I reach down to itch it and there's that string again hanging, floating in my carpet like a bathtub plug chain. I roll over still Jeanie but when I punch my pillow I'm me again. I've got my own dinky hands back, my regular crotch, a pink shell.

Still.

If I shut my eyes and make a fist I can almost grab hold of her. She's somewhere inside my brain stuck in some gray groove. If I sparked on the right spot I know I could bring her to life again, I could set my brain on fire with her, maybe for good.

I could think Scar and know all her thoughts about it. How the doctor's saw slid between them, how much it must have hurt. I could think Mombie and see her sister, think Her Voice and hear her talking. Hello, Sister, she'd be saying, I've been waiting for you.

EIGHTEEN

Three weeks later and Jeanie's saying weird shit all day offhanded. She says If I could be an animal I'd be a lemur with a big dick. This during the Grand Prize Game on *Bozo*. We watch it every morning, Jeanie loves WGN. Next when we're stuffing Monthly Mailers she calls my dad a fagatron, but the stunner's after Sweetie calls to tell us when Helen's Celebration of Life is.

I put the phone down and Jeanie looks at me and I swear I'm not fucking crying.

Too bad for her, she says. She says The only one who ever really loves you is your mom.

But she's still got one, I tell her. Her moms are lesbos, I say. I make a V with my fingers and wiggle my tongue between them.

She asks me what kind of cancer and I say it was the mouth kind.

My mama had the blood kind, she says. Before it spread to her bones.

Shit, that sucks hard, I go.

Don't tell me how it was, you have no idea, she tells me and I say Two dead moms between us is better than one.

Your dead mama can suck my dead mama's tits, Jeanie says. She says I took care of her day and night for six years. Mombie was long gone by then and I was all she had.

Bozo's over so now Jeanie's flipping channels, eventually settling on *One Life to Live*.

Princess Crotchtard, you may find it hard to believe but I was as good to her as she'd been to me, she says. I went with her to chemo and kept the trailer picked up. Cleaned up her puke and got groceries and kept her mind off things.

Did you ever play board games? I ask her, hoping maybe she could teach me some.

No, she hated games, shut up, Jeanie goes. No, I got out her tools and bought her bricks of wax. Sitting up in bed she could still do people in parts. Like Bill Cosby's ears or Boss Hogg's fat fingers, or she'd go on a Bible jag and do Billy Graham's nose.

For a long time it was like Mama was only sick in bed and not dying, Jeanie says, but in April of 1986 shit got real. Her skin went yellow and started flaking off in patches. She slept all day and then the times she wasn't sleeping she talked crazy. The hospice nurse said she still had a few months left maybe, but I was a dumb bitch and hadn't learned that nurses were liars.

Well you're definitely not a dumb bitch now, I say to be nice to her and she says Fuck no, Kittentits, that's what you are.

Anyway that May Candlemass goes on tour, she says, and they were my boyfriend Mangus's favorite. I was seventeen and he was almost fourteen so the only way he could go was if I took the Caprice and drove him. By then it had been six years of chemo, six years of shit and puke, six years of watching Mama's tears drip-dry all over Billy Graham's nostrils. All I wanted was one day of Euro doom to snort crank before June because in June I knew grief was going to hit like thunder. I get Terry to take care of Mama for the weekend and I drive me and Mangus to St. Louis for the show.

Bitchface, she says, are you even listening?

I am listening! I am! I say. Which is a lie because how could I be listening when in my head all I can see is Jeanie and Mangus.

Were you in love with Mangus? I ask her.

I thought he was top shit for a kid, she says. His drawings of angels grinding grim reapers were pretty fucking cute. Anyway, we go to Candlemass and it's just okay, then afterward Mangus starts acting like a shit because I won't take him to McDonald's. He's all butthurt and pouty and I'm like Fuck this shit, I'm taking you home. So I drive four hours back to Kansas City and drop him off at his stepmom Brenda's then drive back to the trailer thinking how everyone's alone.

Everyone *is* alone, I say.

Yeah, I fucking know, she says. I get back to the trailer and open the door and guess the fuck what? Guess what crazy bitch it is sitting by Mama on the edge of her rented hospital bed?

Mombie, I say. It's got to be.

Well who the fuck else, Jeanie says then finger-thwacks me. And what is my bitch sister sitting there doing?

Smothering your mom with a pillow, I say.

No, she says. My bitch sister is pretending to be me.

What the fuck! I say. What fuck! I go.

I'm so excited I jump off the couch. I'm so excited Jeanie has to shove me.

The bitch has on my Jucifer shirt and the dog collar Mangus made me. She's got her bangs exactly like mine, she says, and she's feeding Mama ice chips from a bowl Mama gave me.

Oh she better not fucking be! I say.

So I walk in and of course I'm like What the fuck, what the fuck? Who the fuck do you think you are coming back to this trailer?

Fuck yeah! I say.

And do you know what comes out of this bitch's mouth right then?

Shut the fuck up or I'll shoot you both, I say.

No, Jeanie says, her voice rising high and cracking. No, she turns to Mama in her bed and points at me and she says: Look, Mama, look! Mombie came home.

In the House of Friends living room everything goes quiet, me and Jeanie and even somehow the TV.

And my mama, Jeanie says after pausing a long time, her words backing down a ladder all slow and careful, my mama who can barely fucking speak, she says, who lymphoma has fucked over body and soul, who smiles at me now like the dying saint she is, who holds her arms out fucking Christlike to me, clear as day she says Baby I knew it, I always knew you'd come home.

And you played along. You loved her so much you played along, I say.

No, I did not, shut the fuck up, Jeanie says.

No, I'm shaking my head and pointing at Mombie and I'm like, No, Mama, that bitch is not me, *I'm* me. But Mama won't hear it, she's happy and smiling and waving me over and Mombie's patting the bed next to her like Come give Mama a hug, come sit over here.

So I go over and bend down gentle so as not to fuck her tubes up. I lean in and whisper Mama, it's not Mombie, it's me. It's me, it's me, it's your Goldaline, I say.

Jeanie's real name is Goldaline. Goldaline, Goldaline, I can't stop thinking it.

But at that point Mama was too far gone, Jeanie says. All she wanted was to touch my hair and ask terrible questions. How bad did the evil porno men hurt me, she wanted to know. Did I have to sell my body and live on the street? Then my crazy bitch sister looks me straight in the eyes and says Did you hear that, Mama? Her first night in New York a Puerto Rican girl tied her shoelaces together then stole her Paraguayan harp and kicked in her head.

Jeanie, can I call you Goldie? I say.

Mama died a week later and fuck no, Jeanie says. She wipes her eyes and grabs her pockets like to get her smokes out. You may never ever fucking call me Goldie, she says.

Jeez, just kidding, I wasn't serious, I say and she sniffs in hard and says Will you let me finish this fucking story.

She says Those last days before she died she thought the both of us were Mombie. Side by side, she called both of us that name. Then one morning Mombie's passed out in the recliner and me and Mama are watching *Scarecrow and Mrs. King.* Mombie, whispers Mama, could I please have some water, so I go to the sink to get her her water and when I turn back around Mombie's awake standing over Mama's bed, touching her forehead smiling and Mama thanking her for the water and Mombie's saying No problem, Mama, anytime I'll get you your water, me the whole time standing there behind the TV with the water. So I nudge in to say something but then Mama gives a tiny gasp then a big one and then her eyes fix on Mombie, not on me but on the real one, and then she says to her and not to me she says: I chose you out of the world, Mombie. I love you so very much, Mombie, and then she closed her eyes and never looked at me and then died.

And that's when you lost it, I say. That's when you tried to kill your sister.

No, I threw Mama's water in Mombie's face, she says.

It was the funeral, I say. I bet you lost your shit there. As quick as I say it I can see it clear: Jeanie unleashed, lip-curled and snarling, hair-blood-meat in slo-mo on the casket smack-landing.

Listen, you little fucker, she says. If you really want to know, I paid Mang—

Wait, wait, are you crying? I say. Oh shit, Jeanie, sorry! You're sad about your mom, I say. Sometimes I forget people usually get to know them. I'm so very fucking sorry, I say.

Matlock comes on so I get our Cheez-Its for *Matlock*, then it's *The Maury Povich Show*. Evelyn calls his guests Legacies of Poverty but Jeanie calls them either crank addicts or tubby fucking hoes. I sing Hungry hungry hoe bags! when the *Maury* song comes on but all Jeanie says is Shut the fuck up and be quiet, this is a good one.

It so is, it's "I'm Having My Dentist's Baby" so I shut the fuck up and watch super close. By the first commercial I'm bursting to talk, but for once Jeanie beats me.

Bitch, stop interrupting. You're a wound-up little shit, she goes. Don't you have your own public?

I don't even know what that is, I say and she says it's like people of your own kingdom. Like my old guards, Rusty and Jerome, she says. Like my dirt bike friends, like that piece of shit Mangus. Look, Crotchtard, she says, stubbing out her smoke, you are a prairie dog and I'm a dark serpent. This is just where I'm living, she says, then from the heel of her shoe pulls out a new one.

It's not only cigarettes she keeps in her Keds, I've seen the steel toes inside them. She welded them herself from two clawed hammer heads two days before she got out of prison.

So what, you think I should hang out with Sweetie? I say. Because eff you if you do, my public's Demarcus.

Jeanie rolls her eyes and says Molly, you're so fucking dumb. He's just some Black kid you've never met. You're way too fucking Nordic to be his public, she says. Besides, for all you know he doesn't even exist. For all you know that bitch Evelyn invented him.

He does too exist, I say, because he does, I know it. There was that one time he wrote me back.

Well you'll never meet him anyway so who cares, says Jeanie.

He is too my public, I say, my knuckles bursting to fists.

She says she doubts he even opens my letters.

Maybe he doesn't even know how to read, she says and I say Goddamnit, Jeanie, I'll fucking show you.

My face burns hot and my eyes start to twitch.

Dare me, I say. Dare me to prove it.

Okay, Crotchmouth, prove it, she says. Make me eat my words instead of Evelyn's shit, I dare you.

Fuck you, Jeanie, get ready to swallow, I say.

And here she laughs hard like I said something so dumb then next she's lifting up her Dream Death shirt like to flash me. But she doesn't flash me, she stretches the black cotton over my head, entraps me up close against her octopus boobs which smell like spit-yellowed pillows sprayed with Electric Youth. I wriggle and kick but she pins me there, laughing and giving me a thousand airless noogies. She laughs so hard she starts hiccupping bad, and even though I'm super pissed, I can't help it: whenever she laughs, I laugh too.

I laugh but at the same time try not to. Two opposite thoughts swim parallel in my head, the first backfloating in floaties slow and happy. This one says Jeanie, you're so fucking cool. It says Jeanie, I so fucking love you.

The second laps my skull in fast jabby strokes, it's a shark, a piranha, a bullet racing. This one's a voice whispering harsh and low. Fuck you Jeanie, over and over it's saying. Jeanie, you just fucking watch me, it goes.

NINETEEN

YOU MIGHT THINK IT'S HARD for a little white girl like me to get all by herself from Cal City to Chicago, but guess again, it's not that hard. You do what you gotta to prove your pen pal exists. Early that next morning after Jeanie challenges me, after she flashes her tits laughing and calls me Thunderbrow laughing and then says laughing that my pen pal Demarcus doesn't really exist, early that next morning I slink downstairs super quiet and call to activate the Visa that came for Liesel last week.

Outside the kitchen window falls 1992's first snow. I look at it and think not of the snow, I think: Demarcus, you fucker, I'm coming for you.

I find Evelyn in the garden all jumbo puff coat and gloves, her hunched over her onion bed raking dead leaves into mounds. She asks what I'm up to so early in the morn and I say Evelyn, Evelyn, you gotta take me to Penney's! I tell her I'm a woman now, that my boobs have popped in.

She stops raking and smiles, says how about K-mart. I need a new spray nozzle and bird seed, she goes.

I say No, Evelyn, Penney's! It's got to be Penney's! Please Evelyn, pretty please please please Penney's! I say, because Penney's is in the mall and the mall's only three parking lots from the Metra station.

Okey-dokey, she says. Penney's it is, as soon as they open.

To say thank you I stick out my elbows and push my nips out, puff my chest big and march around her like this, like some big-boobed drum major in an onion bed grinning. She laughs, the snow glinting fluorescent off the gray of her teeth, and I think: Like a rapper's fancy grill. How those snowflakes stick.

So my plan's in effect, me and Evelyn are mall-walking, we've passed the So-Fro and the video arcade, the shadowy cave of juvies called the Dark of Zwindon's. This whole time I'm thinking When do I do it, when do I bolt? But also thinking how much I fucking love the mall.

I fucking love the mall! The whooshy spray of the food-court fountains, the white webbed backs of the food-court chairs, how their unfelted feet screech loud on the tile, swipe black marks like war paint on the gridded checks. I love my reflection bouncing off smooth fake marble, the smear of my fingerprints on dirty escalator glass. The sun shooting through skylights like movie projector light where the screen's the floor and the movie's no movie, only a parallelogram of heat and light.

We pass the Dark of Zwindon's and turn the bend toward Penney's, the all-beige butt-end of every mall I've ever known. We pass the giant-pretzel place and then the giant-cookie place, we slow down by the diamond ring place for Evelyn to cluck her tongue.

We're halfway to Penney's when Evelyn stops at Waldenbooks and I'm thinking Molly, what the fuck? I'm thinking Bitch, why aren't you running? Go, go, go, my brain tells me, sprints the word in laps around my skull. But I don't go anywhere, I stay chickenshit by Evelyn. She's slow-reading the back of an Amish romance novel and it's like, Evelyn, come on. The lady on the cover. Her undone bonnet, the hay behind her. What the fuck else do you need to know?

She finally puts the book down and tilts her head and looks at me. You're an awfully good egg today, she says. How are you feeling? Is something wrong?

She goes like to touch the back of her hand to my head but the thought of a touch like that starts me flinching. Her face goes frowny because this makes her sad, so I stand up straight and clack my legs together, salute her American-style, not the Hitler.

Respect for my elders is no disease, I say. Remember: I know all the ways to make Evelyn smile. To make her doubts fall like snow through a carport roof that's rotted.

But by Yankee Candle I start dragging my feet. By Fancy Nails I hide behind the photo-booth curtain. In front of Hallmark I pretend I'm drowning in quicksand and Evelyn finds it not even halfway funny.

I mean it, Miss Priss, I'm not kidding, she says, patting her little warning pat on the side of her leg. I mean it! You better hopscotch right now, she says, grabbing my arm hard enough to drag me. The violence of it surprises her and she pulls soft instead, makes her voice go all throat-coated and syrupy. You're a good egg, but you're so difficult, she says. Why be a thorn in everyone's rear, she says, when you could be a sweet-smelling daisy or a pretty China Doll rose!

Better a thorn in someone's ass than a China Doll, I say, because China Dolls are Evelyn's favorite roses.

I meant in people's eyes, she says. Your father's and your poor dead mother's.

Then say what you mean, I tell her, but what I'm thinking is by now my dead mother has no eyes.

We go through the mall like this, me passive-resistancing and Evelyn soft-scolding, and in no time at all we've passed Hot Topic and Claire's, each step a step farther from the main food-court entrance. I stop us again at the drinking fountain outside the bathrooms, sip the cold water slow like to fill an empty pool.

If I run now the crotchface bitch Jeanie will eat her words forever.

And my days of being leashed to Dad and Evelyn? Over for good. Because after I take the train to the city, after I go alone by myself the half hour to Bronzeville to prove to the crotchface bitch Jeanie that my pen pal exists, after that watch some Quaker mofos try to tell me what to do. I say no more home-school, no more Math Mondays, no more dinners forced to eat at the table. No more too young for the dirt-bike track and no more not cool enough for the Dark of Zwindon's, all its juvie kids leaning on the glass cases of prizes when the sign says big Do Not Lean, when why the fuck not? I was born to lean.

No more wondering why I'm me and them them, them badass juvies living off the dark of the arcade, eyes slit blind like cave bats' eyes, stolen tokens jingling in their ripped jeans. I see them seeing me and waving me in, me the top ever *Alpine Racer*, the *Die Hard 2: Die Harder* high scorer, the Bitch Queen Nasty who's got what they want, who knows the secret to the claw machine.

Watch your hair! Evelyn shouts, snapping me out of my vision. The ends of my hair are soaked wet from the fountain lake I've made.

If I don't run now it'll be too late.

It'll be Evelyn outside my Penney's dressing room door, her passing dinky bras on dinky hangers to me over the top of the door. And it'll be a gutless me I see in the mirror. A shittier me, not early-titted, just fat. A no-courage girl who lets cotton triangles be strapped to her, two tiny white tarps like to cover something tiny and dead.

This is where I do it.

I turn and I run.

Hey now! Evelyn shouts, but I'm not looking.

I'm going fast by Claire's and the Hallmark store, fast past the photo booth and the Dark of Zwindon's. People are watching, but I don't care, I'm rounding so hard the food-court fountain, I'm fixing my eyes to its six brass-barred doors, to the monster gray ocean of parking lots beyond.

I shove through the doors and boom, I'm unleashed. I'm swimming in the parking lot sea and I swear to you, I swear, in the air I hear sea birds cawing.

2

THE LONELY

ONE

Bronzeville and its piles!

In Bronzeville there are awesome piles down all the streets and sidewalks and in the empty lots between buildings where other buildings used to be. Piles of brand-new roller skates and piles of VCR parts and in the empty lots between buildings giant wrecking balls swaying chain-dangled from giant rusty cranes.

I walk by: a pile of fancy ceiling fans, a pile of novelty key chains, a pile of nonstick cake pans taller than me. Into some piles a few old white people lean bent-knuckled and darty, their fingers curled and thrusting like playing piano or plucking a harp. If they've got big enough pockets they put their pile stuff in their pockets, and if not, in cardboard wagons made from jumbo Fresh Step boxes, janky shopping-cart wheels rolling loose underneath.

And this whole time does anybody notice me? The little white girl in the badass jean jacket? The badass white girl in the Blood Farmers T-shirt skipping so happy down the street?

No, not the pile-picking white people and not the regular Black people on the sidewalk. Not the bus-flattened gutter squirrels, their claws like broken pencil leads pointing stiff to clear blue sky.

And I'm not dumb, I know Bronzeville's big. That I can't tug on whoever's sleeve and be like Oh please, sir, can you tell me where my pen pal lives?

But I don't know what else to do, either, so I slap down my hair and rub the crusties out of my eyes, tug the sleeve of the first old Black lady to walk near me. Mrs. Lady? I say, I say it very kitty. Mrs. Lady, I'm lost, will you help me find my friend?

The lady steps back fast, her face pinched like she stepped in crap. Like my voice was not even a voice but only some turdy drifting, a curb-scraped shit mystery afloat in her air. Finally she looks down, sees me holding up Demarcus's address.

Please just please will you look at it? I ask.

She says Who are you and what do you want? She shakes out her sleeve like I'd wiped all my boogers there.

I'm trying to find my friend, I say, my voice high and ripping. Should I take the bus? Which bus should I take? Where are the buses and the taxis? I say.

Here the old lady puts her hand on my head and I don't flinch, I feel a warm pulse, a hot soothey throb, her Black grandma wiseness sinking through to the meat of my brain.

What, are you a retarded child? she says.

And I think: You old stupid bitch. You dumbass hag.

But I sniff in my anger like snot through a straw, I cross my eyes and stick out my tongue. I wrist-slap my chest and go Dur dur dur and wave the address up in her face again.

She shakes her head, she's like Poor retarded thing, she's like, Tsk tsk tsk, where's your white-trash mother? Then she reads the address and looks all surprised, says Why you poor stupid kid, this is the last Robert Taylor! Your poor ass wants The Lonely, she says.

Dur? I say, which means: Bitch, do I look like I speak your gibbershit?

The old lady doesn't answer, just points a long way down the street where a fire-scorched high-rise stands all alone, two lots on either side, open-spaced demolition prairies dotted by snow-tipped cranes.

The Lonely's a cement fortress sixteen stories high, sixteen gray floors of thirty windows each floor, some tinfoiled and some broken and most painted black. The sidewalk in front's got cracks a half foot wide, ankle-twist canyons cut by rivers of trash. Loud metal scraping like rusty seesaws fill the air, air conditioners falling out windows to top the construction rubble like cherries.

When Demarcus sees me he's going to crap his pants in delight! Just the thought of surprising him keeps me grinning and grinning. Which fuck, I can't be grinning, how dumbshit of me! Grinning like a tard through a housing project lobby. What a little dumbass I can hear Jeanie say, like I'm in a crystal ball that she's at home watching. Way to sign up for a gang bang, she'd say.

But it turns out The Lonely has no lobby, only a flickering stairwell, a pay phone swinging. An elevator spray-painted Don't and Beware. I start up the stairs super excited and giddy but force myself to go slow so I can read all the signs, they're like: Have You Visited Your Elders Today? Wash Your Hands or Someone Else Pays!

On the sixth floor landing three Mexican guys lie inside a circle of beer cans napping. I almost poke one to ask him if he knows Demarcus, because who knows, maybe he lives next door to him. Maybe he's heard him talk about me before. But no, I'm chickenshit, I tiptoe over them and keep going.

On the ninth floor I pass a fancy-dressed Black guy and lady and I don't know why but I say Good afternoon, sir, good afternoon, lady. The lady's all attitude, all sharp bitchy huff, she says Hey now, girl, you better watch yourself now, but her husband's cool, he's like Wassup, my kickin' lady.

The top floor, Demarcus's floor, is not what I'd imagined. No sassy Black girls in the doorways double-Dutching, no boys in Air Jordans finger-spinning basketballs down the hall. There's no one in the hall, it's empty and dim, a narrow longness of cement and foot-dented doors. So I skulk mouth-shut and tiptoed to the very end where then there's a left turn and then another hall, a short one this time, one window, one door.

K16. Demarcus's door.

I push my hair behind my ears and lick my lips to shout Surprise but before my knuckles touch the door something unexpected happens: all on its own, the door opens.

Hello? I whisper into the dark apartment. Hello? Hello? Hello? I say. It might as well be Meow, meow, meow? because now my voice is a kitten's for real, high and scratched and ripping.

Demarcus? I say, stepping into the room, Demarcus, your door opened so I came in. I promise I won't touch your shit, I say.

I find the light switch and a lamp flickers on. Instead of a living room with a couch and TV, there's nine folding chairs in a circle. There's a Casio keyboard on a fancy black stand and a weird tang in the air, something warm and waxy. Like the taste of ear crust stuck under your nails. It's like: Don't lick these walls, don't lick this dank wallpaper, these up and down stripes of teacups marching.

Outside it's snowing but they must have the air conditioner on because in some other room there's whooshings.

I tiptoe to the kitchen and look in their fridge. Nothing but Kool-Aid and red-ringed bologna. There's an open box of straws on the counter next to the sink and on the stove a half pot of cocoa that needs stirring. I stick in a finger and swirl it then lick it. The cocoa's cold, but I like it that way.

But what a loud air conditioner, jeez!

Whooosh-Mississippi-whooosh-Mississippi-whoosh, it goes.

I follow the sound to a short hallway with three doors where one door's a bathroom with a spray hose for a shower and one's a closet filled with boxes marked Feathers. The third door's got to be the bedroom, I'm thinking, expecting a peed-on cot with licey blankets, maybe an Ice-T poster on the wall and dried stab blood on the floor, but holy shit, holy shit! I am wrong about everything.

The whole time I thought I was alone I was not even alone because here's this old white lady inside a machine.

A mostly bald white lady in a machine like a coffin, this long metal box, tubes and hoses on each end. Red velvet curtains hang to the floor from its bottom and all of the old woman fits inside the box but her head. It sticks out one end asleep on an attached pillow while above a three-sided mirror's angled over her head. The mirror shows everything in the room behind her: a yellow-flowered couch, a rabbit-eared TV, a cowboy hat on a carved wooden dresser, a box of syringes, and best of all, wide-eyed dumbshit me.

Whoosh-Mississippi-whoosh-Mississippi-whoosh.

I'd thought it was the air conditioner but it's the sound of her machine.

The lady's eyes are closed and she's totally still and unmoving, but here I notice the straw in her mouth, the suck between whooshes, the cocoa slowly lowering in the Who Killed Laura Palmer? mug on the TV tray next to her machine.

I am not expecting her to speak.

What—honky tonk—let—you out? she says, the words slow and divided between the machine's whooshes. Her voice is low like a man's voice, like a woman pretending to be a man or a man pretending to be a woman.

Are you—my rodeo—queen? she asks me, and I'm thinking Lady, oh my god, for hair you've got no hair and you live in a machine. Movie curtains hang down from you, a coffin skirt, a coffin skirt, and then I'm thinking Oh my god holy hell, where the fuck is Demarcus?

But what I do is I curtsy. I bend at the knees and lift the corners of my Blood Farmers tee like it's not Jeanie's shirt but a lace skirt that's fancy. I say Hi I'm Demarcus's friend, I'm his pen pal Molly, he asked me here what time is he coming back do you think he'll be back soon?

You are not, says the lady all gaspy-low, a transmission?

I don't know what that is, I say. I came to see Demarcus.

Then one at a time she opens her eyes and one eye's normal and one eye's not, that one's snot-clouded and unblinking.

Oh you—you—sweetie girl, she says. She says girl gair-yl and sweetie sweeteee, talks like some secret wind blows her sounds up and down. I thought—you were—a transmission, she says. Molly, she says. Whoosh whoosh whoosh. Molly—I've read—all your letters, she says.

I don't know what to say. Are you like his social worker? I say. Do you live here too?

Poor Molly, she says, her straw dropping onto a pile of old *TV Guides* on the tray, her mucky eye rolling clockwise in a circle. Don't—you—know?—Demarcus—whoosh whoosh whoosh—Demarcus—whoosh—has left—whoosh—the rodeo. So sorry—you're—too late.

Too late? I say. What do you mean, where'd he go?

To-the-Summerland, she says in this fast breathy way, her machine whooshing in at the stop of each syllable. Like her machine's not a machine, it's like her machine's her lung. He's a beautiful—phantasm—idle, she says.

She tells me she's been waiting for his transmissions for months then asks me how Evelyn and Dad are doing. Molly, she says, would you—place—my straw?

They're okay, I say and step closer to her, stand tiptoed to look through the Plexiglas top of her machine. Inside her nightie's bunched up over her knees, old-white-lady blue like Evelyn's, bruisy sagged folds swirling to peaks.

What a little perv, I can hear Jeanie say. Quick I bend down to pick up the straw and when I come up again the old lady's snoring.

And then I hear something else, another voice. Someone else in the room with me.

She drinks oceans, the voice says.

Here I am, it says.

Look down look down look down, it says, and then the machine's red velvet curtains are parting.

TWO

DEMARCUS IS A BOY BUT NOT A BOY, he's a ghost sitting Indian-style under the old woman's machine. He's see-through and chalk-colored and his toes and fingertips are on fire, twenty tiny flames burning bright in the dark. When he waves like to say hi his flames wave too, they lick the air between us, these orange-blue glows.

I'm Demarcus, he whispers, I'm not a boy anymore, he goes and I say Oh my, just like Evelyn, just like Sweetie.

You're a ghost, I say.

Ghosts aren't real, he goes.

Yes they are, I say.

Call me a thought form, he goes. Call me post-physical abstract expressionism, but don't call me a ghost. Ghosts aren't real. I don't believe in them.

Hold on a minute, wait a minute, are you a hologram? I say. Because one time I did a science unit on holograms and this all could be some trick.

Demarcus puts a see-through fire finger to his see-through lips and shushes me, says Shut up for a minute, don't wake up Marlene.

And you lied! I say. You're a liar, I go.

The one time he ever wrote back to me he said he was my age but his ghost looks at least two years older. You look real fucked up, I say. You're a boy, but only formerly.

To this he hoos sadly and moves his mouth like to speak but stops when he sees me staring. Instead of a tongue and teeth he's got a black hole, electric sparks buzzing where normally tonsils should be. I think: This is his hum, his electric Rice Krispies, the snap-crackle-pop where his ghost voice is made.

People who don't know one think ghosts are angel-food things. That they're white wispy floaters moaning soft for their crap, like O where is my golden trumpet? O where is my lost love? But now I watch Demarcus unfold and see all the jagged angles he is, all kneecaps and knuckles and sharp corners jutting. His skin's not skin, it's chalk that's transparent—in some places it's filled-in but in others it's way lighter, in some places it's disconnected lines and zigzags unfilled, the kind of coloring Sweetie's lesbo mom Leslie calls lazy to which I say Fuck you, Leslie, that's how I color.

He's ghost-white all over so his hair's the only place you can tell he was Black: heavy chalk curlicues scribbled thick and hard, like how Jeanie scribbles in the notebook where she keeps her dirt-bike friends' phone numbers, fat jaggy doodles of cobras striking drippy angel-winged dicks.

While I stand there jaw-dropped he floats out the room, one fire finger curling behind him like telling me to follow. So I follow him—not too close!—and poor Demarcus, god! Besides living in The Lonely dead and on fire, he's lopsided too, one ghost leg's longer.

Outside the bedroom his flames light up the hall and now I see all the things I missed before: a framed photo of cowgirls sitting sidesaddle on horses, a calligraphied diploma from Reverend Zetluna's Mystery School. In the living room he float-walks straight to the window, looks down forlornly at the old white people and their sidewalk piles.

How are you able to see me? he goes. No one has so far.

I see ghosts sometimes, I say and he says Please, call me a thought form.

But not all of them, I say. Really only one. How can you talk, how can you do things? I go, remembering how the apartment door opened on its own. Sister Regina doesn't open things and definitely can't speak, all she does is float through the walls trying to hug me. She also has no fire coming from her fingers and toes, only the smoke from the ghost fire that follows her.

I told you, I don't believe in ghosts, Demarcus says. I simply think about things and things move, he goes. I think certain things and my flames get bigger or smaller. If I think about things the right way I can do stuff with my mind.

What certain things, what do you think about? I say and he says Western mythology. Art history and its failings.

You're so weird, I say. I say You better not be a fucking hologram.

I swear on the blood of Pontos, he goes. Pontos, he says, is the mythological god of the sea.

I'm no dumbshit, I know he could be lying, but the feeling in my bones says Molly, believe. It's a feeling like twinkly Christmas lights wound around my gristle, a warm water feeling, a hot tub turned on inside me. For a moment I almost love the dead, that I'm made from their dust, my mom's stretch of yellow bones.

Okay, I believe you, who's the lady in the box? I say.

Here his ghost eyes roll to the top of his head. Madame Marlene in her Polio Machine, he says, Famous Spiritualist Medium in her Iron Lung of Otherworldly Vision. He says it with his voice all dumb-dumb old lady, almost as funny as me doing Evelyn.

I've been lending her my powers every Friday night since becoming post-physical, he says. She thinks she's legit now but she's still a sham, only now she doesn't know it.

Here his face goes all sad again. He turns and looks back out the window.

Lately it's really going to her head, he says.

So how does Marlene go to the bathroom? I ask him and he says Don't call her Marlene, call her Head On The Pillow.

Whatever her name is, I say, her life sucks shit bad, and right as I say it Demarcus turns back fast to me, his finger fires flaring.

Never feel bad for her, she loves the lung, he says.

Jeez, okay, don't have a cow, I say while outside the sky goes orange to night all at once. I look at him a long time then, like Is this shit for real, but he doesn't speak so finally I ask it.

Is this really for real? I say super serious and he says Why? Do you want me to show you?

I say Okay and here things get so fucking weird, he shoots fire out his eyes and into mine. Instead of my eyeballs catching fire or me falling down dead what happens is this entire new place appears. It's like this place I never noticed that's always been there now jumps itself fully formed into my vision. And at first it's all misty but then the mist clears and motherfucker, I'm not lying, it's the courtroom from *Night Court*. It's the empty *Night Court* set, no one except Roz by the bench, her in her regular bailiff suit except not black, it's golden.

And for real, I'm not lying, it's more vivid and beautiful than anything I've ever seen ever and even though I'm no lesbo I truly get now Helen's thing for her. Right now Roz is the most beautiful being I've ever seen, but the feeling underneath is that *everyone* is this beautiful.

Then it gets weirder, it's like somehow my mind gets tickled separate from my body and shut the fuck up, don't fucking make fun of me, but I feel a love like I've never imagined, so much and so hard and it includes me even. So I'm crying now, fuck! because I don't know, I'm that fucking happy apparently, and then Roz goes Order, order in the court. She goes Someone's here to see you, Molly.

My mind scans the possibilities—Bruce? my dead mom?—but then who comes out in judge's robes but freshly dead Helen.

She doesn't look dead, though! She looks like herself but better. She's like Hello, Molly, good to see you again, meanwhile I'm all What the fuck? Is this heaven?

Helen winks at Roz. It's not hell, she says smiling. Roz says Better hurry, Helen.

Helen turns back to me and says she'll get to the point quickly, she says she really needs me to tell Leslie and Sweetie she loves them. Tell them I love them the way you're feeling it right now, Helen says. They won't understand, but try to tell them.

Before I can say Okay or Hell no or Whatevs, the courtroom starts glitching like cable going out and Demarcus in his living room breaks back into my vision. The last thing I hear Helen say is that I should watch out for myself, but before I can ask why she's gone and I'm back with the ghost of Demarcus in The Lonely.

Was it real? I say and he says I don't know. Maybe some of it, he says. I don't know, he goes.

It was my friend's dead mom, I say. She was like Molly, Molly, you're in danger, girl. She must have been trying to warn me about something.

That's from a movie, that's from *Ghost*, Demarcus says. That's magical negro Whoopi Goldberg warning trust fund artist Demi Moore grieving the gentrifying capitalist Patrick Swayze.

No it's not, I say.

Whatever, I don't care, was there anyone else? he asks me.

I tell him Roz from *Night Court* which makes him smile. Like Ha ha, yeah right, that's a good one.

Seriously, I say. Helen had a thing for her.

Usually the first person white kids see is Santa, he says.

Who did *you* see, I ask him, then remember he's here and not there.

At first I *was* there, he says, which I guess means he can mind-read, thought-hear.

I saw artists, he says. Basquiat and Schiele. I saw Francis Bacon and Victor Brauner and Andy Warhol.

Who the hell are they? Are they art gods? I say and he says

No, art monsters. They didn't know what they were in service to, he says. He asks me again if I saw anyone besides Roz and Helen, like maybe was it possible I saw my dead mom?

No! I say, surprised at my voice, out of nowhere hiked-up and back-off-ish. I told you, just Helen and Roz, I say.

Okay, he says. I believe you.

Why do you ask? I say. Can you make me see her?

I've never been able to control who shows up, he says. All I am is a receiver. I don't make the rules but my mom's dead too, and she's never haunted me either.

Wait, she's dead? What about all your brothers and sisters? I say. What about everything you said in the one letter you sent me?

Lies, he says. Untruths for Pontos, he goes, then he floats into the circle of the nine folding chairs and sits on his hands in the center. When he sits his finger fires smash down and burn low, ten birthday candles that now barely flicker.

I'm an only child, he says. No brothers or sisters. I used to live with my mom and grandmother on the fifth floor, my grandmother was Head On The Pillow's helper. Head On The Pillow let us stay here after Grandma died when I was four. My mother died when I was seven.

Why didn't you go live with your dad? I say. Oh wait, was he in prison?

Here he stares death at me and at first says nothing. Then he says I can't tell if you're racist or just dumb.

I'm definitely not dumb, I say, but why didn't you go live with him? For real, is he a gangbanger? Or what? I say.

That's a fucked-up thing to say, he says. He's a painter specializing in scientific illustration. Astronomical illustration for NASA, he goes.

So he's an artist too! I say and quick he says No! He's a fucking illustrator, he goes, his finger flames rising.

Jeez, I go. Touchy? So why didn't you go live with your fancy artist dad?

I never knew him, Demarcus says. He was in grad school when he met my mom. He had a side job doing manual illustrations for an iron lung manufacturer and came to do sketches of Head On The Pillow's lung. It's one of the oldest still in operation.

La-di-da, so how come you never met him, that's so weird, I say.

Let's talk about something else, he tells me.

So I ask how he died and he says he's killed living things. When I ask was it a gang fight or an AIDS needle or a drive-by, he calls me provincial and bigoted and shakes his head sadly.

Demarcus, you need my help, you're so mothereffing sad, I say. I say I promise I'll help you find the light. Here I drop my voice soft and shushy, tell him everything's going to be okay. I go to pat his hand how Evelyn patted mine one time, but with him mine falls through and I pat the floor instead.

Now that I'm here, I say, things won't be so crappy. We'll still go to the Fair, I say. Because in all my letters I promised.

Seeing him like this, so sad and ghosty, it's hard not to turn his face into the boy I'd imagined, all the little movies of him I'd made in my head. Him switchblading Vice Lords and stealing their drug money, him mouthboxing sick beats while braiding his sisters' hair. Now all those movies break apart and disintegrate the same way your dead mom in a photo you soaked in puppet glue disappears. How soaked in anything a picture will eat itself and eat itself until it's the same thing as there never being the thing in the picture there.

Thanks I guess, he says, his face like he doesn't believe it, and here I go with my finger to touch his hair. In part because I've imagined before having someone touch my hair, but also in part to see whether it feels like real Black person's hair.

What happens is I erase him some. Only a little and only in spots, but enough to see through to where his brain should be. Instead of a brain there's a fist-wad of sparks, tiny burning fires like gnats set ablaze. I think: This is how his ghost thoughts are made. His voice is electric but his thoughts are flames.

Don't touch my hair, who does that, what's wrong with you? he says. Then he says Listen, I need to be working right now. You can read me my book while I work, he says, then yawns so big the corners of his mouth fade away.

What work, what book? I say and he points to the kitchen.

Under the sink, it's my studio, he goes, then like to show off he uses his mind to open the cabinet.

I get up to look and he's right, there's art stuff there, Big Gulp cups of brushes and Miracle Whip jars of turpentine. There's a pillow and blanket and a book called *A Hundred Myths of the Sea*, a drawing of a crocodile-man taped to the ceiling. A fat brass ring goes through its green-shingled snout, but its muscled man-arm raises a sword skyward.

That's so fucking awesome, I say. Before I can ask if it's traced or freehand Demarcus is there next to me, folding himself smaller and smaller. He drifts into the cabinet the size of a cat, unfurls halfway and pulses his flames.

Time to make art, he says then sees me staring at the crocodile-man. He says That's just my dumb juvenilia. Your job is to read this book, he says so I squish in the cabinet beside him, hang my foot out the door.

At first this is going to be really bright, he says pulsing and I'm like Okay, shut up, give me the book.

It's going to be really, really bright, he says and then he does something I'm not at all expecting. There's a wumph of ignition and he explodes himself in light and somehow he makes himself into his own lantern. It dumps the cabinet dark in blinding white light and only now do I see what he's really painting: foam-mouthed Minotaurs and bare-titted mermaids, oiled-chest cyclopes riding the shoulders of sea gods with horse crotches. It's a kind of mural, an under-the-sink mural, all blacks and pinks and corals and blues. And scattered all over's painted the same black stick-figure, sometimes holding hands with a grinning goat that walks upright, sometimes riding on top of a crawling skeleton. Wherever the stick figure is there are tiny words underneath: Bleeding Bloodletter, Orphaned Herbivore, Bag of Wounds Who Deserves This.

Demarcus, oh my god, this is badass supreme! I say while his flames small down until they're burning regular. It's just like Jeanie's T-shirts, I say.

Listen, he says, I just need you to read the book, he says, pointing to *A Hundred Myths of the Sea*, which now is pulsing this green-blue color. I go to pick it up and he says Careful! Watch it! Don't crease the pages. My mom gave that to me.

Whatever, I say and start at the beginning, Chapter One, Oceanus: The Titan God of the Great Earth River, the horse-crotched fount of all clouds, lakes, and streams. I settle in and read to him about Oceanus plus his little incest kids the Oceanids, how they ruled every river that separated Earth from Hades.

The whole time I read he hovers and listens, it's like he's waiting for a certain word, for something to ping. I read him a story about how Orion, son of Neptune and Euryale, got drunk and raped Merope, daughter of Oenopion and Helike. Then Orion fell asleep and that badass Merope stabbed his eyes out, left him blind to search the Earth for a child to guide him.

The only cure for blindness is to stare into the sun, Demarcus says and I say What the fuck does that even mean?

But he doesn't answer because here he finally gets to painting. Using his finger flames as brushes he paints and I read, but still even now I'm secretly watching.

He flame-paints a house with fire bursting out the windows and in front a girl with her hair wind-machined like in *Firestarter*. The girl's got a hand up like Bitches don't fuck with me and on her hand he adds a flaming red scar the shape of infinity. At the bottom he writes Molly Never-Ending, the Horrifying Daughter of Sharon and Steve. I'm practically crapping myself I'm so fucking happy.

That is the best, that is so awesome! I say and he says I don't know, it's actually kind of stupid. I'll probably paint over it tomorrow, he goes, then asks me why I stopped reading.

By the end of Chapter Two, Amphitrite, the goddess-queen of fish, snails, and dolphins, runs away from the perv-moves of her future husband Poseidon. Demarcus's finger flames are burned down to embers now, flicker orange-black-orange, on and off slow. His eyes are half closed and his brain sparks are tiny—flashing pinpricks of light, faraway stars.

I think: This is how a ghost artist falls asleep when he's tired.

I think: This is how easy my best friend sleeps when I'm here.

And now between her whooshes Head On The Pillow's snores come through the wall, floating. Her machine's hypnotic, it's why she sleeps and sleeps. It's why now even me, nap-trapped under this cabinet and yawning, my eyes start fluttering and I'm falling asleep.

When I wake up I'll ask Demarcus to come home with me. I'll take him home on the Metra back to Cal City, tell Dad and Evelyn I got snatched at the mall in the parking lot, how a pervy thug kidnapped me all the way to Bronzeville and then how Demarcus's ghost rescued me here. That thundercunt Jeanie will eat her words but for now I'll close my eyes because this pillow, it's like a real pillow (it is a real pillow), and because now Demarcus is a pulsing light drifting next to my head. I'm yawning and there's drips from the sink faucet above us and the snoring whooshes floating through the wall behind us and together the both of us, the glub-glub of our hearts (but there's only one heart, it's mine, it's under a sink and I'm thinking Words, Jeanie, Eat Them and I'm seeing Jeanie with a plate of them, her with a fork and me yawning at her) and now I'm thinking Now you sleep, Molly, now you go asnooze, so I pull my leg inside the cabinet and rest my knees against the pipe and even before Demarcus shuts the door with his mind, before his mural around us goes dark forest dark, in my head I'm thinking I'm sleeping now, I'm sleeping, and then all at once I am.

THREE

It's late at night when I get back to House of Friends. Demarcus doesn't come with me, he doesn't like fun and adventure. I woke up stiff under the sink and said Hey over and over while his ball of light got bigger until it was finally him. Hey, I said, hey, you should come back with me. You should come to my house, you don't have to stay here.

He shook his head no and so quiet I could barely hear what he said, he said Her séances are Fridays. I have to be here.

Séances? Fuck those. Séances? I said. You're dead, you can do whatever. It's not like she's your mom, I said.

Friday night's séance night, he said, his fingertips sparking, and I said Well if you won't come with me at least tell me how you died. And if they hid your body tell me where it's hid, I said.

He floated to the living room and spun circles into smoke and then when the smoke settled back into him he thanked me for coming. He said Sorry, Friday night's séance night one last time then disappeared in a flash of tiny fireworks and then the apartment door ghost-opened.

When I get home Dad and Evelyn are fretting in the kitchen, Evelyn by the phone, a raggy Kleenex snaked through her fingers. She sees me walk in and thanks God a thousand times while Dad shuts his eyes and puts his sunglasses on.

Of course next they're in my face, all Where were you, where have you been? and I'm like, Guys, shut up, calm down, I'll tell you the whole story.

My story is genius, I thought it up on the train: in the mall I'd bolted only to pee but then got snatched up by this crazy lady. This lady, I tell them, had had a daughter my same age who'd been murdered one year ago on this exact day. So when she saw me by Orange Julius the lady snapped and went crazy, she snatched me up and took me home with her and fed me Jell-O all day. She called me Little Sheila and gave me presents and baked a cake, then she made me hold her hand until she passed out from crying. That was a few hours ago, when I sneaked out and got away.

Hey, where's Jeanie at? I say, but all they do is look at me.

I say Don't worry guys, I'm okay. Hey, where's Jeanie?

At the dirt bike track, Evelyn says suddenly grumpy, grabbing the phone to call the police. She doesn't even tell them about the awesome crazy lady I invented, only that I came home safe.

But who cares if they believe me because, what, are they my public? Are they an awesome ghost artist with a studio in Bronzeville? Are they my new best friend, see-through and floaty?

Next Evelyn comes over next to me and asks do I want any ice cream. I tell her no, say I'm so full from all the cake and Jell-O that all I want is to go to bed.

Upstairs Sister Regina's ghost bobs up and down, frowns on the landing. I check her for tiny fires, but there aren't any there. She gives me a scoldy look and doesn't try to hug me, then in my room I draw crocodile-men and eat Doritos while I listen for Jeanie's bike.

It's after midnight when I hear her, the vroom of her engine, the slam of the kitchen door. Her Keds on the stairs fast and heavy then her boom box switched on.

I'm out of bed so fast, knocking on her door with orange knuckles. She answers with eyes like machine guns but I don't effing care. I say Thunderbitch, I found Demarcus! He's a ghost but it counts, I got you!

I put my hand on my hip super sassy, tell her even dead he's still alive.

Jeanie grabs my arm and pulls me into her bedroom. She shoves me and then kicks me then points to her open closet door. I told you never touch it! she hisses, pushing me to the floor.

Ked on my throat, she whispers Motherfucker, tell me. Tell me right fucking now where my black box is.

I say I don't know, I didn't touch it! Please don't hit me, Jeanie! Please don't! I go.

She says If you're lying I'll kill Evelyn and pushes her steel toe down.

I'm not lying! I say, choking. I'm not an effing liar! I go.

The Lord detests lying lips, she says and I say But he delights in people who are trustworthy!

She lets up and I push her Ked off and I'm like Jesus fucking Christ. You could have hurt me! I go.

I walk back to my room sore, disappointed in Jeanie's sportsmanship. Maybe tomorrow she'll want to hear about Demarcus. Maybe she'll find her box wherever she left it. Maybe in the morning she'll feel better, but until then I'm locking my bedroom door.

FOUR

We go to Helen's funeral, splendid and bleak. We go again door to door about community gardening, speak to ladies in their apartments about organic community dirt. Every day Jeanie goes out dirt bike riding for hours then comes home again each night mud-flecked and mean. She wears sunglasses now, even at nighttime, the kind with mirrored lenses you can see yourself in. One night I'm side-crouched to spy under her door crack and I see her still wearing sunglasses as she gets into bed.

The day before Thanksgiving Dad comes up from the basement. He's smiling with his sunglasses off, it's all him and his face. Why not let's all go for ice cream, he says. I'm feeling good, no clouds in my vision!

So me and Jeanie and him and Evelyn head to the carport. What a sweater! he says to Evelyn when it's just her dumb cat one.

Evelyn gets in front and Jeanie takes the back, puts her legs up on the seat so only she can ride there. I take the middle row and sit the same way, expect Dad to yell about it, but he doesn't, he's so happy.

It's because of his new puppet concept, George Fox the fox. George is the founder of the woodland animal Quakers and lives in the Forest of Quiet where he teaches kids about where God dwells. Dad says the grant people are going to love it so bad. George is going to buy us a new roof, he says, then all the way to Dairy Queen he sings "Wayfaring Stranger."

Outside it's almost dark, but the dome light's stuck on and I wonder what we look like to all the things we pass. To the stray sidewalk kitties and the Mexican lawn guys are we a brightness? A thing to notice? Something glowing on patrol? Or are we just see-through, dumb and unmattering, a box of not-afire ghosts ghost-driving an empty van. When we get to Dairy Queen the guy says they're closing, so we take our cones out to the sidewalk and lick them braced against the blow.

Dad asks Jeanie how things are going with Debbie and Jeanie says Debra and he says Yeah, her.

Jeanie scratches her arm and says things are fine. She's got her cone held close and her sunglasses on. She looks over her shoulder again and again.

No one's going to steal your stupid ice cream, I say, then Evelyn wants to go for a drive so we go home the long way, by the fancy brick houses then the field with the cows. The whole time I've got my head against the van window thinking: What's in the future? What will tomorrow hold? Will Evelyn have a heart attack, might Dad be re-struck blind? If I had a Ouija board would the ghost of Demarcus write me and will I ever really go to the Fair with him and Jeanie? I try to picture a day where all this happens, one thing then the next, like dominoes. The thought of it makes me so delirious my eyes cross from the smiling.

Then, to my left, above a field with no cows, there's something big, lit, a bright bulb of neon. The hot air balloon! It's the hot air balloon! The one from the zoo, the same flamed monster trucks beneath it.

A sign says Tethered Balloon Rides $5.

Dad, Dad, PLEASE! I say and he winks at me in the mirror. Sounds like fun to me, he says and then to Evelyn, How about it?

Evelyn grins girly and goes Okey-dokey while Jeanie rolls her eyes and Dad parks the van. I jump out so fast, fly to the one-armed man selling tickets. He's got a beer koozie in his hand and around his stump twirls the wheel of tickets.

Are we too late? Are you closing? We'll pay extra, I say, the whole time checking over my shoulder to make sure Jeanie's coming. The one-armed man asks how many and I say Four please, extra polite. The one-armed man sets his beer down carefully then puts his hand out for the money.

I point at Dad coming up behind me, say He's got the cash because already I'm moving toward the light of the monster trucks, letting the Guns N' Roses from their roof speakers wash over me.

While we wait for the balloon to come down Jeanie's all weird and keeps checking her jean bag. She takes out a smoke over and over again but never lights it and instead drops it back in. Each time she pulls it out Evelyn makes a face like Nasty nasty but Dad doesn't notice, he's whistling "Welcome to the Forest of Quiet" to the one-armed man.

Finally the balloon comes down for our turn, gets almost to the ground but hovers a few feet off it. The basket's full of assholes, cheery-cheeked, windy-haired. The assholes wave like assholes while a bearded man unlatches the basket.

When one of them steps out, one of you of approximate equal weight steps in, he says, and on my turn it's this preteen kid I stare down as we trade places.

Inside the balloon basket it's way bigger than it looks. There's a bench all around the sides plus the whole thing's carpeted. In the middle the bearded guy stands at the control panel, puts on a white cap like a sea captain's hat. He jiggers some knobs then winks at Jeanie then bows and says I am your pilot, Madame.

His face is cool and wind-chipped, his beer koozie grip-torn, but I wish he wasn't here and that Dad and Evelyn were gone. That it was just me and Jeanie up in the night, no monster trucks lighting the earth below us, no nylon ropes tethering us to the ground.

After Jeanie sits he latches the basket then starts fussing with the knobs that control the flames. Evelyn and Dad act all thrilled and giggly, devil-may-care is what Evelyn would say. Jeanie holds her jean purse close to her body, watches the pilot closely, shakes her head.

Isn't it too windy? Isn't it too cold? she asks him.

Well maybe you should have worn a heavier jacket, I tell her. This isn't Kansas anymore, I say.

Dad's all Girls, girls, let's enjoy God's beauty! then the balloon begins to lift slow. I close my eyes and pinch my wrists, think Remember this, remember this. Remember this night, the fire of it, the float.

The pilot turns the flames higher and the heat blows warm on my neck. Evelyn grabs the edge of the basket next to me and says Tomorrow for science unit let's do something on balloons. When I turn to say Evelyn, shut the fuck up, don't ruin this, I see Jeanie in back of us in the back of the basket, her pulling Donna the bolt cutters out of her purse.

I'm the only one who sees what's happening.

The pilot's busy with the flames and Evelyn's watching them, probably remembering the last time she saw her Bruce, him crying Mama on the stairs, him on fire running down them. Dad's tapping his foot, his bare eyes shining, him not even here, him in an imaginary fox forest singing.

By the time the balloon's five feet in the air, Jeanie's got Donna through the first of the three tethers.

Everyone out! Jump the fuck out! she shouts, but it's windy and no one hears her so she says it again louder.

I'm grinning so big, I'm thinking Fuck yeah! then Evelyn sees what's happening and then the pilot goes Abandon!

Evelyn unlatches the basket and jumps to the ground which makes us shoot up another five feet like a rocket. Then both Dad and the pilot hop over the side and by now Jeanie's cut the second tether. She comes toward me for the third and I tell her I've dreamed this and now she's grabbing me under my armpits, lifting me high.

Goodbye Kittentits, she says. Goodbye, Thunderbrow.

And the next thing I know is I'm falling.

FIVE

THANKSGIVING DAY ALL DAY they find scraps of balloon and burnt wicker, mostly in the fields near the zoo, sooty black and tattered yellow. But still no sign of Jeanie. The one-armed man and the pilot went after her in the monster trucks but lost sight when the balloon went over some trees on a hill. Like she'd been swallowed by the night, the one-armed man said. Like the night ate her, the one-armed man told me.

Now they're searching trees and bushes for a dead broken body, even Dad and Evelyn out in the van. Even the guys from the dirt bike track ride low along ditches and gullies. Debra her P.O. was cautious and put out a three-state alert: armed and dangerous white female, possibly injured, approach with caution.

I want to be out looking, but I don't get to. Instead for Thanksgiving Dad makes me go to Sweetie's. When Sweetie's mom Leslie says to say what we're thankful for, Sweetie says gymnastics and Leslie says love from beyond the grave and then they both look at me and at first I don't say anything. Then I say I don't know. Flames. Bolt cutters.

I definitely don't give them the message Helen gave me. I'd sound so crazy. I'd sound fucking dumb.

After the turkey I sit back and puff a carrot stick like I'm smoking it. I'm thinking Jeanie's probably holed up in the zoo. I'll go there each free day and check for dirty Keds under the toilet stalls. I'll count the number of chickens in the petting zoo week to week. Maybe not the first time, but if I keep going I know I'll find her, badass among the wolves, maybe, or with the zebras or giraffes. She'll be a new wilder Jeanie: Jeanie of the big-dick lemurs, Jeanie of the poisonous snakes. Jeanie not of the dirt bike track anymore. Not of House of Friends, not of people anymore. Her finger snakes will pulse with rats, she'll be lit up, she'll glow. Come here! Come here! she'll say when she sees me, and I will, I'll come there. I'll do whatever.

Probably we'll run away together then.

Leslie claps her hands to bring me out of my dreaming, says Okay, you guys, you two layabouts you, now it's time to move your bodies!

She gives Sweetie a look like Tubs get to it, then turns to me like she's going to say something but then doesn't say it. Instead she says if we need her she's scrapbooking in the den. She's working on a giant new one of her and Helen.

Move your bodies is Leslie's code for Sweetie to do Cats in Motion. It's Sweetie hopping around their family room to a tape of jumping pervs in neon cat costumes. Leslie makes her do it every day. There's a tabby cat and a black cat and a prissy white one with a bow. They skip in place and hold their hands like paws and twitch their tails a lot between the songs.

Cats in Motion! Cats in Motion! Cats in Motion! Sweetie says, and I say Bitch, you know I'm no fur burger.

I follow her to the family room anyway and help her with the VCR. I'll watch from over here, I say, pointing to the pink monogrammed beanbag in the corner. I'll be the judge, I'll score you, I say, and she says Okay, but you have to score me!

Sweetie gets out her pink exercise mat and puts on the cat mask that came with the tape. I flop sad on the beanbag and sigh and groan, chain-puff Leslie's carrot stick. The first song on the tape's "How Much Is That Doggy in the Window," so for fun I hiss when the cats go Bark then Sweetie fake-claws at me like to cat-claw my face and it's all I can do not to tell her she's a no-talent pussy. That if I put my mind to it I could dance like a dumbass cat. That I could do gymnastics, even. But no way would I ever because my mom was a Real Artist who I'd want to be proud of me, not work-for-hire hacks like Leslie and Helen.

But if I said that it'd be Time For Me To Leave for sure, so instead at the end I give her all nines and eight point fives, add one point extra for difficulty.

On the coffee table they've got the same Fair brochure I've got, so when Pepsi waddles in later to sniff my crotch I sit her upright and move her paw around the Fair map.

Pepsi, look, here's Autotopia, I say. And over there, that's Arcadium. And look, I say, pushing her wet snout to the center, That's the World and the Sea. That's where each different country has a fancy pavilion.

I tell her how the pavilions go around the Sea of International Waters and about the glass elevator going down to the Submarine Palace. I tell her about the live corpse reanimation they're doing on New Year's, that they're bringing back to life the Sleeping Silent Princess. I keep talking and talking and soon I'm telling her about the hot air balloon, how I looked up to the darkening sky to watch it disappear from where I landed. I tell her about Demarcus and Head On The Pillow in Bronzeville, her whooshing in her machine, him blinding me with his ghost light in the cabinet.

And the Submarine Palace has to be pressurized, I say, squinting because suddenly my eyes are wet. If I wanted to cry I would, I'm no pussy, but what if somehow Jeanie is watching? What if where she's hiding she's got her brain tuned in to mine, knowing everything I think, seeing everything I'm doing? What if she's about to send me a thought message but sees me crying and is like Fuck it, I'm not wasting an important thought message on a baby like that.

One tear gets away and trickles down my nose, but I sniff it in fast, a snot rope recoiling. Now Pepsi's asleep and drooling on the map, breathing soft snores, butt-puffing spongy farts. Sweetie's doing her knee-lifts, she's meowing to the beat, and finally I understand something about the Fair: I'm the only one it even matters to. I'm the only one who even cares about going.

SIX

THE NEXT MORNING IS FRIDAY morning and Evelyn doesn't give me my math test. Dad and her get to go be interviewed at the police station instead. On their way out Dad tells me to bag up Jeanie's things, but as soon as they're gone I fill the trash bags with my own shit: stuffed animal bats and pop-stained tees, the Adolescent Lamb Holy Bible Dad gave me.

Then everything in Jeanie's room I put in my room. I shove it all in my closet, no one looks there. I'm hauling the last of her T-shirt bags through the hallway when I hear it: the vroom of dirt bike outside near the carport, her trademark triple rev.

I run downstairs fast, Sister Regina flying above me, fling myself out the kitchen door barefoot, no coat. I peel out toward the carport shouting Jeanie! Jeanie! but it's not Jeanie, it's this guy, so I yell Get off her bike!

Here out of nowhere this guy's trying to steal it, this fat kid in a Packers jacket, not even eighteen. He doesn't hear me, just keeps revving and revving, so I shout Stop asshole, stop! and throw snow clods at his feet.

Little girl, what the hell? he says when he sees me.

That's not your bike, I say. Get the fuck off it right now.

It was stolen from me, he says and I say You're a liar. I say It's Jeanie's bike and I'm calling fucking Debra. I'm calling the pigs right fucking now.

Cool it, little girl. That bitch is my ex, he goes. This bike was never hers, it belongs to me.

Mangus? I say, at first not believing, but then he's like What? Does she talk about me?

Mangus is not at all how I'd pictured. He's not tall and skinny, he's tall and fat. Seeing him for real is like seeing an imaginary creature, like going to the bathroom and finding the Loch Ness Monster taking a crap.

I say Jeanie says you're an asshole and he says Jeanie's a motherfucking liar. Jeanie's not even her real name, he says.

I'm serious, leave the bike or when she gets back we'll come after you. It won't be pretty, it'll be ugly, I say.

She's never coming back, the witch is dead, the lying fatass Mangus tells me. Sorry for your loss, he says backing into the street. Before he drives off he shouts something but I can't hear it. I think maybe what he shouted was Jeanie's real name.

When Dad and Evelyn get home Debra comes in behind them. I'm supposed to bring down Jeanie's things for her to put in her trunk. She says to call when we're ready for a new Resident Friend from the Department of Probation and Dad says Will do! but Evelyn's shaking her head.

I carry the bags to Debra's car where she turns to look at me. She snaps her gum loud and says Girlie, I've got my eyes on you.

Well ha ha, Debra. It's sacks of *my* crap in the back of your red Ford Festiva. You're a lady Santa in reverse, the joke's on fucking you.

After soy burgers Evelyn gives me a new Civil Rights Word Find, all the words in bold from *Hello, World!* Unit Ten. *Hello, World!*'s the one real textbook Evelyn uses for homeschooling, she got it used from Leslie when Sweetie's school bought the new one. She likes it for the Teacher's Guide that comes with all the word finds and I like it for what's drawn in the margins in colored pen: humping cartoon cats and springy penis bunnies, fat bubble letters spelling Fart-Fart and Mr. Poo. Inside the back cover is a stamped grid with each kid who's ever used it: Tammy Donahue, Misty Morris, Steve Hassback, Stephanie Nguyen.

I finger down the names and see at the very bottom Molly Quacker. My heart skips a beat. I'd recognize Jeanie's writing anywhere. For Date Issued she wrote The Past and for Date Returned she wrote The Future. For Condition she drew a skull and crossbones and wrote Kittentits Was Here.

When did she do it? Before Halloween or after? But who cares, it doesn't matter, reading it makes it like she's right next to me. Like she's poking my kidneys and messing my hair up, whispering Molly, you're so bitchin' super close in my ear. I can smell her, she smells like motor oil, and now she's lighting *Hello, World!* on fire. She's whispering Molly, come find me, we'll *kill* that fucking fair.

I can hear the paper burn and I can feel her lip twitch. Dad and Evelyn can talk about her in the living room as if she's not right here, but as long as I see her words I feel her whispering.

I finished my word find! I shout all the sudden to the living room. I'm going to Sweetie's! I yell, because wherever I am no one seems to care.

I grab my coat and Liesel's Visa and then I'm out the door running. Until I find Jeanie, I'm not coming back here.

SEVEN

By two o'clock I'm on the top floor of The Lonely, but this time Demarcus doesn't open the door with his mind. I turn the knob myself and hear Head On The Pillow's windy whooshing which means I didn't imagine it: there's a psychic lady in an iron lung inside. Meaning somewhere nearby floating is the ghost of Demarcus, his finger flames turned way down, no doubt, on pause until I arrive.

Demarcus? I say, because where the fuck is he? I check behind the living room curtains and in the cabinet under the sink. I'm about to tiptoe to the bedroom in case he's hiding under Head On The Pillow when suddenly through her door bursts this really big Black guy. He's fat and wearing scrubs and pushing a cherry-red vacuum cleaner. He doesn't see me in the dimness, he's bent over to plug in the cord. He's vacuuming the hall while I'm shouting Hey and waving my arms at him, jumping up and down doing jumping jacks shouting Hey, over here!

After a while he looks up, cups his ear like going Sorry? Then switches off the vacuum and says Sorry, the vacuum was on. Like no biggie for a little white girl to randomly show up in this tragic apartment. No biggie for her to waltz right inside and stand here.

I said hey, I say and he just smiles like Keep going, but instead of asking about Demarcus I say Hey, I heard tonight there's a séance here.

That's right, he says and then I ask if I can stay for it.

Madame Marlene welcomes all, he says bowing. You're early, though, he says. I'm not done getting ready.

What's your name? I say and he says Nurse Le Feb.

And you're early, he goes. You here to contact a dead grandmother?

Sure, I say. I don't say a word about Demarcus. Sometimes the smartest thing you can do is play dumb.

Nurse Le Feb looks over his shoulder to where Head On The Pillow's room is loud with whooshing. Those are the sounds of Madame, he goes.

Then slow and soft like he's speaking to a tard he says Madame's a very special person with a very special lung. He says normally lungs pump inside you but that's not how it is with Madame, that when she was just a little white girl like I am, polio broke her lungs. He goes on and on about iron lungs and intubations, says her lung will be in a museum after the Summerland calls her home.

She's a very important person, he says in summary, super serious. I'd let you meet her now but she's resting, he goes.

That's okay, I say, I met her once already. Because no way I'm going back there with Nurse Black Guy alone.

I helped her with her straw, I say, but Le Feb's gone back to the vacuum, popping the handle now.

Like I told you, you're early, he says. Make yourself at home.

I look around for signs of Demarcus, a ball of white light, flickering flames.

I haven't even bought the donuts yet, Nurse Le Feb goes.

I've got so many dead people to talk to I had to get here early, I tell him.

Madame will do her best, he goes.

I take a seat in the folding chair circle while he vacuums the room fast and another time going slow, sucking up each one of the orange rug's tassels then pulling them out smooth and flat. Then he dusts the folding chairs and the Casio keyboard, then from Head On The Pillow's room a bell tinkles and he goes to get her her tea.

Madame's feeling strong today, he says when he comes back a few minutes later. The transmissions will be clear! he says, a smile frozen on my face like I'm effing Little Debbie.

Because who cares about transmissions when where the fuck is Demarcus?

Why didn't he tell me about this Le Feb guy and where's the mystical séance shit? The crystal balls and Ouija boards, the donuts Le Feb keeps saying? My belly's snarling, I'm so effing hungry, but I keep sitting here all quiet watching this gaytard Le Feb walk around with his dust cloth spraying Pledge on shit.

After an hour of this finally Demarcus phantomizes in front of me.

He looks much better than the last time I saw him, the white scribbles of his ghost body way more filled in. I say Hey! real loud because the sight of him phantomizing surprises me, but also because I'm happy to see him again.

Le Feb stops stringing Christmas lights around the chair circle to look at me, his face all Hmm? What did you say?

Then it's true, I'm the only one who can see him. Demarcus's finger fires are flickering bright, but Nurse Le Feb looks only at me.

I wave a little white-girl wave, this wave like Oh, nothing. Le Feb goes back to cleaning and Demarcus floats to the window to stare at the piles.

He's not a real nurse anymore, he's her servant, he says. Tell him a vision led you here.

His face is serious, like You better fucking do it, so I say Hey, Nurse Le Feb, did I tell you a vision led me here?

Here Nurse Le Feb stops what he's doing, which is wiping his huffed breath off a dark purple vase. Visions are important, he says, almost whispering.

I didn't say anything before because I didn't really know you, I say, but yeah, it was this awesome vision that led me here.

Le Feb looks at me, waiting, so I turn to Demarcus, but he just stares out the window like in some sad trance. I close my eyes to think better and then all at once it comes to me. I was sitting on the porch of my orphanage, I say.

I was sitting on my orphanage porch counting my blessings, I say, when suddenly the sky went all purple and thundery and then everywhere it smelled like donuts and then everything went black.

Then I saw this apartment, I say, and here I point to the carpet. And then I heard the iron breath of Madame Marlene.

Whoosh-whoosh-whoosh, it went, but I understood it in words, like her speaking. And the words said Little girl, come see me in Bronzeville. Come visit my magic ghetto apartment where the donuts and séances are free.

Here Le Feb's eyes are wide like he's legit considering what I'm saying.

And in the next part of the vision, I say, I saw you, Nurse Le Feb. I saw a tall strong African American male nurse being so nice to me. It was this same apartment, these same Christmas lights, I know it, only I was eating donuts and bacon and drinking SunnyD. And you were over there, I say, pointing to the kitchen. I think you were over there frying more bacon for me.

Le Feb nods then says A vision is a vision. He grabs his jacket and his wallet and Demarcus says See?

EIGHT

A SÉANCE IS NOT WHAT I THOUGHT it was. I thought it was a round table draped with dusty rugs, old-timey people holding ringed fingers in the dark. Maybe a scarfed gypsy, swoony or growling, probably the table going up and down on its own. Probably shadows on the wall the shape of trumpets or bats maybe. But that is not a séance at all.

After I eat the donuts and bacon Nurse Le Feb brings me, without thinking I ask if I can see some of Demarcus's things.

You knew Demarcus? he asks, his head whipping fast to look at me.

He was in the vision, I say. What a tragic tragedy, I go.

Le Feb nods slowly but tells me nothing. There's some of his stuff in the hall closet, he goes.

From the closet he pulls out a grocery sack holding paint tubes and colored pencils, some sea god doodling on used envelopes, two sea god books. There's a sketch pad where over and over he was drawing a pirate and a cartoon turtle, his application for grading by experts at the mail-away Art Instruction School. But the most interesting stuff of all clinks together at the bottom: a handful of glass eyes, mostly brown, a few blue.

Demarcus hovers close here, his fires high and glowing. Don't touch those, put those back! he goes, but I pretend not to hear.

What were these for? I ask Le Feb and he says Those were his mother's. She worked for an ocularist, she painted glass eyes, he says. Those small ones there are Demarcus's.

I find the two small ones—dark brown with flecks of black. I didn't know he didn't have eyes, I say and Le Feb laughs. He did, he says, she made those for practice.

Put those back, those aren't yours, Demarcus ghost-shouts at me, but I don't, I ignore him, look only at Le Feb. So how exactly did Demarcus die? I ask him.

Here of course strange noises start up from Head On The Pillow, high twangy yelps between the normal long whooshing. At first I think Oh my god she's dying! but then realize it's her trying to sing.

She's ready, Le Feb says. Time to get going, he goes, then switches the Christmas lights wound around his Casio stand to blinking.

Right after that a lady shows up at the door. Not some neighborhood lady, but like a bank lady or a real estate lady. Like maybe a lady who works in a jewelry store. She's got black high heels and red sheeny lipstick, thick cushy thighs I bet curve nice into a lap. She folds her coat over the folding chair next to my folding chair then nods hi to Le Feb like she's been here before. Le Feb's fussing with the Casio now and no one speaks except in my head, Demarcus. He's rolling in and out of himself, balling all up then unfolding again and again. Pontos, Pontos, speak through me, he says.

One by one, people show up for the séance. A tubby white guy in a Sonic Drive-In shirt, this old Mexican lady in pink boots. Next another fat white guy with skin near see-through who takes a seat then fast-taps his feet. I say hi to everyone, I'm like Hi, my name's Molly, but it must be a rule or something because people nod but don't speak. Nurse Le Feb passes out orange juice in Dixie cups and Head On The Pillow's weird yodeling gets louder, like she's getting closer and closer when I know that can't be.

Finally Demarcus unfolds for good and stops with the Pontos stuff. He stretches in front of the window and does jumping jacks like warming up for a sport. No one but me sees him ghost-exercising, Nurse Le Feb even sticks his arm through his neck when he pulls the curtains shut. His feet fires keep jogging in place under the curtain hems, but the curtains don't catch, so I guess ghost flames aren't real ones.

With the curtains closed there's no light but Demarcus's fires and the Christmas lights, the pinprick constellations of Le Feb's Casio. Everyone's all hushed and still, watching our wall shadows swimming, us sitting on our fists rocking but our shadows floating steady. Us waiting for-effing-ever to talk to the dead while our shadows hover quiet in dark aquarium light. The Mexican lady rolls her ankle in a circle counterclockwise and the Sonic guy picks his nose like nobody's looking but I am. He bets it's too dark for anyone to see, but my eyes are like cats' eyes, they see everything. One by one he wipes the boogers on his knee and one by one I count how many.

Nurse Le Feb goes to the Casio like Let's get this thing started, puts on a slow auto-beat. He pulls a can of air freshener from out of his back pocket and sprays three shots of a flower smell that makes the Mexican lady sneeze. Next he disappears into the back of the apartment where Head On The Pillow still whooshes and sings. The sound of it sunk into my brain where I'd almost forgotten it, I bet that's how it is all the time for Demarcus and Le Feb.

He's bringing her out now, Demarcus says, either inside my head or from his mouth, I can't tell. For the record, he says, floating out from the curtains finally, performance art is bullshit and I don't believe in it. Then there's the sound of loud clanking and whooshing plus Head On The Pillow's weird singing coming down the hall. Next Le Feb's pushing Head On The Pillow headfirst into the living room chair circle, the iron lung ablink in twinkle lights, the red velvet curtain skirt sweeping the floor. Head On The Pillow's cheeks are pinker and she's wearing a cowboy hat and magenta lipstick. Someone put silver glitter around her eyes.

Here everyone stands and clap clap claps for her, so I stand and clap too, I even shout Hooray. Le Feb jogs her one lap around the clapping circle then parks her in the center and we all wait for Head On The Pillow to speak.

Good Evening—whoosh—my living rodeo—whoosh. Pray tonight's transmissions—whoosh whoosh—are clear—whoosh—and strong.

I look around and see everyone's holding hands now and that Le Feb behind the Casio is looking at me. I grab the hand of the bank lady, her palms are super sweaty, then mumble along to the prayer set to the Casio beat: Lord of the universe, spirit of the pure white light, show us something something and lift us somewhere. I have to hold my mouth closed not to laugh at how stupid and here Demarcus's voice in my head says keep it together.

Next everyone sits but Sonic the nose picker, he pulls a yellow yo-yo from his pocket and sets it on top of Head On The Pillow's lung. She strains her neck forward like trying to see it, then lies back, shuts her eyes, and begins to hum. She hums a minute while Demarcus stares at her, waiting, then all at once aims his flame lasers at her eyes like he did with me. Her eyes flash open then all in one breath she speaks: Daddy, I transmit from the Summerland—whoosh—all is well all is well all is well where I am!

Her voice when she says this is all high-pitched and girly and now the nose picker is crying so bad. Oh, Katie, my Katie! My sweet baby girl! he sobs.

Please don't cry, my forlorn Daddy, Head On The Pillow says, this whole time Demarcus holding the eye-fire stream. Acute lymphoblastic leukemia has no existence in the Summerland, Head On The Pillow says, and now the Sonic guy cries way harder, him throwing his arms on the lung like it's his daughter, not a balding white lady inside a machine. You can tell Nurse Le Feb doesn't like for people to touch her, he moves fast from his Casio to walk the guy back to his seat.

This is how it goes around the circle, Demarcus shooting his eye fire for each person's dead kid. All kinds of crap ends up on top of the lung lid, a gunked-up retainer, a plastic bucket of broken sandcastle shovels, a telescoping crayon storage tower. Each piece of crap makes Head On The Pillow start humming and at some point during the humming Demarcus does his fire-eyes thing. Each time Demarcus does fire eyes Head On The Pillow says something crazy: how great the Summerland is, how beautiful its weather, how everyone jumps ropes made from braided angel wings. Everyone's dead kid dangles open-mouthed from astral jungle gyms to catch spirit-guided licorice floating through the air.

Now it's my turn and everyone's looking. Also now everyone's crying in the séance circle but me. Head On The Pillow's humming and the bank lady's tear-swollen and hiccupping, she puts her hand on my back to push me out of my seat. I don't know what to do so like a tard I say Oopsy. I say I forgot to bring my thing.

Le Feb says It's okay from behind his Casio. Use your hand, she can work with that, he says. I look at Demarcus and he nods like Just do it so I slap my hand down hard on the lung lid.

For whom do you search? For whom? Head On The Pillow asks me.

For my friend, I say, still looking at Demarcus. People think she might be dead, I say.

And duh, I know Jeanie's not dead, she's in hiding. And if she were dead no way she'd hang out in a place called Summerland. No way she'd spend her ghost life with yo-yo fuckers and cancerface kiddies, she'd be somewhere way cooler riding cuss words into the sky. She'd be dirt biking dark clouds into black smoky letters. Fuck You Death You Can't Fuck Me, she'd skywrite.

Head On The Pillow starts humming and right away Demarcus does his fire-eyes thing, but this time Head On The Pillow sings instead of speaks. She goes *Bummm* ba-da-do-dummm! which I recognize right away as the *Night Court* theme. Which means it's Helen who's transmitting and definitely not Jeanie.

You didn't give my message, Helen via Head On The Pillow says.

I'm so relieved not to hear Jeanie but also it's like Fuck, dead Helen's mad at me.

It's hard, I say, feeling all the sudden shy now, all the séance circle people hushed and looking at me.

No it's not—whoosh. You've got a body—whoosh. You've got a tongue—whoosh. Your mouth works.

I'm thinking: Bitch, I didn't come here to get scolded. I didn't come here to be embarrassed in front of my new friends. I'm a serious badass on a rescue mission, not some dipshit messenger of love.

We are all—whoosh—messengers—whoosh—of something, she says.

I am such a dumbshit, I forgot they read your mind.

Just tell them—whoosh. Tell them—whoosh—they are my truest home.

Okay, whatever, sorry, I say, but in my head I communicate to her telepathically: Sweetie told me one mom's as good as two, I thought-stab. And I'm pretty sure Leslie's moving on already.

There's a long moment where all thoughts disappear and then out of nowhere I regular-say Hey. Hey, I say, if you see my dead mom, tell her thanks for fucking nothing.

Now the séance circle goes all atwitter, the Mexican lady going Poor niña, poor niña, the Sonic guy saying that's no way to talk to your mom.

Helen/Head On The Pillow goes Not cool, Molly, not cool, and I turn to everyone and say It's okay, I barely knew her. She was barely my mom.

Here Demarcus pulls back his eye fire all sorrowful sad-looking then does a new thing I didn't know he could do: he wads himself up like a weird ghost Fruit Roll-Up then hurls his whole ghost self into the lung. Like a badass he hurls himself into Head On The Pillow and possesses her, at first she chokes and gasps between whooshes but then she starts talking really slow.

Good wombs have borne bad sons, Demarcus whispers through her, good wombs have borne bad sons, he goes. Good wombs have borne them, I'm so sorry, I'm so sorry, Demarcus inside Head On The Pillow goes.

Then her eyes roll back and there's a long whoosh-whoosh-whooshing, then she croaks like something inside her throat just collapsed. Then Demarcus burps out of her mouth in full-flamed glory and only I see it but I don't care, I clap and clap.

It's okay, this sometimes happens, Le Feb says, but I can tell he's freaking, him shaking his head worried behind the Casio. Tonight's transmissions are over, see you next week, he goes.

He turns the lights on and bends over Head On The Pillow, touches her hair patches softly like It's okay, there there.

Out the door over their shoulders everyone goes Thank you, thank you! See you next time, Madame Marlene!

Do I leave too, I wonder, or can I stay the night if Demarcus invites me? That was so so cool, I think to him telepathically. Now do it to Le Feb! Do it again!

Instead Demarcus slow-floats to his favorite spot by the window then slow-floats through the glass and drops like to kill himself dead.

NINE

OUTSIDE THE LONELY IT'S ALREADY NIGHT, the street blue-black and pile-shadowed. Razor-faced white guys dig through the piles with long-handled knives but they don't notice Demarcus's ghost crumpled on top a mound of almost new bike tires.

I yell and run over, ask if he's okay.

It never works, he says, barely flickering. Let's get out of here, he says and I say Okay because I know now I'll follow him wherever. We zoom through the shadows of people and things, past sidewalk piles and shop windows and bag ladies. I don't know where we're going so I say Hey, where are we going? and he says To the water, I breathe better there.

He flies faster and faster now, getting too far ahead. The lake? I say, because that's where next week the Fair opens.

I'm running super hard now and I'm not even tired, it's like something underneath is lifting me. The wind blows Demarcus all over up ahead and if it weren't for his flames I'd lose sight of him. When we fly by people the people are big and gray, and I know we're in Bronzeville, not a dark scary fairy-tale forest, but something afraid tugs in me. Something says killer wolves might jump out every black alley, that around each corner are definitely piles of dead Russian whores, that around the next one small orphans roast on spits over trash can fires.

I tell myself Molly, don't be scared, you're a badass now. You're a badass you're a badass you're a badass like Jeanie. And because I'm such a badass I look straight ahead and pound down in my Heatwaves, stay focused on keeping up with Demarcus's fast-floating heels. After a block he slows down, turns to me ghost-breathing heavy. There once was a man-God named Oceanus, he says, the Titan God of Okeanos, the great Earth river. Okeanos, the fount of all freshwater lakes, rivers, subway tunnels, and streams.

Then he throws himself down the steps of a Red Line station and I'm running fast after him again. I'm hopping the turnstile and now I'm in the station and there's no fresh water, no river, just a guy pissing in a metal tin.

Demarcus, I say, look at that guy pissing!

But Demarcus doesn't look, he's still and quiet. He's hovering a foot above the platform for the eastbound train. I'm yelling Demarcus, hey, Demarcus! and now people are looking, but fuck them, let them. I've got a public and they stare at little girls waiting on trains.

When the train comes we take the last seat of the last car. It's just us and the giant advertisements framed in plastic. Mark Bogacki, Your Best Dentist Downtown. Cheryl Price,

Chicagoland's Realtor. I read the posters then hang off the pole in the aisle, make my legs limp so when the train turns it throws me.

The whole time Demarcus hovers Indian-style above his butt-molded seat, taps his finger flames through his knees, impatient. His chalk-hair's swirled thick and his ghost mouth is shut so I can't see the sparks I know spark there.

I swing pole to pole saying God, ghosts are so serious. God, I hope you're not this boring when we get to the lake, I say. Then I ask him what we're going to do when we get there and does he even realize that the Fair's not even open yet?

His eyes flash yellow, he opens his mouth like he's got something to say, which I'm one hundred percent expecting to be I'm not a ghost, I'm a thought form. But he closes his mouth without speaking and then closes his eyes and in my head all I hear is him sighing.

Three stops on the Red Line, seven on the Orange, then we get out at Fifty-Sixth where it's a different kind of city: silver gleamy buildings and parks and trees, fancy trash cans every corner. It's after midnight and no one's around and the wind whips at Demarcus, almost blows out his fires. The only noise besides the wind are my Heatwaves thudding the ground and we walk and walk until the sidewalk's lined with orange cones then a tall fence covered in blue tarp top to bottom. All along it are signs saying Coming Soon! World of Worlds! Coming Soon! Future of Futures!

Smell the lake, Demarcus says, his ghost chest rising. I sniff and he's right, there's a green stink floating around.

Next there are some bushes by the fence. Demarcus says Hide in these bushes so I jump in them. Demarcus hovers close, puts his ear to the tarp. Almost, almost, he whispers while I spit bush thorns.

Then there's metal jangling like someone's opening a gate, then the tarp rustles and there's thick man-voices. They're going like Fuck yeah, let's get some tacos, they're like Oh shit yeah, let's get some beer, then on the other side of the bushes six construction dude work boots walk off somewhere.

As soon as they're gone we find the gate and as soon as we find it Demarcus touches it. He flames his finger fires high into one single monster flame and sure enough, that's the right ghost magic to open it.

The Fair, the Fair, fuck yeah! I say.

A blue city within a city where even in dark blackness you can make out the blue: the blue iceberg doors of the marble buildings, the veined blue marble of the marble buildings, the soft sapphire turf we walk on right now.

We walk down the blue streets and boulevards agog and the whole time I'm thinking How will I tell all this to Jeanie? I part feel guilty not being here with her now, but am also part She shouldn't have cut those fucking balloon ropes so fuck her.

Demarcus zooms ahead grumbling about neoliberalism and the commodification of desire while I put Jeanie out of my mind, replace those thoughts with an all-new feeling, something mysterious unfurling head to crotch inside, a tickling like maybe there's something beyond all the awesome attractions we're passing. Something more than Barbara Newman's Aquacade and Uncle Ozmahon's Fabulon. More than The Man with the Electric Eye, more than the World Congress of Ladies of the Seminude. Like something these shows and rides cover up like a blanket, something glowing and hidden: a secret tunnel, a hidden door, the Fair's big secret thing. You can't get a ticket for it, it's not on the map, and the info booth idiots won't tell you. I don't think even a ghost could tell you, even if you had a ghost like I do.

There's white-blue fog thick all around us so Demarcus uses his flames like a flashlight to see. We go by the Observatory Tower and the Parachute Jump, by a stone-columned building called Parliament of Monsters. We go under a giant blue arch where its big sign says Arcadium, where after is a long boulevard of kiddie rides and games. There are food stands and trailers with giant roof corn dogs and cotton candies, giant fizzing plastic sodas tilted like to spill pop on your head. Demarcus floats to one and touches his flames to the counter and all at once its roof corn dog blinks to life. It turns halfway on its axis while four tinkly notes play from a speaker, the janky last notes of a music box wound down.

You can do *lots* of things, I say, and Demarcus smiles at me for real for the first time ever. I smile too then like a dumbass punch him in the arm. My fist goes straight through him to hit hard on the food stand counter, and I lick my knuckles quick and say One day for sure I'll work at a corn dog place like this one.

Demarcus says he'd rather get a boat and go out to sea and make paintings and I say that's stupid, how much more awesome to make corn dogs all fucking day. How awesome to have your head bump cotton candies strung from the ceiling, how at night you'd watch for miles the Fair's million blinking lights. I say Admit it'd be so awesome and want so bad here to pinch him, but for once I'm not a dumbass and remember there's no him to pinch. So instead I keep on saying it, Admit it, admit it! but Demarcus won't admit it and now he floats away.

At night after everything closes you could eat the leftover corn dogs! I say catching up with him. Then you'd check under all the rides to find the best place to sleep, I go.

You'd hide behind the metal skirt, I say because all the rides I've been on have them. You'd hide behind the skirt, I go, you'd look for a crack with moonlight shooting through. You'd find where it shoots through to make a rectangle of moonlight and then that's your bed and you lay there in secret and you suck on corn dog sticks until you fall asleep.

What I don't say is how the rectangle of moonlight is like a holy light to protect you. From rabied killer carnival rats, from pervy carnies let loose in the night.

Instead I say You'd wake up the next morning as soon as the ride started, you'd get up and brush your jeans off and clock in at your corn dog hut. Then for breakfast you'd make yourself a funnel cake and every effing day that would be your awesome life.

All Demarcus says is that he'd rather work on his painting. That he'd rather be a working artist on any ship in any sea.

After this we're quiet, Demarcus floating fast like he knows where we're going, stopping just once to wave his flames over a giant map of the fair. The wind picks up, it's getting chilly.

Eventually Arcadium's over and there's another blue archway, another monster sign saying The World & The Sea. Here everything opens, the blue turf broadens, splits two directions, circles around the special fake lake they made just for the Fair. All around the fake lake are more fancy marble buildings. Some are super big but others are tiny, like little libraries and city halls the size of Evelyn's garden shed. In the front each one's got a garden of bushes shaped like animals: elephants and lions, horses and combo kangaroo moms/baby kangaroos. Standing between the bushes are tall statues on pedestals, naked ladies with big nips and wreaths of arrows in their hair.

I want bad to look close at all these statues and bushes, but Demarcus won't budge from the spot where he floats near the lake. His fires pulse slow now and he hangs there, staring, which makes me think: at the séance how easy he threw himself into Head On The Pillow and how easy he threw himself out the window when the séance was done.

Demarcus, I say, promise you won't jump in the water. Promise me you're not going to jump into the lake.

He says nothing, stays staring at the center of the water where the biggest statue of all rises up out of the lake. It's a giant Viking rowboat three times my height, two Econolines long, two Ford Festivas wide. Four white lady statues are the rowers inside it, naked like all lady statues, flowers and shit in their hair. They're getting whipped by a stone angel dude who looms big and scary behind them and in front of them another angel dude leans out over the water to play his trumpet, his wings so big they dip into the lake.

But the best part of all sits on the marble shoulders of the four rowing ladies: a helmeted Viking queen sitting tall on a badass throne. Her posture's straight and perfect like approaching some fierce enemy, a sword in each hand, her back not touching the throne.

Here Demarcus gets all excited, he floats up and down now. His fires flicker bright while he shouts Pontos! Michelangelo! Francis Bacon! I'm home!

Whatevs, I don't have time for Art bullshit, so I run around by all the marble buildings, up and down their stairs swearing, shouting Crotchface, I'm home! I try all the doors but of course they're locked when I jangle them. Hey Demarcus! I say, jangling the handle of the biggest one. Hey Demarcus, you have to help me! Open this with your mind! I go.

Demarcus floats over and makes this face, very prissy. He says it's not that easy, he can't just open whatever thing.

Can't or won't? I say then go God, you're one faggy mofo and somehow it comes out way meaner than I mean. I go to friend-punch his arm to nicen the words, but stupid dumbshit me, again I've forgotten and my hand punches through his ghost fog and straight through the glass. Now it's inside the building bleeding, my cut-up knuckles bumping a latch.

I open the door all smiley, all See what I did? and inside's a giant lobby filled with Sea Specimens on display. The floor is smooth blue marble with green swirled eddies and the ceiling's definitely got some mural but it's too dark to see. Demarcus floats next to me while we walk by all the Specimens and I tell him which to light up while I pick glass bits from my fist and lick my knuckle cuts clean. Mostly the Specimens are varnished fish either on stands or flat inside glass cabinets. Some are normal fish like catfish but there are monster fish too. Some of these ones have knife fins sharp as triple Lady Bic razors plus gill flaps that puff out when you push a button on the wall. Some are shaped like bicycles and some like weird alien ice cream cones and oh my effing god, Demarcus is so mothereffing slow. He's got to read each and every little thing about each and every one of the fishes.

Tonight's for looking, not for reading! I say. Come on, we have to keep going, there are way more rooms! I go.

After the lobby there's a long hallway of seahorses, big to small in oval golden frames. The first ones are my size which I had no idea could happen. Neither did Demarcus, I ask him and he says he didn't know. The smallest at the end are so small you have to use magnifying glasses to see them, so they've got magnifying glasses hung from strings nailed to the wall. And get this, the handles of the magnifying glasses are shaped like seahorses, those motherfuckers! Too much! I say. Eff no! I go.

Then at the end of Seahorse Hallway there's a door hung with blue velvet curtains. I wonder if they make Demarcus think of Head On The Pillow, of her weird crazy lung or her Summerland show. On either side of the curtained door is a stack of metal poles and two cardboard boxes, the boxes stuffed with what looks like blue velvet ropes. For hooking on the metal poles to make a waiting line for whatever's behind the blue curtain, I'm guessing. I pick two velvet ropes up to wave around for fun.

Look I'm a rabid octofish! I say, try to do mouth foam with bits of spit chunks, but my throat's super dry now and nothing comes. And anyway, look: Demarcus isn't even watching, he's staring down one of the seahorses and calling it Thetis. He's sketching it in the air above him with his finger fire and whispering low.

Fuck it, if he wants to be weird he can be weird alone. I throw the ropes over my head behind me then push through the blue velvet then walk into a dim room two stories high. It's long and narrow and the two long walls aren't walls really, they're two giant aquarium tanks glowing dark blue. A velvet-roped walkway cuts down the middle with the only lights these little night lights all along the floor. It's not until my eyes adjust that I see it: in the water on both sides, Two Dark Vast Things, floating and still.

Then it's like my brain clicks and I finally really *see* it: it's a mothereffing whale that's been split in two! Sliced down the center, gore sides stuck to the glass to show everything. Here Demarcus catches up with me and is too awed to speak.

We're inside a whale, I tell him all hushed and whispering.

No shit, he goes.

All along the whale halves are buttons on the glass you push in. One when you push it the whale's organs light up different neon colors. Another one lights up its circulatory system bright red. Push both at the same time and the veins and vessels web over the organs, everything pushed up against each other in an unholy nightlighty glow. All neon pinks and blues, orange and greenish yellows. Meaty and fishy and circulatory, splendid to behold.

But some parts are no color unless you count light-up see-through a color. Translucent is the word for it. This whale uterus is so filmy and translucent! you might go. Ghosts, I know, are differently translucent. Between Sister Regina and Demarcus, Sister Regina's way less so.

Anyway, with the whale halves the lit translucent parts push up on the colored glowing parts and it's so completely sick and awesome it almost makes you cry. All those veins streaking around like red lightning, that sliced uterus straight from a science book! If I ever need more Art Points I'll paint this mofo and call it "Ocean Mother," I'll sign my name big and loopy at the bottom awesome because by the time I'm good enough to paint "Ocean Mother, Mom of Water" my signature on anything will be that fucking good.

Demarcus is excited like I am, he floats back and forth, head to fin. The aquarium water shines through his own translucence, turning his chalky white to blue, his orange flames to purple and green. It's like the Cross Section of the Human Eye coloring sheet Evelyn made me do one time where I colored the optic nerve midnight blue and the blood vessels pink-orange and the ciliary muscle a mustard rebel yellow and then Evelyn came in and said my colors were wrong and I gave her this look like Back the eff off Bitch and then I said Evelyn, have you ever even once seen a real optic nerve?

Here I realize Demarcus isn't excited. His floating back and forth is him pacing, him worrying. He's working himself into one of his ocean-art-god loops. And it's like Oh my god. It's like What's wrong now? Like Why can't you just be happy for this awesome thing?

So I say Demarcus, how awesome is this? This is probably the awesomest thing I've ever seen. Do you think it's awesome, Demarcus, or do you not think it is?

He shakes his head, points his flames to the empty whale womb, half on our left, half on our right. Glorious mother, he says, what have they done to you?

Yeah, I say, it's pretty fucking cool.

I push a button by the whale's mouth and whale sounds play from hidden speakers, whale clicks and squeaks over water sounds. We sit on the floor of the roped walkway for a long time listening, quiet as Quakers, until finally he seems like he's back to himself.

It's really pretty, I say, and here a bigger wave of sadness overtakes him. He furls and unfurls, lets out the saddest ghost wailing sounds. Mom! he cries, Mother! Mother of Pontos, slayed!

Every third wail of his the whales on the speaker shriek back to him, makes his shoulders hunch and heave double-time. Which makes me think Jeez, poor fucking Demarcus, and then the wailing stops from his mouth and starts up in my mind. First weird sobs and warbles all wet and hiccupy, then not even sounds, just words written out. They fly across my mind like a TV tornado warning, thick typed letters reading Mother Mother Mom!

It makes you tired having captions go through your head like that. You tell yourself to stop looking, but it's not that easy. You can't help but read every word they say.

Finally his brain wailing stops and Demarcus gets quiet, now he sits straight up humming like going into a trance. Slowly his effed-up face starts to re-chalk itself, first his eyes then his nose then his ears-forehead-mouth.

Demarcus, how did you die? How did it happen? I ask him, trying to change the subject from the sliced-up whale. C'mon, Demarcus, tell me, I'm your best friend, I say, flinching. Flinching because saying Best Friend still makes me think of Her, wherever she's hiding, balloon-cut and bruised, probably calling my name.

I blink her away, ask was it bone cancer that got him? Did a gangbanger kill you? Were you raped to death by a perv? I say.

Then something flips on a light inside my brain and I say Oh my god it was *Le Feb*, wasn't it? Because maybe this is part of my mission: to rescue Jeanie plus serve gory vengeance to Nurse Le Feb.

While I spitball wrathful retributions Demarcus stretches horizontal. He sighs super heavy and starts to levitate. I stretch out on the floor next to him, prepare to hear all about Le Feb raping him. Somehow lying the same way as him I think maybe he'll tell me the whole thing.

I pretend the whale halves aren't split, that this Ocean Mother's in the ocean right now swimming, that me and Demarcus are balled up inside, her whale juices dissolving us into a single thing. Until then we'll tell stories of The Things That Happened To Us, how definitely it was Le Feb who killed him, how me and Jeanie once were two beautiful Apaches, how free we ran when we ruled House of Friends.

Go ahead, I say. I'm listening. Tell me the whole story.

Fine, he says, whatever, I'll tell you the whole thing. He rolls his eyes, flicks his fires once or twice like cracking his knuckles, then after a long pause finally begins.

It was the spring of sixth grade and I was deep into Wolfgang

Paalen. Wolfgang Paalen was an Austrian Mexican surrealist painter and philosopher of art. So I was deep into Wolfgang Paalen, his idea that imagination precedes cognition, his cosmogony of the prefigurative New Image as the ultimate expression of modernist art. I began experimenting with fumage, the technique he originated in which the artist uses lit candles to apply smoke and soot directly to canvas. It was revelatory and gave me the permission I needed to see myself in the artist-in-exile narrative so common in twentieth-century European art.

Demarcus, oh my god, you died of boredom, I say.

No, he goes, no, shakes his ghost head sadly. This is how it happened, he goes. One day after school I went to the Robert Taylor next to The Lonely. By then it was entirely vacant except for neighborhood kids who would play in the halls.

Wait, I say. There's just an empty lot next to The Lonely. That's why they call it The Lonely, I thought.

Before I burned it down, there was another one, he goes.

Here my eyes go big. Here my jaw drops.

I kept a studio on the fifteenth floor and was doing fumage one day when I dropped the candle into a can of turpentine and the can exploded, he goes.

You lit the whole place on fire, I say.

It set my easel and oil rags on fire, he says, and the fire spread to everything. I couldn't see, I couldn't breathe. I jumped out the window in flames.

You're an arsonist, Demarcus. A Firestarter! I say.

I'm an artist, not an arsonist. But I am a murderer, he goes. Three boys were playing hide-and-seek on the floor above me.

Whoa, I go. Fucking tragic, I say. I don't say anything else about that part. Sometimes there are things you don't let yourself think about or say.

But too late, he reads my mind, says Not thinking it will never make it go away, Molly, his voice low and heartbroken, ninety-five percent sorrow, five percent disdain.

But the painting you were doing, what even was it? I say.

He sighs, says It was in memory of my mother, of her favorite sea monster, Charybdis. Charybdis was a giant whirlpool with eyes and teeth, a tornadic waterspout mouth spitting out bodies: sailor heads and mermaid hands, scales and ankled feet.

That's so badass, I say and Demarcus says Thank you and then after a few moments I ask the question this whole time I've been wanting to ask.

So what was it like? I say. What was it like dying?

Here he floats close to me, looks me straight in my eyes, my face. He doesn't cry or wail. All his fires burn steady.

What was it like? You can tell me, I say.

I fell from the sky on fire, he says, and when he says it he's smiling.

I was Icarus. I was art, he says. It was fucking amazing.

I GO ONE LAST TIME around the room pushing buttons. Some light up whale parts while others turn the narrator on: a deep deep man voice saying what ocean the whale was from, how she picked her mates, what she ate for lunch. One button when you push it tells you all about her babies, lights the tank both sides where the halved whale wombs stick. The womb's lined with yellow blubber, but if I blur my eyes I can imagine a baby in there, a fishy potpie of bloody squirming, a smooth slimy alien waiting to burst out and swim.

Demarcus, I say, bet her actual baby's in the ocean right now swimming, but Demarcus says No way, shakes his ghosty head.

Oh yeah she is, I say. When they do this to your mom you grow up to be one tough bitchass. Here I imagine my own dead mom netted, caught, and split in two.

We should go, Demarcus says, the first thing he's said in a while. His nose and eyes are smudged. His toes and fingers burn low.

But at least let's find the Submarine Palace, I say once we're outside the fish building.

He says no, he says Let's just go home, so I stop and look at every sign and poster along the way, read every word about IMAX Presents *The Primeval Experience* and *Journey into the Grand Canyon 3D*. By the entrance gate to Autotopia is where I see it. A poster so surprising I almost scream.

Come See Her Sleep! it says over a picture of an old-time movie actress, except it's not really an old-time actress, it's a face I'd recognize anywhere. Black around her eyes like a raccoon bandit, black bangs and black sideburns slicked into stabby devil tails.

A face exactly like: Hello, zombie sister.

A face like: I knew you'd find me, Thunderbrow.

At the top in red letters it says Sleeping Silent Princess! Feel her Cosmic Sex Energy! See Inside her Crystal Coffin! Then at the bottom: The Countdown to Reanimation Begins.

Demarcus oh my god holy shit, it's Jeanie! I say pointing,

though in my head I don't think Jeanie, I think Her Her Her. I think: Here she *is*, it's *her* on the poster. It's Jeanie who's always been the Fair's secret thing.

I turn to Demarcus to make sure he sees what I'm seeing when from the lake darkness in front of us here's another new thing: wild-haired from the shadows, a ragged and swaggery woman emerges. Scratched and bruised all over, rip-toed dirty Keds. Dripping wet jean jacket. Torn Darkthrone tee.

That's not me, the woman goes, coming closer. That's not me, that's my fucking sister, Jeanie says.

3

THE FAIR

ONE

I KNEW IT, I SAY. You're alive, I go.

I want bad to knock her down and lick her face all over. Like a tard I go to give her an actual hug. Her scratched-up arms go up fast like Don't fucking touch me, but she doesn't kick me off and what she says next isn't mean.

Well aren't we top shit, she says and then I introduce her to Demarcus, him a wadded blinking ball floating on my right. I say I know you can't see him but I swear he's right next to me, the ghost boy I told you about, he's an artist, I say.

Demarcus surprises me, he unfolds all the way, says Well well well, it's really Jeanie. Molly talks a lot about you.

But also at the exact same time in my head he says Beware her, Skulla. Beware her fang teeth, beware her fish tail.

And here Jeanie surprises me, she looks straight at Demarcus!

Ghosts are fucking everywhere, she says.

Then she says nothing but like checking for weapons she eyes Demarcus up and down. This is not a safe place, she says super quiet, so quiet without talking we follow her through the shadows and onto one of the blue lanes.

I smile at half-balled Demarcus who floats the whole time next to me. He fades in and out, maybe jealous, probably sad. It's really her, I whisper. It's really effing Jeanie. My best friend is alive, we rescued her, I say.

Do you have anything to eat? Jeanie says and I pinch myself hard for not bringing donuts from the séance with me.

You fucking suck, she says then calls Demarcus Casperass and me Thundercunt and the next thing I know we're halfway to the Cosmosphere, the Space Education building sponsored by NASA where Jeanie's been hiding in the daytime since she got here. We follow her down a blue-bricked path I'd never noticed, cut through an alley marked by an Employee Only sign.

So if you can see Demarcus could you see Sister Regina? I ask her.

Strange-shaped winter birds perch one-legged in the trees, sleeping heads sunk deep in their bodies. The only sounds are our footsteps plus the birds' sleep-cheeping sounds. If you listen close, the hum of Demarcus's electricity.

Ghosts are everywhere, I see them all the time, Jeanie says. That Sister Regina, what a card! she says.

Demarcus says nothing but he's listening, I can tell. He floats awhile ahead of us then falls close behind.

While we walk Jeanie tells how this one time on her cell block this epileptic girl died. She had a fit one night and choked on her tongue. When the prison guards came with the stretcher to get her, out of nowhere an entire all-ghost gospel choir appeared.

They shook and swayed in see-through church robes, they paced the block for hours singing her and her prison sisters to sleep.

I ask what they sang in case there's certain music ghosts like, something special that keeps them at peace.

"Vision of Love" by Mariah Carey, she goes, pausing like she has to think hard to remember. All those sad prison bitches crying to fucking gospel pop. Even the guards, even Rusty and Jerome, she says.

All of them could see the thought forms or only hear them? Demarcus asks her.

What do you mean thought forms? You mean ghosts? she says. Both, I think. Most of them, Jeanie goes.

He's trying to figure the rules out, I say. Why only some people can see ghosts and why then only certain ones.

Demarcus floats in front of us, hovers up close to Jeanie, says In the story you told, why the choir? Why didn't the thought form of the actual dead girl show up instead?

Yeah, I say. And where the hell are our ghost moms? And why can *we* see Demarcus but not Head On The Pillow or Nurse Le Feb?

Who the fuck are they? says Jeanie and I say His public. Demarcus rolls his eyes, says My smaller-minded friends.

I've thought about this a lot, Jeanie says, lighting a cigarette. And I've got a theory, but that's all it is, she goes.

We stare at her, waiting, while she takes a drag slowly, puffs three perfect smoke rings into the cold and dark night.

Want to hear it? she asks finally. Know anything about waveforms? she goes.

Like radio signals? Demarcus asks her.

Yeah sure, she says.

Not really, he says, so I say that too.

I think ghosts are a kind of carrier wave. At least the ghosts we can see, she goes.

What's a carrier wave? Demarcus asks.

Wait, are you making this up? I go.

Shut up and listen, Kittentits, and no, I'm not. For my required eight-week Serve and Learn I did Principles of Radio Communication, she goes.

What's a carrier wave? Demarcus asks.

A waveform modulated by an information-bearing signal, usually transmitting through space electromagnetically, Jeanie goes.

But where does the signal transmit from? *What* does the signal transmit from? Demarcus goes.

How the hell do I know? says Jeanie

Maybe from your higher self? I go.

Anyway, with a carrier wave the amplified signal gets converted to radio waves that get picked up by a receiver. You're a receiver, Jeanie says, looking at me.

But that doesn't explain it, why isn't everyone a receiver? I go. And why isn't every dead person a ghost? Or where is the place the other ghosts go?

Jesus, Kittentits, she says, I don't know. Maybe they're on a different frequency. Like maybe only dogs and cats can see certain ghosts.

I imagine my mom haunting Sweetie's dog Pepsi, her booing the wood-pile's feral cats.

I don't think that's right, though, Jeanie goes. For carrier waves to be transmitted and received, they have to be amplified on both ends. Amplification is what gives them power. So maybe not every dead person transmits here because they don't have the thing that gives them the power. Same for receivers. So there's something we've got that amplifies the signal, that helps us tune in.

Like what? I say.

Grief, Demarcus goes. Grief is the amplifier. Grief is a thing that transmits and receives. Here his unfurled ghost body does this pulse thing, this shimmer.

It's true, Jeanie says. Sadness reverberates like strings on a fucking harp, she goes.

Grief as a harmonic phenomenon! Demarcus continues, all excited. It opens you to sympathetic vibrations, you transmit and you receive and suddenly you see thought forms.

Yeah, it certainly busts you open like that, Jeanie goes. Guilt too, she says, looking at Demarcus. Looking at me.

Bullshit, I say. I don't even remember my mom. You and him might be busted, but I'm not, I go.

Jeanie shakes her head and says Kittentits, you are so totally busted. You are so totally broken. It's all over you, she says. Think about it, she goes. You floated in her nine months which in baby-time is forever. The beat of her heart was the first sound you heard. She was the universe you soaked in and the one you clawed out of and you lost her so early it formed you completely, so completely it's invisible because it's all you've ever known. But I can see it, Crotchtard. And I bet Demarcus can see it too. Demarcus, can you see it?

Yeah, Demarcus goes.

See? We three harmonize, says Jeanie.

Demarcus nods but doesn't look convinced, says That still doesn't explain where all the other thought forms have gone. Why am I here while others are in the place called the Summerland? My mother is in neither, where has she gone?

I don't know, but suck it up, Floatface. I haven't seen my mom since she died either, Jeanie goes. Here she stops a moment, sizes up Demarcus. You're here and you're very powerful, she goes.

Yeah he can totally do things, I go.

Maybe dead you're still busted open, Jeanie says. Maybe that's why you're here and they're—

My mother had enough grief to power ten suns, Demarcus says, interrupting.

Well then I don't know, Jeanie says. Feel guilty about anything?

Demarcus says nothing. His flames pulse brighter and brighter.

Yeah, that's what I thought, Jeanie goes.

What about Evelyn and my dad? They couldn't see Sister Regina, I say. If anyone should receive or transmit, they definitely should.

I don't know, Jeanie says. You're dad's a fucking narcissist. Probably that gets in the way, she goes. And Evelyn's got her Quaker shit to carry her. Us, though? We have nothing. Which also means we have nothing to lose, she goes.

THE COSMOSPHERE'S ALL DOME, all fancy white marble, but also at the same time super modern and edgy too. Jeanie says if the Taj Mahal and R2D2 got it on then this would be their weird fatass baby. I barely notice we've walked up the twenty marble steps, barely notice the giant golden door she unlocks while talking.

Demarcus hovers close and looks at everything, hum-sings "Blue Moon" direct to my head. Inside we follow Jeanie into a big round rotunda, but it's not a rotunda, It's a cyclorama, Demarcus says.

What the fuck's a cyclorama, does it go upside down? I say.

It's not a ride, it's a round painting, he says pointing to the domed three-story wall covered all around with layers of drop cloth and scaffolding.

The mural's almost finished, Jeanie says, taps the Artist and Craftsperson ID clipped to her paint-splattered jeans. The paint splatters are mostly long drips of black and gray but there's some reddish brown here and there and I'm thinking: What if that's not paint, what if that's blood splatters?

I've been posing as one of the artist's assistants since I landed two days ago, Jeanie says. Mostly I eat popcorn in the staff room then at night sleep in one of the maintenance closets.

Demarcus is so interested in the craporama thing he's not listening, he floats along the drop-clothed wall trying to see the mural behind it.

It's all space shit, Jeanie tells him. Some nebula stuff, she goes. The artist is this serious Sidney Poitier douche, the one

Black guy who works for NASA so he thinks his shit's the hottest.

Demarcus zooms to where we're standing in not even a flash. What's his name what's his name what's his name? he goes.

Ghostmunch, chill, it's right over there, Jeanie says and points to a big-ass golden-framed poster.

ARTIST RECEPTION

FOR

PAUL TURNER WILLIAMS

7 PM NEW YEAR'S EVE

I don't know who the fuck Sidney Poitier is, but to me the guy in the poster looks like Malcolm-Jamal Warner. Possibly Sondra's boyfriend Elvin, I don't know.

The second I think it there's a zap in my head, a brain-flick, something Demarcus has started doing when my thoughts make him mad. Ow! I go, ready to erase him, but too late, he's already floating to the poster to stare scary death at it, his flame licks getting longer the closer he gets.

I will tie him to a chair with snakes and I will set the chair and snakes on fire. I will dash his eyes out with rocks and drag him into the sea, he goes.

Demarcus, jeez, what the fuck, I say, embarrassed.

Jeanie blows a smoke ring. Ghosts always slay gently, don't they? she goes.

I will cut open his heart for seabirds to eat, Demarcus says softly. But for now I'll destroy his shitty illustration, he goes.

Then he does the thing he did when I first met him six days ago: ignites himself from inside, explodes again in light, shoots tiny light-balls of himself upward in every direction. Tiny fireballs of Demarcus spark and ping against the scaffolding metal until all at once the drop cloths drop and his free-floating cinders bathe the cyclorama in wild glowing light: red-rimmed black holes and Lisa Frank–colored nebulas, asteroid belts and space clouds, comets with neon tails.

It'd be pretty except for now how Demarcus defaces it, makes words in flame-sparkled letters appear all over the mural: Mother Leaver, Son Hater, Dad I Hope U Die.

After a few seconds an invisible wind makes the letters scatter and fall to the floor near where me and Jeanie stand. The golden glitter swirls together, a tiny tornado all spark and shimmer, then swirls itself back into Demarcus again. Except not the regular him because now he's sobbing. His tears are wet and shiny flames.

I move to him closer but don't know what to do, I can't touch him. If I touch him it will only wipe him away. So I say: It's okay, Demarcus. It's okay.

Paul Turner Williams is his dad, I whisper to Jeanie.

I figured that much, Jeanie puffing her cigarette goes.

He abandoned him and his mom before he was born, I say, still whispering. And I think that's where he gets his artistic ability, I go.

Bullshit, he gave me nothing! Everything I am is from my mother! Demarcus goes.

Same for me, I say.

Same for me, Jeanie goes.

Mother, I'm here, where are you? Demarcus wails before going back to crying, and at that moment a sudden knowledge springs into my head fully formed.

Is that why you stay at The Lonely? I ask him. Is that why you live in the cabinet under the sink? I go. You think she's coming back to get you so you're waiting for her, aren't you?

He doesn't deny it, only balls up tighter and flickers his finger fires hard.

Jeanie says Ghostdick, I wouldn't get your hopes up, and she's totally right, I'm someone who knows. Before last year Sister Regina and this year Demarcus, I didn't think ghosts were for real at all. No dead person had ever phantomized in front of me. My own dead mom had never bothered to say hello. And now that I do see them, where the fuck is she? She's elsewhere, otherwhere, she's motherfucking gone.

I forget Jeanie's there and join Demarcus wailing and like a dumbshit crybaby I cry for my mom. I'm all Where the fuck are you! Where the fuck did you go? Why did you leave me? Show yourself! I go.

After a while of this I sit down on the floor of the craporama. Snot-streaked and teary, my knuckles sore from the broken window from earlier. Demarcus floats near me, ghost-sniveling, hiccupping. Finally after a while his face starts to fill back in.

Your rage is weak, Jeanie tells us while she lights another cigarette. If she was sad about her own dead mom, you'd never know.

She takes a long drag, says Both you two, stop your fucking crying and listen. You never let me finish my prison story from before. What do you know about necromancy? she goes.

What the fuck's that? I ask her, still sniffing.

She means raising the dead, Demarcus says.

Jeanie nods and says she saw it done once. She says later that night after the epileptic girl died from her epilepsy and after the gospel ghost choir came and disappeared, her cellmate, cumguzzler Tina, an actual practicing Satanist, summoned the epileptic girl's ghost in their cell right there.

She wanted to bitch her out one last time, Jeanie says smiling. Tina was the meanest bitch there, she says.

Bullshit, I say. Satanists aren't real. And here Jeanie swings her hand out fast and slaps me.

Dumbshits! she says, if you want to see your dead moms again, listen! I'm trying to tell you fucking crybabies how!

How? Demarcus says, stepping quick in front of me. He says it like not believing but also like almost believing, like Alright then, tell us right fucking now.

I know exactly how, she says.

Tell us! I say because I want so bad to do it. Until tonight I never knew how bad I wanted to see my mom.

You have to help me first, she says. You have to get my black box back. Do that first and then I'll tell you, she says.

Figures, Demarcus says and I say I never touched it, then I flinch, brace for knuckles, but Jeanie says No shit.

It was Mombie, she says. She's been following me, spying. She came here from Kansas to kill me, she says, and now she's the Sleeping Silent Princess of the Silver Screen.

Your enemies are my enemies, I say to Jeanie and mean it and Jeanie says Don't ever forget it, Kittentits. Don't ever be less than my top-shit friend. Give me your arm, she says, taking it from me, dragging her jaggedy nails down my skin. It hurts but I don't care, it leaves something that's worth it: bright blood-dotted lines like lightning bolts. It makes my neck tingle and my hands feel hot.

I thought that's all she wanted but she doesn't let my arm go.

Did you know when you're struck by lightning you get a permanent scar on your body the exact same place where the lightning bolt hits? she says.

I shake my head.

Beware her, don't trust her, Demarcus says in my head.

The scar's the same shape as the lightning that hit you. It means it's claimed you as its servant, she says.

Somehow this flips switches and pushes keys in, turns my regular thoughts off to darkness except certain pictures lit in my head: the wide pink scar under Jeanie's Darkthrone shirt, dead lesbo Helen's chemo-bald head. Demarcus's face on fire and Dad's eyes under his sunglasses, and now, my arm, the lightning bolts she's zapped there.

Listen, Molly, listen, Jeanie says to me.

In my head, Demarcus: Beware, beware.

I see my fall from the balloon two nights ago, the spin of the stars, the monster truck flames. The jangle of my own bones thudding.

I am listening, I say. I'm always listening.

Molly, Jeanie says, for once can you fucking shut up and listen! Then her voice backs down soft again and whispering she says, Molly, did you know that I chose you out of the world?

I shake my head. I don't know what to say when people say weird things. I say I think you're cool, Jeanie. I think you're so cool.

Beware her fang teeth, Demarcus says.

Then you'll help me? Jeanie says and I say Okay.

Beware her kicking legs, Demarcus says.

Am I your lightning? she says and I nod my head.

Are you my servant? she says and I nod again.

Good, it's a deal then. You and your ghost friend will steal my black box back. Then and only then will I teach you how to raise the dead. But first thing's first, she goes, heel-stubbing her cigarette. I need a better hiding place. Like tonight, she says.

TWO

It's both fun and not fun to ride the train with a blood and paint-splattered Jeanie plus a fire-fingered ghost boy only we can see. It's fun because the ghost and the paint-blood are our secret but not fun because the whole time people throw dirty looks our way. But fuck them, let them look is what I'm thinking. It's me who's the center of this awesome trifecta, it's them the sex molesters perv-staring at badass me.

Off the Bronzeville platform and into the city Demarcus floats wadded between my shoulders and Jeanie's, Jeanie for the first time seeing the weird awesome piles. She's like Holy fucking shit, all these weird fucking piles!

I told you, I go. It's exactly like I said, I say.

I'd told her about Bronzeville the whole way on the train, everything I'd wanted to say the night last week she beat the shit out of me. All about the piles and the cranes and The Lonely, the sixteen scorched floors, the sixteen hot dog water halls to run down.

See? I say, See? We're walking up the steps to The Lonely.

Inside by the elevator the pay phone dangles off its hook. I'm feeling so good I feel like doing a nice thing, but when I put it back on its cradle right away it starts ringing.

Who the fuck's this? Jeanie answers it saying, me watching this unfold in awe like Holy shit, you're amazing.

No, this isn't Andre, Andre's not here, she says to whoever's calling. And who the fuck are you to be calling for Andre? We killed him because of you calling here, she says.

Then she drops the phone, lets it swing like a dead man hanging, me laughing and clapping and heading for the stairs, Demarcus next to me very slowly unfurling.

Why take the stairs when there's an elevator? Jeanie says.

I turn around but she's already pushed the button. Don't do that! I say pointing where it's spray painted Don't, Beware. Jeanie rolls her eyes like what a dumbass I am to worry.

I look at Demarcus to see what he thinks, a cursed elevator the kind of thing right up his alley. So I look at him thinking Well what do you think? then telepathically he tells me that it's no biggie.

Then from the elevator there's a sound like boom-clank-boom and then no warning ding, just the doors screeching open. Inside's the napping guys I saw last week on the landing, they've moved their nap circle to the elevator floor.

I scrunch my face like to say *Now* can we take the stairs? but Jeanie walks into the elevator all No matter these sleeping dudes, wedges her Keds in the spaces their armpits make.

Get in or get out, she says, don't be a pussy, so I dart through the closing doors shouting I'm no pussy, hopscotch around the guys as best I can. Demarcus floats through with me, unwadded head to foot, and this is where I realize something: the closer we are to The Lonely the more he shows up, the thicker his whiteness and the brighter his body. Except right now in the elevator, something new: the R&B song he starts to sing.

Hit which floor, Jeanie says and I hit sixteen.

She says Your foot's on that guy's balls, so I jerk up my Heatwave.

We go up floor by floor slow with occasional lurches, fast and bolting. What if one wakes up, I ask Jeanie about the guys on the floor and Jeanie bends down like I'm some kind of tard, whispers in my ear Cocksauce, these guys are zombies.

Oh, I say, not really believing. Oh, I say a second time, a smell sinking in. Then all the sudden I recognize what Demarcus is singing: "It's So Hard to Say Goodbye to Yesterday" by Boys II Men.

At Demarcus's apartment the door's half open but Nurse Le Feb is nowhere in sight. We walk in like stereo system burglars, tippy-toed and slack-wristed like Hamburglars. The apartment's been tidied since last night's séance, the folding chairs are folded, the footprints on the rug vacuumed away.

Right away in the kitchen Demarcus floats to his cabinet, no goodbyes or good nights, no Make yourself at home.

That's where he sleeps and has an art studio, I tell Jeanie. It's like a cave that restores his battery, I say, but she gives no shits, all she wants is something to eat.

Wait, I say shushing her, finger to lips. Listen for it! I say tilting my ear.

And there it is, Head On The Pillow. The sound of her breathing via her lung whooshing in.

Jeanie whacks me for the shushing but I can tell she's listening. I can tell that before she didn't believe me, but now she's seeing how everything I told her is true.

Wait until you see her, I say, grabbing her and pulling. I drag her through the hallway. This will blow your effing mind, I say.

The room's dim, but I can see Jeanie see her, Head On The Pillow asleep in her spangled lung.

What the fuck, Jeanie whispers. What the fuck is this? she goes.

Shh, she's sleeping, I go, tiptoeing into the dimness. I wave Jeanie over, tell her it's okay. I point to where Head On The Pillow's head sticks out the lung like a turtle, tap where through the Plexiglas you can see her blue-nightied knees. Whispering, half-miming, I tell Jeanie her real name's Madame Marlene. That she's a very special person inside a very special lung and then I talk some about the human lung, how it's a pump, a motor, an airbag inflating, except for with Head On The Pillow's because of how polio broke her lungs.

This whole time Jeanie says nothing. Does nothing but run her snake fingers along the bolts of the lung's lid. When she gets to the edge, Head On The Pillow starts sleep-coughing, and right after that Nurse Le Feb walks in. He's got a row of plastic grocery bags hanging off each meaty arm, the look on his face Oh You Again.

I had another vision, I tell him.

And I wouldn't fuck with a girl with a vision, Jeanie says. One hand's on her butt pocket, sliding it up and down like she's got a gun.

Le Feb puts down the groceries and turns on the lamp on the dresser. Well I never ever would, he goes.

Any Jell-O in there? I ask, pointing at the sacks because it looks like maybe there is some.

Who's that—a new—cowgirl? Head On The Pillow wakes up and goes.

In the kitchen I help Le Feb put away groceries, Jell-O and Ding Dongs and Hershey's chocolate sauce. I tell him after last night's séance I went home to my orphanage where right away I got in so much hot water with the nuns. They beat me and called me a witch and made me sleep in the alley where the white dude pervs come to pick out orphan girls to take home.

I say So I'm in the alley on lookout when she (I point to Jeanie) rides in and rescues me from the pervs. Her name is Jeanie (here Jeanie waves and nods) and then riding away on the back of her bike I had my second vision.

Uh huh, uh huh, go on, Le Feb says.

So I'm on the bike behind her with the wind blowing through my hair and at first the wind's just wind but then I hear it speak to me, I hear it say Help him, help him! Help Nurse Le Feb!

No you didn't, Le Feb says like he thinks I'm teasing and I say No, I'm dead serious! No! Yes I did! So I asked the voice of the wind Who the hell are you and the wind voice said: Someone in the Summerland who loves him.

Here Le Feb stops uh huh-ing and looks at me serious. Mama? he goes. Margaret Roberta Le Feb, RN? he says.

I tilt my ear up like hearing her voice right this minute. Yes, yes, I think it was your mom, I say. So your mom's speaking to me through the wind saying Go with this woman Jeanie back to my boy Nurse Le Feb. Help him take care of the white lady, she says. Then she shows me us living here helping you with Madame Marlene, us helping you clean before séances and getting things ready so that you can take breaks and not feel guilty when you leave to get groceries.

Mama, Le Feb says. Mama, he goes, smiling.

Yeah, she says she loves you so much, I say.

THREE

Turns out Nurse Le Feb doesn't like how I wipe things. Or the way I vacuum the orange rug. My sweep strokes he says are too short and uneven, when I wipe stuff all I do is spread the dirt around. Instead of cleaning I spend the next week feeding Head On The Pillow pudding. Reading to her from *Deadwood Dick's Doom; or, Calamity Jane's Last Adventure: A Tale of Death Notch*. Her very favorite part's when someone tells Jane that Deadwood Dick's drowned in quicksand. Jane won't believe it, she says "Dead—you dead, my brave, true friend? No! no! no! I will never believe it—never, until when my own life shall have ebbed out."

I also like the part in the same chapter where when the bullet-proof dwarf comes at Jane she outruns him, where it says "She didn't run toward the town, but up the gulch, and as fast as her feet could carry her, for she was aware that it was now a matter of life or death to her." I like the life or death of it, the way it says what it says, how she runs up a gulch. Whatever a gulch is, I'd run up it too.

So each day my job's to read to Head On The Pillow and feed her her pudding while Le Feb cleans the apartment and Jeanie paces the halls of The Lonely, planning me and Demarcus's mission, she says. Demarcus spends most mornings asleep under the sink in his cabinet and sometimes I curl up to his wad of light and nap next to him there. Afternoons and evenings he hides behind the living room curtains or follows me around drawing weird things over my head, the flame of his pointer finger smoking out weird little pictures: winged skeleton kids flying out the mouths of black-fanged snakes, skeleton kids in hot air balloons floating through giant fire clouds. Sometimes the clouds or snakes have words drawn into them: Beware the Water. It Bleeds. Beware.

Each night Le Feb goes out to do errands and Jeanie goes downstairs to smoke with this guy she met named DJ Toad. Neither one lets me go with them and I have to stay behind in the apartment with Demarcus who won't let me in the cabinet at night because he's working on something new and therefore needs to be alone.

What are you working on? I go and he says Some sketches.

Sketches of what? I go and he tells me I'll know when I need to know.

So those nights I read Calamity Jane to Head On The Pillow until she settles and starts snoring. When finally it's just me and the whooshes I crash on the living room couch, watch sparks from Demarcus's mystery project shoot out from behind the kitchen cabinet door.

Sometimes during the day Demarcus and Jeanie have free time and we play a game I call The Lonely Explorers. It's me and Jeanie and Demarcus running up and down the sixteen floors, us yelling Fire Fire Fire then when whoever still lives there goes down the stairwell cussing we go inside their unlocked apartments and dig through their shit.

We find all kinds of things in shoeboxes, shoeboxes full of weed and shoeboxes full of nothing. Shoeboxes with Happy Birthday cards with folded cutouts of giant boobs. We find unmailed letters to congressmen, to pissed-off girlfriends, to chip-shouldered brothers. Letters from Save the Children, fly-eyed pictures of them taped on refrigerator doors. One old lady's apartment's filled with photos of individual hedgehogs, the one same hedgehog over and over or each time different ones, I don't know. But the photos are everywhere, framed on her walls and on her radiator, on top of her TV and taped inside her medicine cabinet when you open the door. Some are black and white and some are in color, but in the bedroom next to her mattress is the nicest one. Here in front of somebody's rose bush is a hedgehog in an Easter basket. It wears a giant velvet ribbon tied in a bow.

Wednesday we're playing Explorers when an apartment we think is empty isn't.

The living room's dark, VCR boxes everywhere. I trip and bang my knee and Jeanie and Demarcus both laugh so I say Fuck you, Ghost Twat, fuck you, Jeanie. I give them both the finger and for the first time Demarcus gives it back.

Want to try the bedroom? I say but neither of them hear me, Demarcus too busy staring in the aquarium where Jeanie's finger-flicking the fish into the air.

I say Well screw you both, I guess I'll go all by my fucking self exploring.

Then by myself I find a little girl's room down the short hall. It's layered in VCR boxes and Barbies and pink plastic ponies. There's a sheet curtaining off the closet so I yank back the sheet.

Inside on a pile of shoes a tiny Black girl's sitting.

Hey girl, I say, trying to sound friendly, but the girl's face is like Motherfucker, put that sheet fucking back!

I don't want to scare her but also I sort of do, so when she starts throwing the shoes I walk backward, float my arms zombie-like in front of me, and it's like I'm so fucking ghostly, I'm like Ghost of the Little White Girl, like Woo woo woo.

FOUR

Thursday night Jeanie calls bullshit on Head On The Pillow. Le Feb's telling her about tomorrow's séance when she rolls her eyes. Bullshit, she says and Le Feb stops restringing Head On The Pillow's guitar to look at her. His eyes are perfect circles, like Oh hell no.

I was only half listening, I was thinking about our box-stealing mission. I was thinking about what I'll say to my mom when I necromance her from the dead. I stop pretend-reading *Deadwood Dick* and even Demarcus comes out from behind the curtains, his ghost face all Oh shit, oh shit.

Bullshit, Jeanie says again because now we're all watching. Bullshit, bullshit, bullshit, she goes.

Le Feb puts the guitar down and at first stares and stares at her, then he closes his eyes like he's got the worst headache he's ever had. Then still with his eyes closed he goes It doesn't even matter. It doesn't even matter if you believe or not, he says. But there is a Summerland, Miss Young White Lady, and even *your* departed loved ones live there eternally, he says.

Oh snap! I say.

Oh Christ, Demarcus goes.

Don't ever talk about my departed loved ones ever, you fat fuck, Jeanie says.

Here Le Feb gets up out of his chair.

Don't you ever belittle what relief from heartache and grief Madame Marlene provides her clients for an extraordinarily reasonable fee! he goes.

His eyes are flashing now, brown with bits of golden-flecked lightning in the center. His scrubs are this weird eggplant color I hadn't noticed before.

Don't you ever speak ill of her, you know nothing, he goes. I'm a third-generation nursing practitioner and nurse educator, licensed and registered in the State of Illinois. More importantly I am the son of Margaret Roberta Le Feb, RN, and Jeanie—if that's your real name and I doubt that it is—I have seen more people healed in this room you smack your gum in than in any hospital I've set foot in in my twenty-five-year career.

This is the closest I've heard Le Feb to pissed, each word an egg cracked hard over a bowl's chipped rim.

It's all bullshit, Jeanie goes, smacking her gum louder. You're such bullshit, it's all bullshit, Jeanie goes over and over again. She rubs the left side-seam of her jeans a little, I notice. I wonder if it's because her scar itches there.

If you believed less bullshit, she says, maybe you'd see what's real.

Le Feb's eyebrows go high like he cannot even believe it. There's a long, long silence before he speaks again.

When my mother retired I took her to Disney World, he says. Margaret Roberta Le Feb, RN. She'd lived a life of perfect virtue, was a living jewel, as every Black woman is. It was the canonization I owed her and I took her to Disney where we drank milkshakes and rode Thunder Mountain again and again. For three days we dissolved ourselves in the Magic Kingdom and each night at the Polynesian Village Resort holy rest reconstituted us again.

But the one thing my mother wanted most of all was to ride Space Mountain, to be blasted into a dark universe of some larger creation, but each day my mother's feet were too blistered and tired and the line for Space Mountain always too long. So on the final day we got there thirty minutes before the park opened and when we got to Space Mountain there was no line at all.

Space Mountain is glorious! It's well worth the wait. But something happened to me on that ride that I'll describe for you now, Jeanie. We were speeding around a dark turn, the fake stars twinkling above us, Mother's hand on my hand, her arm linked in mine, and at that moment I had a thought: My mother is happy! And at that moment our car stopped on its track and the lights turned on. This is something that occasionally happens on Space Mountain, but of course I didn't know that at the time.

So there I am, looking all around at the truth of Space Mountain, at how space is just darkness, this coaster just scaffolding inside a giant metal shed. So I'm looking around and see a car paused on the track beneath us and this is the moment my spiritual experience begins. Inside the car's a Black man with his mother, hand in hand. Slowly I realize that the man is me, his mother my mother, that I'm outside my body now, that I'm floating overhead.

At first all I see are the things immediately around me, but then there's something I can only describe as a holy expansion and suddenly, simultaneously, I see a thousand of me. A thousand Nurse Le Febs, each through the eyes of another. I saw how you see me right now, Jeanie. I saw my fat fuck of a self. I saw my patients at the hospital seeing me, hating me and loving me, a hundred times mistaking me, not one ever once understanding who I really am.

I saw little white girls seeing me and thinking I was dumb. I saw my father the week before he died swaddling me in a baby blanket and I saw my mother seeing me graduate from nursing school and I burned with the love.

Then I stopped seeing me and I saw everyone. Unattached from my body I was the body of the world. It only lasted a moment, but it felt like eternity, then just as fast I was back in my body and the Space Mountain lights started flashing off and on. The car started moving again, but it was too much for my mother, says Le Feb. Most likely it was the flashing lights that gave her the seizure. She'd crossed to the Summerland by the time the ride was done.

Bullshit. Total bullshit, Jeanie says. Normally I'd side with Jeanie any day over Le Feb, but I don't know, something about Jeanie's face tells me she's not winning. Something about Le Feb's voice tells me his is.

This *bullshit* is sacred and I have made an energetic contract to honor it! Le Feb goes. He slaps his hand on the table, is almost shouting now. We live in a world of infinite ecstatic possibility, Jeanie! You dwell in the body that receives you! Don't you see that you're bullshit too?

Then it's like he stops himself, climbs back down from something.

And despite my feelings telling me otherwise, I will honor your bullshit. Under that weird eyeliner and your heavy metal hair, you are but a smallness, he goes. A white trash smallness. And your white trash smallness is holy too. I honor the place in your white trashness where the whole of the universe resides, Jeanie. I honor your cheap darkness because it holds the true light. And I honor and celebrate my Black fat fuckness and I ask that you honor it too. It holds a transgenerational memory of luminous suffering, of pain there is no existing language for. It's a pain that saturates and a pain that embraces, and so I embrace you, Jeanie! I embrace you and I celebrate you and I collapse the distance between us until there is only light.

Here Jeanie looks horrified and Le Feb's voice turns thick and heavy, a pile of pancakes where the syrup overflows.

I see the light inside you, I project the light inside you, I sing praise to Spirit for you, white trash Jeanie! he goes. I sing praise to the Summerland for the wretched smallness we know as Jeanie, for she, too, will live eternally in its light!

Magical fucking negro, Demarcus says in my head.

Who's the ghost fucking thought-talking? I go.

After that Jeanie goes to bingo with DJ Toad and Le Feb leaves to do errands. I run back and forth outside the closed kitchen cabinet doors saying I reflect you, Demarcus! I project you, Demarcus! while inside them Demarcus settles in to work on his mystery sketches all night.

Eventually I get too dizzy and sit, check for whatever bag of Cheetos is in reach. Maybe Le Feb's right, I say. Maybe everyone's holy.

I seriously doubt that, Demarcus says from inside his cabinet.

That night I dream it's Halloween. From the neck up I'm some kind of Cleopatra Egyptian Queen, from the neck down I'm myself but also this weird Candy Killer. I dream Demarcus and me trick-or-treat through The Lonely where at every door he hides behind me, floating and moaning. Sometimes answering the doors it's nice old Black ladies with pet chickens, but mostly it's dudes in pit-stained tees, tiny scruffer dogs springing between their tube socks yapping. Into my bag each person drops nothing but crap: scratched lotto tickets, Wendy's mustard packets, a bottle opener shaped like a bowling pin.

Then one guy gives me ten French fries hard as rocks, each one from a different restaurant, he tells me. Like a collection, he says. Antique, he goes.

One by one he puts them in my hand, counts off each one, one through ten, then at ten Jeanie walks up tattooed and naked behind him and somehow I sense that it's her place, not his, that this is where *she* lives, not him.

FIVE

FRIDAY MORNING'S THE MORNING BEFORE me and Demarcus's mission, one morning before opening day at the Fair. I wake up almost forgetting that tonight there's a séance since I've been so busy thinking about the Fair. I get up and eat Twinkies, look out the living room window, go squinty from the glinty metal scraps in the piles. Demarcus is still under the sink sleep-wadded, pulsing. Jeanie went out to shoplift smokes from somewhere.

After I finish my Twinkies I jut my elbows and do a tap dance, say Guess what, guess what? to Nurse Le Feb. He's at the table stapling new info sheets for the séance and I'm tap dancing around him going Guess, Le Feb, guess! Guess who's going to the Fair opening morning of opening day! I say.

Oh really? he says. Now he's getting ready for dusting. He's getting out his dust rags and his big can of Pledge.

Yeah *oh really*. I've got an important mission, I say. I do a kung fu move and pull Liesel's Visa from my pocket, wave it around like a prize in the air.

I haven't told Jeanie yet about Liesel's Visa, but somehow I know I can trust Nurse Le Feb. Like how he vacuums around my bare feet fast but careful not to hit them. It makes me want to show him all the things I have.

You can come if you want to, I say without thinking then right away call myself a dumbshit tard in my head. Tomorrow morning me and Demarcus have *got* to be sneaky, we've got Mombie's dressing room to bust into, Jeanie's black box to steal. There's no time to skip around with even the nicest big Black guys, no time for riding rides with every male nurse friend.

That's okay, he says. I hate crowds, but thank you for asking. You should probably keep that credit card to yourself, he says.

Relieved, I follow him with a dust rag and help him. Every third thing he hands me the Pledge and I get to do the spraying, the whole time me tricking him into telling me things. Like: I bet Demarcus was a really clean boy, I say. I bet he always picked up after himself.

Nurse Le Feb stops dusting and laughs. Not at all, he says. Demarcus was so messy.

Yeah but I bet you and Demarcus were like really good friends, I go. I bet you guys did stuff all the time together. Like those piles, I say. I bet you guys dug through them together.

Demarcus was a loner and those piles are filthy, Le Feb says. Here he stops to look up, like he's thinking. One time before his mom died we all went out for ice cream, Le Feb says. I remember it like yesterday, it was right after Marlene hired me.

You knew his mom? I say.

Lisa? Of course, he goes. She and Demarcus had moved in with Marlene right before I did. I was hired to replace Miss Rosemary, Lisa's mother.

Demarcus's grandma they lived with? I say.

Her name was Miss Rosemary, Le Feb goes. Marlene's caretaker before me. She had a heart attack and left for the Summerland when poor Lisa was only twenty. Her and little Demarcus were living in Miss Rosemary's place on the fifth floor. Demarcus hadn't even started school yet and Lisa had nowhere to go and she'd only just started her apprenticeship.

Apprenticeship? I go. I thought apprentices were from olden times, Deadwood Dick things, etc.

She was an apprentice to the ocularist right off the Green Line on Thirty-Fifth, he says, as if that might mean something to me. An ocularist is someone who makes glass eyes, he reminds me. Lisa would have been one by now had she lived. She was extraordinarily talented. When she wasn't taking care of Demarcus she spent all her time painting people's irises, he says. That and reading classical mythology.

How did she die, what happened to her? I say and Le Feb says she had an aneurysm two days before Demarcus's seventh birthday.

Her brain exploded, I say and he says, No, an aneurysm. Anyway, Lisa's mother, Miss Rosemary, was one of Marlene's oldest friends, so when Miss Rosemary died leaving Lisa and her four-year-old nowhere to go, Madame invited them to live here and hired me so Lisa could keep her apprenticeship. For a few years we were our own little family, he goes.

Sometimes I miss it, he says almost sadly.

It's lunchtime when we're finished cleaning. Jeanie's still gone but Demarcus wakes up, materializes by the living room window. I can tell by his face he needs time for his sad ocean thoughts before speaking, so I go to the bedroom and help Nurse Le Feb feed Head On The Pillow her lunch. I load the baby spoon she likes best with onion noodle soup and then with every third spoonful Le Feb wipes under her mouth while I re-stir the noodles.

Head On The Pillow isn't as scary now as the first time I saw her. Because I know how really out of it she is, all the weird wonky shit she says between whooshes. Sometimes she doesn't even remember who I am. She'll smile and say And who are you, young scoundrel?

Other times she's agitated and thinks I'm hiding a pistol in my pocket, that I'm the Devil Dwarf from Death Notch there to drag her to hell.

Today she says it's closing time when lunch is almost over.

I say Okay, Marlene. I say Finish your soup.

Come back—and—transmit—tomorrow, she says and then I start spooning her her pudding. She loves chocolate pudding, she swallows it fine even when she thinks I'm Devil Dwarf. Today her eyes are bright and wet and she's got me fixed in her vision, but her tongue still folds like a cat's tongue to lap up the pudding.

You wonder—how I do it—don't you? she says.

Do what? I say and she says Receive them.

What I do is I—go—into my ear, she says. There's a bench—near my sixth chakra—where if I sit—I hear them.

That is so cool, I say. You go, girl, I go.

ARE YOU READY for the Fair or what? I say when finally Demarcus comes out from behind the living room curtains.

Beware her. Beware Skulla, he goes. This is not a good idea at all, he goes.

First thing's to find out where Mombie is, I say. Where she'll be and when, where her dressing room is.

Beware her fang teeth, her kicking legs, Demarcus goes.

I'm so effing hungry, where's the taco chips? I say, then I'm getting up to go find them.

Look in my book if you want to know, Demarcus says, then wads up to float behind me. Skulla has twelve legs and six serpent necks with six heads. Six snapping dogs tied to her waist, he tells me.

Where's that fucking chip dip? I go.

Molly, I'm trying to help you, Demarcus says.

Demarcus, I'm trying to find our ghost moms, I go.

Molly, who on earth are you talking to? from somewhere else in the apartment shouts Nurse Le Feb and I look at Demarcus the ghostwad and shout No one.

SIX

AN HOUR BEFORE THE SÉANCE and Jeanie's not back yet. I'm feeling real sickish, I've got the craps bad. All afternoon down my hatch it's been licorice whips and taco chips and now my gut's killing me with red and black licorice shits, twirling barbershop poles asplash out my ass.

From the living room Le Feb shouts at me tonight's séance theme after I ask him. Contact Those Who Died Before You Met Them! he says.

I shout through the bathroom door how it won't be so bad. Better than last week's Kleenex Clutchers, I go. Them crying and shaking and all so professionally sad.

But oh no, I'm so wrong, Le Feb tells me. These people mourn just as hard, sometimes harder, he says.

I leave the bathroom already arguing, the toilet flushing in full color.

Did you wash your hands? Le Feb says. He's setting up the folding chairs for the séance circle, lining the legs up perfect along the orange rug's edge.

Le Feb, oh my god, you're effing crazy, I say.

If you're really that sick go lie down then, he goes.

I was going to help him, but fine, whatever, I slo-mo moonwalk to the bedroom holding my stomach instead.

Head On The Pillow's asleep as I lie on the couch and listen to her whooshes. They're like ocean waves going back and forth over jaggy rock, ripped-up land. They sooth my sore guts, they're like a blanket put over them, they send me straight into a deep swimmy nap.

I'm sleeping so good until Le Feb comes in, loud-breathing and brick-footed. With one eye open and one eye still aswim, I watch him lift Head On The Pillow's lung window. I watch him hike up her old lady blue nightie then I watch him shoot her in the thigh with a giant syringe.

Oh be—joyful! all the sudden she wakes up gasping and here Le Feb sees my one eye seeing him.

It's okay, he says. This is okay, Molly. In everything I do I feel the divine hand.

He twirls the syringe and says this time would I please stay here until the séance was over? Could I please stay in here quietly without moaning until the séance was done?

But what if I'm dying, what if I'm dead? I say. He'll go to the store and get me Pepto-Bismol he says.

Don't bother, I say, I'd rather die than drink pink shit. But he's already out the door and I'm off the couch already, I'm already moving through the hallway looking for wherever Demarcus is.

Demarcus, where are you? Where're you hiding? I say.

I check behind the living room curtains but that's not where he's hiding. I know probably he's wadded under the kitchen sink doing art stuff, but fuck him, I'm tired of being the one always looking for him. Head On The Pillow's awake for real now, she's warming up her vocal chords, she's singing scales up and down like on a staircase with half the stairs missing. La la la, she goes upward. Mi mi mi, she goes down. Now she open-throats the opening of "Home on the Range."

I note a few things here: that Nurse Le Feb left the syringe sitting on top of the iron lung. That the bottle he stabbed the syringe in before stabbing Head On The Pillow with it sits on top of the dresser in a nest of dead kid shit from the séance last week.

I walk over to the dresser like Hey look at all this kid stuff! but instead of the yo-yo I pick up the syringe bottle and sniff it, ask Head On The Pillow how much it hurts getting stuck with a syringe.

Not hardly at all! she says, her words shoved fast together without whooshes. I've been doing it—once a week—since 1952, she says.

From just the way she's talking I can tell that it's for real, whatever's in the bottle. The sudden crystal clearness of her words and thinking.

I ask how her stomach feels and she says Marvelous! Rooty-tooty!

That sounds good to me so I pull down my jeans and slap my butt red. Eyes closed and counting I stick the needle in on three. Then for fun I walk around the bedroom zombie-armed and pants-down, laughing and crying and but mostly laughing.

I'm addicted, I'm addicted, I'm addicted! I say. To be honest sometimes I'm just so fucking awesome and funny.

TELL ME ABOUT YOUR SEA GODS, I whisper when I find Demarcus. Like the day I met him, he's hiding under the lung. I pull back the red spangled curtains like the first time I pulled them and there he is, all white-glowing fuzz.

I want to know every last one of them! I say.

Before the syringe my brain was slow gray sludge and never ever never a high-speed train, but now it's whistling and chugging and hiss-whispering to say: Sea Gods, Sea Gods, learn of them now!

And fuck, it's like Fuck, I'm a genius girl now! And everything's new, even every smell, I sniff my pits and even my pits smell like brains.

Oh my god, Demarcus, *c'mon*. Sea gods, Demarcus, tell me!

Demarcus's face lights up but when he talks he talks so so so slowly. Welll whaat doo yoou waantt tooo knoww, he says.

All the sea things, all of it, everything, I say, then I crawl under the iron lung to sit beside him. When I pull the spangled curtains shut I knock over a stack of *Omni*s and my arm shoots through the ghost smoke of one of his legs. Shit, shit, shit! I'm so fucking sorry! I say.

Demarcus says There's nothing you can do to hurt me.

Tell me everything, I say. Start at the beginning, I go, and he says In the beginning there was only Pontos.

Yeah yeah, good good, what's after Pontos? I say, my toes twitching fierce like having to pee. And my socks, my Heatwaves, where did they go, those fuckers? When and why did they leave my feet?

In the beginning there was Pontos, Demarcus says, his ghost hand raised up like he wants to high-five me. I wind back like to slap it to him good, but he jerks his arm higher, jiggles his fire fingers under the lung like to heat up the metal, set it aflame.

Close your eyes twice, he says.

I close my eyes once and all I get is eyelid blackness, but the second time I close them then it's flames. Then after the flames there's a picture flickering, then this warbled, muffled sound. Then the picture unflickers to hold steady—the picture's the ocean, Demarcus's voice the sound, him reciting the Cycle of the Great Deluge to me. Somehow with my eyes closed I can see the whole thing, how it destroyed the first and fourth mankinds, how in the Great Deluge I wild mermen fought Satan's Giant Waves.

How for weapons the mermen sharpened spears on the jaggy lip of Ditmar (a bottom-water volcano and the birthplace of Pontos, destroyed in the Great Deluge III). How then the mermen threw their holy spears at the Waves sent by Satan and how the Waves didn't die from the spears but instead they caught them, how when they pitched them back in the mermen's faces, the mermen turned their backs, faced away. How spine-stabbed and spear-heavy the mermen watched the first sunset smiling because mermen backs are barnacles and spears are like thorns they pluck out and throw away.

How in the end the Giant Waves got the mermen anyway, flooded their secret coral cavern and cut each merman in two. They ate the screaming man-tops during their nighttime dinner war-chanting, sent the dead fish bottoms floating bloodless out of the cave.

By the time we get to the Great Deluge IV, I myself am ocean-floating. No spangled curtains, no twang-sung scales, no ghost boy hovering in the lung's underdark around me. Just me backfloating on clean green waves, somewhere in the air seabirds cawing.

Suddenly the wind shifts to float me the other direction and slow like a dumbshit I remember I'm not actually in the ocean, it's the iron lung that's moving.

I sit straight up and open my eyes (the seabirds in the air are still cawing). Demarcus in one corner is re-wadding to light, trying to fold himself inside the red velvet curtains. I lean over to flick him, lift the curtains to peek: it's not water or waves or the Great Deluge V, it's two giant white nurse shoes, velcroed and pumping.

Wait, wait—I'm not ready! Head On The Pillow goes from above me. My lipstick! she says. Tangerine Dream—please.

Le Feb stops the lung and I stretch my ears to listen. At first all I hear are the lung's steady whooshes, Head On The Pillow smacking her lips, but then when my ears settle the Casio's auto-play fades in, a robotty bossa nova faint from the living room. Then I hear whispers and now loud clapping, the people in the living room excited for the séance to begin so that they can contact their loved ones who died before they met them.

You're my someone to ride the river with, Head On The Pillow tells Le Feb.

You're my Deputy, she says and Le Feb says he knows.

He takes his place behind the lung again and suddenly we're moving. We're out the bedroom into the hall and then we're circling inside the circle of clapping, no one but Demarcus knowing I'm under the lung, that I'm a hidden part to this circus, a daredevil girl who folded herself into a cannon for fun.

Good Evening—my living—rodeo! Head On The Pillow says to start the show. Pray—the transmissions—this evening—are clear—and strong!

I look at Demarcus, wait for him to do his eye lasers, but this time he just sits there like he's meditating, just staring ahead.

What's the deal, aren't you going to help her? I think to him and telepathically he says No, I'm going to sit this one out. I need to save my energy for the studio, he goes.

Whatever, I think to him. It won't be as good without you, I go.

Head On The Pillow's first customer's an old man whose mom died giving birth to him. He jumps out of his folding chair to set something of hers on the lung. His old man feet tap impatiently only a few inches away from me, tap faster and faster the longer Head On The Pillow hums. She hums forever, for at least five minutes, then Oh—too—bad—your mom's—reincarnated, she says. She says his mother's no longer in the Summerland because now she's this New Mexico pawn shop owner's son.

The lady going next wants to talk to her miscarriage and I want to know so bad what she sets on the lung. Whatever it is, she down-plunks it like it's heavy and this time Head On The Pillow doesn't even bother to hum.

Your spirit guide—is on—vacation, says Head On The Pillow. Your substitute—is a—singing—cowboy, she goes. That's why—you've been—crying—lately.

It's true, I've been pretty dreamy and lonesome these days, the woman goes.

Le Feb sets his Casio to Church Bell Tower, plays "Bury Me Not on the Lone Prairie" while Head On The Pillow and all the séance people sing along.

It's all so boring I have to pinch myself to stay awake now. I pinch myself and pinch myself and think of all the jokes I'm not pulling. I could be jumping out from the lung giving everyone the finger. I could be jumping out shouting Motherfuckers, ghost alive!

I've almost worked myself up to it when the apartment door opens. I'm thinking it's Jeanie come back from shoplifting, but no, it's some man and woman, I can tell by their shoes. Them and their navy New Balances stride to the center of the séance and Le Feb says Oh shit and everyone gasps.

Le Feb quick halts the Casio but Head On The Pillow keeps singing until finally she clues in and then everything is silent. Me and Demarcus and everyone.

We want to talk to Anthony, the lady says, then on the lung there's a clanking, her setting something on it, and whatever it is starts Demarcus folding and unfolding over and over again.

Then there's a long hush in the séance circle but for Head On The Pillow's whooshes. Finally she clears her throat and says, Those are—Anthony's ashes?

Who the hell else's? goes the man.

Head On The Pillow says she'll do her best and here Demarcus starts shaking, shoots his eye flames into her like rockets from where he sits under the lung. At first there's a jolt and then the air changes to something denser and that's when Head On The Pillow begins to speak:

I'm—rewired—here—it's different.

Baby, we won the civil suit, says the lady.

Tell Lardo—hello. Say hi—to—Bugface.

Tell me Demarcus the arsonist isn't where you are, says the woman. Tell me he's somewhere on fire, that he's burning in hell.

He's not—in—the Summerland—Mama.

That's good to hear, baby, that's such a relief.

Take care of yourself, son, says Anthony's father.

And here Demarcus does the thing he did last week. He hurls himself into Head On The Pillow to possess her. I'm sorry, I'm sorry, I'm so sorry! he/she shrieks.

And I swear to you, I swear, I try not to do it. I try to swallow the red-black rumble coming up my throat but can't. I lift the velvet lung curtain and barf licorice all over Anthony's parents, cover their nice sneakers and the orange rug in my chunks.

Tonight's transmissions are over! Le Feb says, hurrying to his cleaning closet. See you next week! he says for the second time in two weeks.

SEVEN

The Fair in daytime's different than at night. Opening day the crowds drown out the blue everywhere, douchewads in the thousands snarfing giant turkey legs, waiting hours for rides in lines that zigzag for blocks. I'm not worried, I've got everything I need on my body. Liesel's Visa in my left pocket, directions hand-drawn by Jeanie in my right.

Way late last night when she got back from shoplifting she left a Fair map unfolded on my head while I slept. This morning I woke up in the living room and found it, hard-penciled arrows pointing the route to Mombie, tiny bird tracks she must have scribbled.

Then right before we left she said Don't fuck around, Molly. To Demarcus she said Better fucking help her, Ghost Tard.

Get in and get out, she said. Don't fucking dawdle. Get the box and bring it straight here.

But now that we're here her words seem super far away from me, the pinch of her shoulder grip gone, a dream I had.

We've got enough time to do stuff, I say to Demarcus.

We've already passed the Observatory Tower and the Parachute Jump and now we're plowing through the crowd near the blue archways to Arcadium.

Ride some rides, I say. Corn dogs if you want one. On me, I say smiling, patting my jean pocket where Liesel's Visa sits.

As usual Demarcus ignores me, he says Let's take a different way. Let's cut through World Religion Showcase instead.

I remember last week how he freaked when we were close to the lake and he saw the water, so I'm all Whatevs, Demarcus, you lead the way.

Cutting through World Religion Showcase should be a shortcut to the Submarine Palace, but inside Demarcus slows down to browse the booths of every religion there is: Baptists, Hindus, Fire Eaters, you name it. Each booth has an Ambassador of Faith sitting behind a table to recruit you, your priests-monks-nuns in heavy black costumes, but mostly white ladies in slacks and angrily bobby-pinned buns. Sometimes old guys who look like city tree-trimmers. Sometimes young pimpled white dudes with their short-sleeved shirts tucked in.

Dorkfest Deluxe, but there are some cool things. The Pentecostals have a glass box of writhing snakes you can stand in. For five dollars they'll wave the snakes around and holler in wild tongues at you, but they don't take Visa and I've got no cash.

Tapes of actual exorcisms loop on TVs at one of the Catholic tables, of course Demarcus floats over there first thing. The most awesome one is the possession of this dumb rural farm kid who over and over again growl-whispers that he's the demon Akabor, that he squirts the Precious Blood and fucks the Five Sacred

Wounds. All this while he spits and rolls his eyes to the back of his head.

This is so badass, I say while we're watching.

Molly, it's so fake, Demarcus says.

Down from the Catholics is a table with no TVs, only some pamphlets and papers in front of a white lady with wet hair. It's the Quaker table, I know it, I can tell just by looking. I'm afraid to walk by, afraid one of the old Resident Friends might be lurking near.

Molly, I tell myself. Don't be fucking silly. It's just a white lady and a card table and her Historic Peace Church fliers. It's just some For More Information sign-ups and free postcards listing Outreach Campaigns.

I turn to walk the other way but in my head Demarcus goes Where are you going?

He's floating steady in front of the Quaker table, the wet-haired lady oblivious.

Young lady, are you interested in becoming a Quaker? the lady says. I look away from Demarcus who's now grinning at me, waving his finger fire Hi, like Look what I did. So I go over and pretend to look at her fliers.

No, not at all. I really believe in war, I say.

Next to her elbow there's a flier taped to a coffee can, a slit cut for dropping money through the plastic lid. And guess what, guess what?

Guess whose face is on the flier?

Motherfuckers, it's me! *I* fucking am.

My photocopied face under the words QUAKER GIRL MISSING! then after that Evelyn's name and phone number.

And I won't lie, when I see me and then her name and number I see at the same time her in the community living room making piles of this flier. I see Dad in the basement rubbing his dumbfuck eyes over dumbfuck Delores and Petey, but Evelyn upstairs on the couch, trying to find me. It makes my heart ping—not a lot, just a little. Evelyn's no monster, she hasn't been terrible to me.

But. The picture she picked for the flier is super fucking awful: me last Easter, before Jeanie came. Me standing on the scorched front porch before they rebuilt it in the dumbshit yellow dress Evelyn made me wear the whole day.

I was a stupid girl then, but I'm not one now. Now I'd never wear a dress like that ever and even if I did it wouldn't fit anyway, my looks have changed big time since then. I'm taller with more freckles plus there's more space between my eyes now. No one looking at that girl would think she was me.

I'm so sure of it I'm fearless. I say How sad about that missing Quaker girl, tragic! I say.

Little Quaker girl, what? the Quaker lady asks me.

I point to the coffee can, to me on the flier, and the Quaker lady blinks and blinks like for the first time seeing it.

Oh, yes! That little girl. Bet she's dead, she says.

At the Sea of International Waters Demarcus unwads from his laughing to salute the Viking lady statue rising up from the lake. Her naked slaves and the angels' wings are water-dipped, glinting. Mombie's dressing room is in the Submarine Palace under the lake. That's where her ride attraction The Sleeping Silent Princess is. To get to the Submarine Palace there are three glass elevators where you pick one to take, before that three red-roped lines where you pick one to wait in.

I pick the line moving fastest and wipe my face with a moist towelette from Le Feb. I don't want to be grimy should we ride Sleeping Silent Princess, I'm thinking, then I'm looking close at the towelette when Demarcus starts whispering weird shit in my ear: The nymphet daughters of Pontos bathe on rocks and braid their hair. They gaze at the naked wrestlers of the Games, he says.

I say Demarcus, oh my god, that's fucking pervy, then the lady in line ahead of us turns around and stares, looks either side of me like looking for my mother. My mom is dead, I say. You can turn back around, I tell her.

After almost an hour in line it's our turn. It's a long ride down, but the elevator's see-through. Everyone oohs and ahs over the lit schools of fish, the fake coral, etc. The guy standing next to me pinches his nose and swallows, nudges me like saying I should do it.

That's stupid, this place is pressurized, you're not gonna explode, I say. The man moves him and his kids to the less crowded side of the elevator.

Demarcus floats away too, runs his ghost fingers over the glass, and to my amazement the fish outside can see him. They swim to his flickers, fish-nose the glass where his flames tap.

Hello, my sisters, he says to them. Hello, my sadnesses, he goes.

The elevator dings and we're let out onto a long glass walkway. Blue carpet covers the floor. Somewhere water sounds are piped in. People file out the elevator and walk triple-file down the carpet, heads craned up to look at the lake above. I'm sure everyone's thinking the same thing as me: What would happen if this glass tube shattered? Who would drown and who would swim?

In the walkway Demarcus lags, floats horizontal like a fish behind me. Quick, hurry, you're not an effing fish, I say.

I can already see at the end of the walkway the arched golden doors to the Palace where behind them I'm expecting all fancy Palace things: white-wigged ladies and trumpets and carriages. Sea things carved in marble, harps lining the halls.

But when you walk through the golden doors all it is is a giant food court underwater. A mall inside a giant greenhouse, fish overhead. People everywhere pulling their white plastic chairs out, piling food trays on tables while triumphy space movie music trickles down invisible on your head.

Part of me is disappointed and part of me is I should have known better and part of me is Fuck, this is one kickass mall. What Demarcus thinks I don't have to ask. Art is dead, enjoy your late-stage capitalist buffet, he says, then starts wadding himself into a glowing ball.

If it's so bad then why's it also so awesome? I ask him.

Here he pauses his wadding and looks at me so serious. It's not awesome, he says. You are cloned from cartoon DNA, Molly. You are a symptom of something larger, he says.

You are a symptom of something larger! I say in a high whiny voice to make fun of him but it's too late, he's already a ball of ghost light wedged in my armpit.

Demarcus in my armpit, I walk through the Palace, which besides the food court is mostly kiosks selling shirts-candy-keychains. Where in a normal mall there'd be a fountain they've got fourteen near-nude ladies on horses, it's called: *The Fourteen Godivas: An Equine Burlesque.* No way I'd touch my naked crotch on a giant horse bareback, but the fourteen Godivas love it, they ride around the mini arena blowing kisses while their horses do these intricate steps. The big finale is the head Godiva blowing her whistle then the horses lining up to do the can-can while the fourteen Godivas chink tiny finger cymbals and jiggle their sequined tits.

Jeanie said Go straight to Mombie's dressing room, but I think it's only fair I get to see Mombie before stealing back her stupid box. So we find the line for the Sleeping Silent Princess ride, it starts outside the fake front of a marqueed movie palace where once inside you get to an even longer line. At the end of that line red-vested usher guys usher you into a tiny boat, red or golden. Then the red and golden boats glide on a track through the shallow waters of a dark canal where on either side the life of the Sleeping Silent Princess is depicted on giant IMAX screens.

We're well into the line on the inside, the boats and ushers and canal in sight, when Demarcus unfurls from my armpit, spins clockwise, pushes bits of fire through his eyes. I tell him right there to stop acting like a pussy.

When it's our turn the usher guy asks how many, looks around behind me for a dad or mom. I say two, for a moment forgetting that Demarcus is invisible. One! Just one! Just me! I say, correcting myself. I only ride rides alone, I say.

The guy's like Whatever and points to my boat, it's plastic bench seat big enough for three people. We get in and sit down and the guy pulls a black lever and suddenly we're moving, motoring through the first dark tunnel alone.

I tell Demarcus to use his fingers to light up the water. I expect him not to listen but he leans over the boat and shines his hand down. Opening day and already Mountain Dew cans and gum wrappers float on top of the water. Litterbug motherfuckers littering, I say and Demarcus says Mankind is a parasite. He says One day the ground will open its mouth.

Soon the dark tunnel widens and IMAX screens dome the walls and ceiling where a dozen flickering silent movies loop the same actress in different scenes. The actress looks sort of like Mombie from the posters but also not really. The same black circled eyes and powdered face but with hair overall less angled and stabby—more frizzy and soft, fluffed out like a nest. And the real Silent Princess's nose is smaller than Mombie's (and Jeanie's!), the tip of it's rounder, plus her lips are twice as thick.

I look at Demarcus to see what he thinks, but he's not craning his neck like I am, not looking up and sideways and backward to watch all the clips. He's jackknifed over the boat shining fire on all the litter, splashed-up ride water erasing his arms, his chin.

Put out your fires, you're ruining it, I tell him. You can't watch movies with the lights on, I say.

I didn't tell Demarcus, but at the end of the ride is the real-life Sleeping Silent Princess, her real unrotted corpse inside a crystal casket they let you see. It's on display until New Year's when at midnight they'll reanimate her, but for now these movies are the only place she's still alive, tied down to train tracks, gun-pointed to corners, hijacked by Indians crossing the Continental Divide.

Our boat turns a corner, slows for the biggest screen of all: her as Cleopatra, all snake bracelets and eyeshadow. Shiny black geometrical hair. Let it be done! she mouths dramatically, the words in fancy lettering beneath her. The people in the boats in front and back of us all hush like it's holy.

We turn another corner and float out of the tunnel so that now we're facing a darkened stage. At first nothing happens and then lights turn on to show a fancy bedroom: a white canopy bed, the posts wound in feather boas, a dresser covered in pill bottles and Oscar statues. On the bed's a mound of peach frill and at first it tricks you, at first you think Fluffy pillows but then it moves. It rolls over and lengthens slow to show it has a body: black hair, red lips, Jeanie's eyes.

Mombie, I know it, even in my little boat far away.

She's wearing a peach kimono and reclining, one hand on her forehead, the other resting on a peach princess phone. Suddenly it rings loud and everyone jumps in their boat seats. I jump too, my guts twisted and confused. I want both to spit and cuss at her on behalf of Jeanie but also to see what will happen when she answers the phone.

What happens is this: she answers without speaking! She *mimes* saying something! Then her face and hands mime sadness while from surround-sound speakers violin music flutters and swells.

Then over the speakers a booming narrator guy speaks. Oh no, can it be? he says. The phone call from Metro-Goldwyn-Mayer she's been dreading?

Mombie listens on the phone while pacing the stage kimonoed and fretty, winding the phone cord and heaving sighs every which way.

Poor Silent Princess, your career is over! the narrator goes. MGM says you've peaked, that your working days are numbered!

Mombie grips the phone in one hand and bites the knuckles of the other. The people in the ride boats begin to boo. Fuck MGM! Fuck Samuel Goldwyn someone goes.

Alas, Hollywood movies are silent no more, says the narrator. And sadly, Silent Princess, your voice sounds strange. Poor Silent Princess of the Silver Screen! he goes, almost wailing. Born Louise Grobacheau to Oklahoma farmers without a penny. You've done so well and come so far, he goes. But Miss Grobacheau, let's be honest, you're not getting any younger. In fact, at twenty-six, your legendary beauty's beginning to fade.

Here things get big. Mombie slams the phone down on its receiver. Then she stares out at us in our little boats. Her face goes stone-cold, her face like You are the audience who betrayed me. Then super slow from her kimono pocket she pulls a pistol out.

The people in the boats shout No, no, no! Don't do it!

Yes Yes Yes! I shout. I want to see you do it!

Demarcus rolls his eyes and mutters something about fake beasts making fake offerings, then Mombie puts the pistol to her chest and mouths Let it be done!

Then there's a loud bang, then sparks and blue smoke, then the smell of gunpowder over the canal water wafting. The stage goes dark and the boats begin moving then we're taken through a white light tunnel into the ride's big finale: a gold and silver cathedral split down the middle by the track where above us instead of stained-glass Jesuses and Marys it's stained-glass Silent Princesses in scenes from her movies. Instead of priests there are ushers helping people disembark in two lines. Both lines lead up to a seven-step altar. On the altar's a white platform encircled by a thousand silver roses and on top of the platform's a frosted crystal coffin with golden hinges that twinkle in the light.

The line takes forever, Demarcus gets bored and floats around the cathedral, flies up to the stained-glass windows and pretends to set them on fire. When it's my turn to pass the coffin I put my eye right up to the crystal, but before I see anything from some hidden speaker the ride's narrator comes on: Please do not disturb the Sleeping Silent Princess! Please do not touch her crystal coffin! The Sleeping Princess will rise again soon, her cosmic sex energy restored for all to behold! Will she have her revenge on Hollywood at last? The countdown to Reanimation begins New Year's Eve, tickets on sale at all ticket locations.

God I wish I could see her dead each day before they reanimate her.

I want to chart her non-rot and then I want to see them reanimate her. My guess is it has to do with electrifying her somehow, jolting her alive again, her heart back into beating. Probably jolting one by one each and every dead part.

EIGHT

Jeanie's map says that to find the staff dressing rooms we need to go back the way we came. We leave the Crystal Cathedral's gift shop exit then bird-step Jeanie's arrows past the T-shirt and candy kiosks to the food court blinking bright white, blue, green. Her instructions say find the metal swing door between Fish Licks and Sbarro and I'm looking super hard not seeing it but then all the sudden I do. We wait until no one's looking then push through the door into a bright hallway, I feel like Encyclopedia Brown, like Nancy Drew.

Down this hall we find the costume warehouse Jeanie marked in Sharpie, wild outfits on racks ceiling to floor. Boxes of feathers piled on shelves next to spools of shimmer fabric and the walls hung with wigs, row after row of bloodless scalps. A half-costumed actor comes up to ask who the hell I am and I say Fuck off, one of the Godivas is my mom. I say she needs more sequins to cover her boobs up then dart fast through the racks to the opposite wall's door. This door, according to Jeanie, leads straight to the dressing rooms.

And she's right! It's a long hallway of doors with different crazy names on them: Squire of Poseidon #5, Funtime Bear #2. Hottentot Venus, Young Lady Tremaine. Demarcus hovers at each door to take in the name on it, but we don't have time for that crap, Come on, I say.

The nest of the beast is down there, he says passing through me. He floats down the hall straight to her door: Sleeping Silent Princess #3.

The nest of the bitch, home of Jeanie's mortal enemy. The buzz-sawed twin, the evil twin, the black-box stealer Mombie.

Demarcus, if you're my friend, open this door, I say.

He takes his sweet time while I look up and down the hall. He hums the hum that means he's thinking then wads a finger flame small enough to stick in the lock of the door. It's taking forever and it's pissing me off, but right as I pull back a Heatwave to kick the door in, there's a click and some smoke and the door swings open.

Fuck yeah! I say, my hand up to high-five him, but Demarcus leaves me hanging, floats into the room.

Hurry up, he says. Let's get it and go.

Don't be a chickenshit, I say, switching the light on like I live here. Jeanie says Mombie's shift's not over until three.

It's nothing to me, but you're still living, he goes.

Mombie's dressing room's got one floor lamp and an old ugly couch, a messy counter beneath a lightbulbed mirror. Next to the couch there's a blue Igloo cooler with various hairstyle magazines fanned out on top: *Celebrity Hair*, *Wedding Hair*,

Short Hair Tomorrow. On the counter are three Styrofoam heads, two with wigs on them, a Cleopatra one and a wild one, ratty backcombed spirals just like Jeanie's. Plus a billion million tiny things: lipsticks and eyeliners, face creams, eye powders. Half-empty packs of gold-tipped cigarettes. Full packs of gum.

I know I'm here just for her box. But I can't help it, I like it here and want bad to linger. It's like sometimes on Outreach with Dad and Evelyn, seeing inside other people's houses, their ashtrays, their pizza boxes, their R-rated rentals sticking out their VCRs.

On the wall facing the couch are three framed things hanging: a floorplan of where to go in case of a fire, an autographed Whitney Houston Greatest Love tour poster, and a black-and-white yearbook page. Stella Adler Studio of Acting, Class of 1985, it says, each smiling turtlenecked person's hand tucked under their chin all dainty. Jeanie'd ride mud into all these assholes' nice teeth, but I can't help but go through each row of faces looking for Mombie's.

There she is.

Gritted and pinched at the bottom, looking almost but not quite like Jeanie.

In the corner next to Mombie's photo a narrow newspaper clipping's folded, stuck in the frame:

Missing Balloon Girl

Presumed Dead, Search Continues

In Treetops, Ditches

Ha ha, stupid fuckers! I try to picture it and can't: Jeanie dead, bird-pecked and blue, bone-tangled high up in some death tree's branches. I can't even picture it, what stupid fuckers.

Demarcus floats off his high horse to look at the newspaper clipping too. That's cute, he goes. See what they did? He points one of his flames at the newspaper headline.

Right away I see what he means. They called her a girl when she's a woman, I say.

No, Dummy, it's a haiku, he says then flicks his flames against my arm to count out the syllables.

Yeah, no shit, I say. That's how they do headlines. Listen, Demarcus, we've got to stop fucking around.

So we stop fucking around and look for the box. It's not hard to find, it's next to the couch behind the cooler.

I found it, I found it! I say, pulling it out. Demarcus says Let's go and I say Goddamn, I really fucking found it!

And even though before we left this morning Jeanie said Don't you guys fucking open it, here I whisper to Demarcus Hey, Demarcus, let's look inside.

We should leave, Demarcus says but I stare him down like No way, nuh-uh.

Let's go, Demarcus says but I'm already testing the lid.

Admit it, I say. You want to know what's in here as bad as I do.

Okay, you're right, he says, so I rip off the lid.

Inside's just one thing and it's long and narrow and wrapped in tissue paper, like a tissue-wrapped baseball bat for toddlers or elves. I rip where it's taped and tiger-shred the tissue then hold in my hands a sooty girl's arm made of wax.

The arm's the size of my arm except my hands and fingers are fatter. Also there's a miniature Bible glued to its palm. Holy Bible in gold letters runs melted across the blackened plastic cover, but the pages are still clean, still totally flippable. Like the white snakeless fingers, still perfect and unscorched. Holding it's like holding either something impossibly beautiful or beautifully impossible. A butterfly's wing. A unicorn's horn.

And I know what this means, that Jeanie trusts me as her only apostle. How many people would I trust with the video of my mom?

THIS MORNING WHEN WE LEFT, Jeanie said to come right back when we got it, but we don't go right back because how would she know when we got it? She won't, so we stay at the Fair awhile, take the elevator out of the Submarine Palace.

Walking around Arcadium with Demarcus wadded in my armpit, I think: One day I'll tell my granddaughters about this, how the Observatory Tower looms like a haunted lighthouse over the lake, how the most awesome midway prizes are silvery grids of goldfish in baggies. How I take the one fish I win to the ladies' room to flush it, but how every time I flush it somehow he swims back so I let him live. I tell him good luck and lock the stall door to keep him safe as long as possible, crawl out underneath it then crawl right back under again: I almost forgot the box, Jeanie's wax arm, her Bibled hand! Dumbshit me left it sitting on the lid of the toilet.

Now we follow fat-cheeked security guards strolling slow into Night Town, mustached man-tubs whispering secret codes into walkie talkies. Every time we pass one his mustache twitches, no doubt him getting overcome with the fear of me. Me, the no-good girl punk not even security guards want to fuck with.

No one now will ever fuck with me!

I'm the ghost-friended badass who snuck into Mombie's dressing room, I'm a preteen hellion who emits her own scent: the awesome stink of a girl who bites, the blood-muddied funk of the bramble cats! In Grandpa Hack's Horror Mirrors each mirror shows you killed a different way, but no matter the mirror, no matter the wound, no matter stabbed all over, tractor-crushed, or drowned, I look wild and dirty always, a dirt bike gang's kitten. Someone waiting to sink rabies into the steak of your neck.

NINE

We get back to Bronzeville gut-soaked in grease batter. Demarcus is grumpy and my ears still tin-tin with roller-coaster sounds. I've got hold of Jeanie's box with both arms super careful because what if I tripped and it landed on a pile? It wouldn't matter tonight anyway, the piles are empty, lonely of pickers. Or maybe the pickers lonely of piles.

When we get close to The Lonely my heart pounds one way, but what I see when we get there makes it pound another. In front of the front steps: Jeanie's dirt bike, chained to a streetlight. Sparkling like it just got washed.

It couldn't be, I say. Lots of people have dirt bikes, I'm thinking.

But upstairs when we open the door to Demarcus's apartment Le Feb's nowhere to be seen and there in the living room are Mangus and Jeanie. Mangus bent over hooking up an old banged-up TV, Jeanie standing bossy holding the remote behind him. Mangus the doom metal lover, Mangus the dirt bike stealer, Mangus the fatass trailer park kid. He tracked Jeanie down to bring her her bike back, to hook up this pile-snatched TV for her.

Why? Because he loves her?

Or maybe she called him up and said Bring my bike back or else. Either way, he's here, mint dip packed deep in his cheek, him going through the channels saying Amazing, amazing.

Saying Babe, lookit, I got you HBO and CNN. I got you motherfucking *Dateline*, I got you fucking *Larry King*.

Fuck yeah you did, lover, says Jeanie.

Then she goes to high-five him and that's when she sees me standing there. Or at least sees her box that I'm very carefully holding.

Kittentits, you did it! Fucking A! she says then takes the box while her words bob up and down on the lake of my brain, the nicest words she's said to me ever.

Demarcus this whole time has been a ball of light by my side, but here he unfurls all the way while speaking weird myth shit in my mind telepathically: If she shows you her dog legs, cut one off. Scratch out her eyes with its claws, he says.

I ignore Demarcus's bullshit and say to Jeanie, Hey, Jeanie, what's he doing here? Isn't he our enemy?

Mind your own business, go play with Ghosty, she says. Go find Le Feb. Tell him we're out of hot sauce.

Okay, in a second, but what about our moms? I say. We got you your box back, now you tell us how to necromance our moms.

What's the little girl talking about? Mangus says. He's on the couch now watching *Star Trek: The Next Generation*, the lump of him the hunched slump of someone taking a shit.

Jeanie knows how to summon the dead, I say. Her cellmate Cumguzzler Tina from Cincinnati showed her.

Wow, super fucking cool, Mangus goes. I had no idea you had friends in Cincinnati, Mr. Shit For Brains says.

Shut the fuck up, Mangus, Jeanie goes, then kicks him in his shin medium-lightly. He keels over whimpering like she kicked him way hard and then I remember: the sawed-off hammer heads in the tips of her Keds.

And now she turns to me, smiling. Wolfy.

Kittentits, you're such a little dumbfuck, she says. Necromancy's not real. There's no Cumguzzler Tina. I only said that shit to get you to help me.

Huh? I say, because what she's just said hasn't quite hit me but also at the same time it hits me right effing away, like my heart's already dropped dead into the basement of my stomach while my chickenshit brain stays a few steps away, stays sounding her words out like some ultra dumbass, slowly.

What the fuck, I say, and my eyes start to water. Cumguzzler Tina was a Satanist, you said. You said she summoned the girl who died of epilepsy!

Thanks for getting my box back, but Fun Time's over, Jeanie tells me. Now it's time for little girls to go home.

I brought her fucking box back and it wasn't easy.

I did what she wanted and she fucking lied.

Here Demarcus's apartment fades, recedes to background, fogs over. Everything goes fuzzy and then I'm back on the Sleeping Silent Princess ride. I see the pile of peach frill on the bed stretch and straighten into Jeanie. I see the peach frill rip to show the jaggy scar going down her side. I see a stained-glass window of us sitting under a junkyard moon quiet. I see an open casket on an altar and my dead mom inside.

Tell me, I say. Now I'm bawling like a baby. You have to tell me how to do it, you promised, I go.

Molly, fuck her. Cut off her dog leg! Demarcus mind-shouts at me.

Jeanie puts the box down to grab the phone, dials 911 with a snake-twined finger. I'm calling to report the whereabouts of a missing person, she goes.

It's time, Demarcus says. Run right now or stay and claw her eyes out.

I grab the box, my heart bangs hard, then fast I'm running out the door.

Bitch! You lying bitch, I shout. You betrayed me, you motherfucker!

Then I run with Jeanie's box through the dark longness of The Lonely's sixteenth floor. Inside is Jeanie's wax arm, her tiny girl hand stuck to a Bible. A hand on a Bible means the truth, it means to swear you're not lying, so now I've got this honest fucking arm but I'll never see my mom because Jeanie fucking lied. Well fuck Jeanie, fuck mothers, fuck dads, those motherfuckers. I wanted to see her so bad. I wanted to see her so bad. I was never what she wanted and then she fucking died.

4

THE MOTHERING HEART

ONE

I RUN BACK THE WAY WE CAME, Demarcus flying above me. Past the pawn shops, the three Bronzeville Family Dollars, past smoking trash-can fires and towering piles. We get to the Red Line, we jump the turnstiles, and when we get on the train Demarcus whispers he's sorry.

You were right, I say.

I'm sorry, he says.

I want my mom, I say.

He says Me too.

The train's full of people going to the Fair, parents yawning into paper cups and kids clutching stuffed animals. I sit down facing posters for Mark Bogacki, DDS, and Cheryl Price, Chicagoland's best real-estate bitch ever. I know they're only posters but I'm sad and don't know what to do so what I do is I pretend I'm their daughter.

Mark Bogacki, my dad, says Come home to me now, and when he says home I picture House of Friends, dark on the outside but inside lamplit. Evelyn's fresh out of her bath and even on the train I smell the Epsomy fog of it, the White Shoulders powder sprinkled onto her skin like salt on mashed potatoes. Now she's in bed snoring, the heft of her quilted, a Prairie Girl romance split-spined, rising up and down on her chest. And Dad in the basement with Delores and Petey, him restitching their eyes, him blowing up my old baby floaties.

Back on the train my mom Cheryl winks at me, she's like Oh my dear sweetheart, don't listen to your dumbfuck dentist dad.

Okay, Mom, you can tell me what to do, I think-say.

And then, in a voice I've heard a thousand times but will never once remember, my real estate mom's lipsticked poster-lips say: Molly, look in your pocket.

I reach into my pocket and pull out Liesel's Visa, my ticket to the Fair.

TWO

The Observatory Tower in nighttime looms big and shining. The Sea of International Waters outstretches like sparkly tar. I'm a dead wild animal, a road-killed kitten, Demarcus barely even a glinting now. Jeanie's a bitch traitor who I'll hate forever but I've got Liesel's Visa and I've got Jeanie's wax arm. I would ride rides now, but I'm too sad and tired to be jostled. I want to stab Jeanie's guts out. I want to jawbreak her eyes.

Demarcus floats ahead of me, goes straight to the Cosmosphere, the white marbled space building where his asshole dad's art covers the walls.

We'll stay here for now, he says, fast-floating up the steps to the entrance. We'll find a maintenance closet like Jeanie did. This actually works better for my plans.

Plans? I say.

The project I've been working on. It's nothing, he says. Just some art things I'm going to do, he goes.

I BUY MYSELF FIVE corn dogs for dinner and eat them in the cyclorama while Demarcus wads and unwads himself waiting for the Fair to close. All the drop cloths and scaffolding are gone now. The fancy ARTIST RECEPTION FOR PAUL TURNER WILLIAMS sign is still standing. At first Demarcus floated past it without looking, but I see him watching it super close, giving dirty looks to anyone who reads his father's name.

Before the last visitors leave and the security guards lock the doors, we find a third-floor maintenance closet and hide there until ten fifteen. Demarcus unwads and I hide the black box behind a Wet Floor sign and when finally outside it goes completely quiet, I tiptoe out the closet while Demarcus fills himself in.

Back in the empty cyclorama he propels himself upward, floats high in the NASA-funded space-painted dome. His finger flames burn extra bright now, he says I need to get to work now, I say Demarcus, was I a total dumbshit for believing Jeanie could raise the dead?

Hovering, he looks down at me, drips ghost paint on my head. Maybe, he says. But I wouldn't feel bad about it. I almost believed her too, he goes.

He goes back to painting his weird painting but I can't make out what it is yet. Lots of crosshatched lines, a giant messy grid.

I expect him to stop talking now. I expect him to shoo me, but he doesn't.

I'm the one who should have known better, he says. Like Jeanie's ever read *The Odyssey* or the *Aethiopica* of

Heliodorus. Like she'd even know the Necromanteion if she walked right in.

What the fuck is Heliodorus? What the fuck is a Necromanteion? I ask him.

The Greeks and Romans thought necromancy was real, he says. I never believed in it, but becoming a thought form has forced me to reconsider certain things.

But what the fuck *is* it? A Necromanteion, tell me, I ask him.

A portal for spirits at the meeting point of three rivers. The Joyless River, the River of Burning Coals, the River of Lament, he goes.

I don't know, I say. That sounds like bullshit.

It probably is. It probably won't work, he goes. But you don't know what works and what doesn't until you try it. Like Isaac Newton. People think he was this rational scientist when really he was an alchemist nutjob who came up with the laws of physics while trying to turn rocks into gold.

So the necromancy people are nutjobs?

Totally. As bad as the Neoplatonists. Does "the hidden thing of our stone is nothing else than our viscous celestial and glorious soul" sound reasonable to you?

Fuck no it does not, I say.

But we can still try it, he goes. Here Demarcus squints one ghost eye closed, leans back to check the grid lines he just painted. The only problem is we don't know the rituals, he goes.

What do you mean? What rituals? I say. You mean like magic spells?

Spells are for children, Demarcus goes. Rituals are symbolic rites that activate the spheres of sensation. You'd have to get a book on it. *A Hundred Myths of the Sea* doesn't have that kind of thing.

I know who to talk to, I say the exact moment I realize I know.

I so seriously doubt that, Demarcus goes.

I know who, I promise, I say. This time tomorrow you'll have the spells, I go.

THREE

You might think it's hard for a little white girl like me to find out all by herself how to make a portal into the spirit world, but guess again, it's not that hard. The next morning I wake up super early on the floor of the maintenance closet, Demarcus sleep-wadded beside me, dripping ghost paint on the floor. At first I think we're in The Lonely, in the cabinet under the sink in the kitchen, but then yesterday comes back to me, every last feeling renews.

I don't wait for Demarcus to wake up before leaving. I really want to impress him with how competent I am. I get directions to the nearest Metra from strangers outside the Fair gates and am at Cal City Community College's JFK Memorial Library by nine ten. On Sundays they don't open until ten thirty, so I find a nice bench outside to sit on and wait.

For forty-five minutes I let my brain shuffle, the outside-sitting riffling thoughts and memories loose. At first it's the basics: Jeanie, you bitch, how I fucking hate you, you're not as badass as you think you are; dead Mom, what will I even say to you when I necromance you? And where the fuck has your ghost even been? Also, should I major in theater when I go to community college? Do you think I look like you?

Behind these thoughts there's this slow echo of pipe-drip, the ambient sound of my mind, I decide. For a while my thoughts run out and there's the lone pipe-drip then from nowhere a new thought floats in: Demarcus, his fire, how he died in flames falling. Part of me feels very on-his-side about it, feels really really super bad for him, but another part speaks up, is like Well at least he got to do an outside activity. Then another part chimes in, like God knows you never did.

Here's a secret I've never told anyone and never will: I've always wanted bad to go to summer camp. The kind where you do things like camping and horse riding and swimming—Sweetie things, I admit it, but imagine: big-ass squares of green grass surrounded on all sides by woods, ghosty. Cabins you sleep in with other girls where you all wear shorts and sports bras with teenage counselors at night who braid your hair.

I could have gone to camp for real once. The summer before the fire Evelyn showed me a brochure for a Quaker girls' camp in Pennsylvania. I could go there on a bus, she'd said.

I was very excited, I turned *COPS* down on the TV to look it over while Evelyn sat in what she called her parlor chair, parlor chair because it had belonged to her Quaker grandmother who back in olden times had a parlor with this chair. Now no one sits in the parlor chair ever. It doesn't exist, it burned in the fire.

But the camp brochure, the Quaker girls: they wore their hair in beautiful smoothed ponytails and carried what I discovered later were lacrosse sticks. Behind them were some other nice-haired girls eating apples, like they had gotten back from picking these apples then spread out these blankets to sit. Their teeth were big and white biting into the apples, two or fewer cavities in those mouths for sure.

In real life I'd never seen girls like this before, all cereal with no sugar, no marshmallows. Girls I knew were white girls like me, all ratted hair with pebbles sunk deep into the skin of our knees. Or Black girls, cleaner but lippy. Not afraid of anything. Or Sweetie, who's her own kind of thing.

And I saw too looking at that brochure that it wouldn't be cool to be my kind of white girl among this kind, that if girls like these were strange to me, I'd be even stranger to them. Like imagine me walking up to one and saying Wow, nice fucking stick you've got there.

You don't even know what this stick is for, the perfect white girl'd say. You know nothing about the sport of Lacrosse, she'd say.

So I turned *COPS* back up and told Evelyn no way, that the camp was for golden lezbutts and why couldn't I do a summertime independent study right here?

Which is what I did. Instead of going to camp I did a summer-long unit on regional paranormal occurrences whose big finish was a poster presentation I called Unexplained Mystery or Hillbilly Hearsay, You Decide: UFOs, Phantom Lights, & Pond Monsters of the Great Plains. I learned way more that summer than I would have at a snotty camp for rich girls, and also, look at me now! Here I am in a paranormal situation myself with someone who's *died*. It's like My god, my splendid prudence is punching me lightly on the shoulder, it's tugging my sleeve saying Molly, earth to Molly. Molly, are you there?

But silly effing me, it's not my prudence, it's the media librarian Goth Roger. Exactly the person I came to see.

I HAVE TO TALK Goth Roger out of calling the police on me. He knows I'm missing, he saw it on the news. I tell him I'm totally safe, that I'm so close to doing what I've been preparing for, that my years of trials and suffering have all led to this quest.

I say You can call the cops on me or turn me into juvie, but please please wait until after New Year's, please don't call them yet.

He looks at me a long time like really considering, then says I myself was once an initiate in the mysteries of life and death.

Thank you! Thank you! I say, then go behind the media circ desk and hug him. Instead of hugging back he beeps his scanning wand on my cheek.

But, Molly, what you're wanting isn't something a community college library would have, he tells me.

Fuck, I'm thinking. Fuck. I thought this would work. What will I tell Demarcus? What will he think of me?

But you're in luck, he says, leaning down to whisper. I have something at home that's just the thing you need.

Yeah, okay, I say. That sounds good, what is it?

He pencils his address on library scrap like a call number.

Come over around six, he says, and I'll show you the world.

FOUR

I WALK AROUND THE LIBRARY, I watch my dead mom in *The Seagull*, I walk around outside and take a nap on the bench. All this gets boring and suddenly a pang takes over me. Suddenly I want to check on Evelyn, see what's going on at House of Friends. I decide I can go there as long as I'm sneaky. I'll hide in the brambles by the carport and see what I can.

It's four by the time I get there, the sun's already setting. I dart behind the abandoned neighbor house to make sure Evelyn and Dad aren't outside. When it seems safe I go for it and sprint to the carport, wedge myself between the brambles and Evelyn's Econoline.

Soon it's dark-dark, the windows yellow-glowing. The living room lamp's on and I can see Evelyn inside. She's on the phone on the couch sitting on the far side, listening. Probably to detectives, maybe Debra, who knows. The basement light glows too, so Dad must be down there. Probably working out a new sad puppet song about me.

I blur my eyes to explode the window glows, to make them more like fireworks, a light show, make them spark like the night I left the hot plate on and two people died.

There. I said it.

It's not true that I'm not a liar because I lied about Bruce starting the fire. I'm the one who nearly burned down House of Friends.

And now here I am, on my belly in the brambles, watching. It's like crossing not my eyes but my whole entire body, like all at once I'm in every single place I've ever been. Like right now I'm Now Molly while inside House of Friends it's still Then Molly, stupid fucking Then Molly dicking around with the hot plate like tra fucking la. Now Molly and Then Molly and Watching Bruce Get Put In The Ground Molly. Dumbshit Baby Molly Barfing On Her Mom The Night Before She Died.

They're all alive at once, every single Molly.

I hate them and love them and they're all so fucking dumb.

I smell the smoke from the fire and see Evelyn smiling on the porch the day I met her. I see me chasing Jeanie around the carport and Dad pushing baby me on a swing. I see Sweetie, Leslie, and Helen the one time they went with us on Outreach and I see me in our old basement apartment picking my nose and reading a *TV Guide*.

Something pulls me out of it. A smoky warmth around me, some ghosty tightness.

Sister Regina.

Somehow in the dark darkness she snuck up behind me to give me a hug.

But.

I'm no Dorothy visiting Professor Marvel. Evelyn's no heart-clutching crystal-balled Aunty Em. I take the hug then I wipe up my nose snot, shoo Sister Regina away as best I can. I've got an appointment with Goth Roger in half an hour. I dart backward through the brambles and pull out his address.

TURNS OUT HIS HOUSE is a nice duplex on a street that's super non-Goth, lit Christmas trees in windows, Buick LeSabres asleep in driveways lined by trimmed and faded grass. When I ring his doorbell an old Mexican lady answers. Sorry, little girl. We bought cookies already, she says.

Then like a bat Goth Roger swoops in behind her, takes her elbow gently, says Linda, *Dateline*'s on.

Linda shuffles away toward a plant-potted living room. Who the hell is Linda? I say.

Linda's my stepmother, she's from Puerto Rico, he tells me. She's a lovely woman, I don't know where I'd be without her, right this way.

He takes me through the kitchen then down a short hallway. Framed pictures of a man and Linda with little Goth Roger line the hall: them at the Grand Canyon, them at a Cubs game. Them at Epcot Center, them on some boat. From the pictures you can tell when Goth Roger went gothy. Toddler him wears yellow, seven-year-old him black, head to toe.

We get to his room and the place is fucking awesome, dark walls and no windows and bird skulls hanging from strings.

Where do you get all the dead birds, I ask him and he says Their bones somehow come to me. Here, have a seat on the divan, he says patting it. I'll go ask Linda if she has any treats.

I sit down on his velvet couch and wait for him, wondering. What secrets of death are about to be revealed?

Roger returns with milk and a plate of Fig Newtons.

Have a snack while I find the right book, he says, then opens a closet that's been converted to bookshelves. I keep my Black Arts collection in the back, he says.

You can never be too careful with dark shit, I tell him, eat five Fig Newtons before he finds the book he's looking for: *Arcana Mundi: Magic and the Occult in the Greek and Roman Worlds, A Collection of Ancient of Texts*, 1st Edition.

He lets me hold the book, it's super heavy but I can flip through it. I won't lie, though, it's disappointing, mostly a textbook with every now and then drawings and boring diagrams.

I expected it to be different, I say. Like made of human skin, like ink made from blood.

Goth Roger goes Oh, sweetheart. Trust me, he says.

He says First we'll start with Chapter Three, and he sits down beside me and begins to read.

FIVE

I RETURN TO THE FAIR WITH vast necromantic knowledge, find Demarcus working near the cyclorama's ceiling, ghost paint sprinkling the heads of fairgoers unaware.

Demarcus, I got it! I say telepathically. There are lots of people still around and I don't want to be weird.

Cool, he says without even looking. Show me later when I'm not working, he says.

Demarcus, did you hear me? We can raise the dead now, we can find our moms!

I know, I heard you, he says. But I need to concentrate right now.

It's not even that hard, I say. All we need is to get some stuff and write these letters.

Molly, shut up, I'm working, he says.

It's fucking awesome, I say. Goth Roger totally came through. Here I expect him to ask me who Goth Roger is but he doesn't.

Probably I should write it all down, I say. But I guess it's not too much to remember.

Fine, Demarcus says. What did he say? What are we supposed to do? he goes.

First we write invitations to the spirits we're trying to summon, I say. Then we do some cleansing rituals to prepare our bodies and minds. Then we sacrifice some livestock and then we descend into a temple and then at an oracle's altar we use our necromancer wand and recite a magic spell.

We don't have a temple or an altar, he tells me.

Don't worry, I say, on the train I thought it all out.

This is ridiculous, Demarcus says. He says I should never have said anything.

I say Whatever, you're a fucking ghost who doesn't believe in himself.

And then something weird happens: I feel like crying.

I don't want Demarcus thinking my feelings get hurt so I go to see whether my fish is still in the toilet where I left him swimming, stand outside the locked stall door almost too nervous to crawl inside. I decide if the fish is there that things will work out, that Demarcus will pay attention and summoning our mothers from the spirit world will turn out just right.

I crawl under the stall door and oh my goodness motherfucker!

The fish is swimming his little swim. I stare at the toilet like What the fuck, I can't believe it, then I don't know what comes over me, suddenly I'm sick and have to barf really bad.

You need to throw up, little girl? a lady at the hand driers shouts to me while I'm in the stall barfing.

I'm okay, I'm okay, I'm just barfing, I say.

I finish and feel better then realize Oh fuck, my poor fishy! He's swimming in Fig Newton gag, but I can't bring myself to flush.

You're okay, you're okay, fishy, I say putting the lid down. I let the feeling of good fortune return and wish him the best.

My fucking god, what a day, I need to think, I need some fun time, so I head back out into the Fair throng to wander around.

The World Religion Showcase is extra bustle-y with its bustle, crowded with puff-coated tourists buying cotton candy and souvenir crucifixes. A bearded Jesus goes around blessing people, flicking fake holy water from a plastic cup. He gets to me and I think of the Pentecostals and their awesome snake boxes. I think of the Catholic demon Akabor and I bare my teeth and hiss.

I'm motherfucking Skulla, beware me! I say.

The Jesus guy freaks and I make my way to the Quaker table. The same lady from yesterday is there except this time she's eating Long John Silver's, pinching the fried crumblies off her fish planks, licking both thumbs.

Well hello again, she says, swirling a pinkie in her golden crumblies, staring me down like Don't fuck with me, little bitch.

But finding my fish swimming has made me bold. I tap the coffee can with the Missing Girl flier and say That girl, I don't know, she looks familiar to me.

Well it's kind of a fuzzy picture, isn't it? she says. It's hard to see.

It's the dress that throws you off, I say. I'd never wear it. Only if someone made me, like for Easter or Halloween. Like maybe if I was going as a zombie priss or something.

The Quaker lady says nothing, keeps staring at me.

I'd never wear anything like that, or my hair brushed like that, I say. I'd wear *this*, I say, wanding my hand up and down like one of the models on *The Price Is Right*. I'd roll in the dirt then run around in the wind until my hair looked like this, I go, showcase showdowning my wild ratty hair for her. I even shake it around and smell it and yes: Twizzlers, crowd farts, smoky wind.

Everything about the lady's pocky Quaker face is Go away, let me eat my fish planks, but I won't go away, I've barely begun. I bet that girl's been through a lot, I say. Fires and ghosts and meanness. Probably a dead mom six feet in the ground.

What are you talking about? the Quaker lady says.

Only a real asshole would judge her for that outfit, I say, pointing at the picture, and I can tell something's happening now in the lady's head. Something's shifted, a thought unfolding. Watch your language, she says, but she says it squinting, head hooked to the right, a question mark lowering down.

I wouldn't judge her if I were you, I say. If she's called people names, she's been called worse. If she's set fires, if she's killed tards, I bet she's been ass-grabbed by those same tards too. Don't judge her, I say. It's not very Quaker.

And here I think she gets it, who I am and what I'm saying. She reaches out sort of like to touch me on the arm.

I jerk back fast, but not because I'm afraid of her. Not

because I'm afraid of going home to House of Friends. Or would I go to juvie for running away? Maybe I could go to juvie, I start to thinking.

No, that's not the reason I jerk back at all. I jerk because just then I hear this high crackle laughing, a familiar-sounding laughing, a noise like someone lighting a fire in my brain.

SIX

IT'S NOT JEANIE. Is that what you thought?

It's not Jeanie, though it sounds like it is. Jolting from the Quaker lady (she says my name now: Molly?) I turn and there's Mombie at the Catholic table. Jeanie's Siamese twin sister, standing there, watching the taped exorcism of the demon Akabor, laughing.

Never mind, I tell the Quaker lady. See you later, I say. It's the last time I'll ever see that Quaker lady alive. I should have looked longer at her nice Quaker face.

I go over to the Catholic table and pace behind Mombie, the woman who via Jeanie I'd sworn as my enemy, the woman who for so long made my ex–best friend's life hell. But after what Jeanie did I figure all blood pacts are over. I figure my public's got an empty spot ready to fill.

Walking back and forth behind her, watching her shoulders shake at Akabor, you can tell Mombie's a different kind of badass than Jeanie. She's Jeanie's same height, her same shape and hair color, but she's wearing sandals in December and her toes are painted light blue. Instead of a jean jacket she's got on a cropped coat made of feathers and under the feathers a green sequined dress. The whole thing's very carefree, like tra la la fuck you, but something else too, like something hidden inside her feather jacket might at any time jump out.

I'm sad to report that I'm chickenshit here. I don't go up and tap her on the shoulder, I pace back and forth watching from behind, watching her watch Akabor's exorcism on the Catholics' dinky TV. The pushy nun at the table tries to get her contact info, but Mombie laughs, waves her away.

The tape's on a seven-minute loop but she watches for twenty, me skulking like a baby dumbshit behind her the whole time. Then suddenly she walks off and leaves the building and I follow her outside.

It's colder now and windy. I zip my coat to the collar and blow hot air out my nose and follow her through Arcadium into the Ugly World then Night Town. I follow her past Grandpa Hack's and up the Spookhouse ramp are Frankensteins and Draculas ushering people into clanky black cars on a clanky black track.

I follow her up the ramp and get in line behind her, five people between us so I'm not too close. I look around like I'm some normal kid standing here but breathe real deep the deodorant fade, the cotton candy fuzz. The false front of the Spookhouse is shaped like a mansion but painted all over with the scariest shit: ghosts and guys with chainsaws wearing masks made from girl skin, evil fanged clowns biting down on burnt skewered cats. Right where I'm standing a naked lady's strangled by a giant anaconda. It's wound up her just right to cover her crotch and nips, squeezes her throat so tight her eyeballs dangle out on her cheektops, their ropey tendons limp licorice sticks.

And even though it's all so awesome and exciting, I put a frightened face on, act how Sweetie might act. I tug the sleeve of the elbow in front of me and say all sniffling that my sister's in line way ahead. That I'm scared of rides that are this super scary, that I don't want to ride alone and may I please cut ahead?

I do this two times then I'm right there behind her, my face so close to her feathers I can smell the bird's nest. This in combo with the chainsaws and ghost moans from the speakers makes me want to shut my eyes and soak everything in. Instead I watch one of the Frankensteins put people in cars two by two. Like a cuckoo clock a car shoots out the top of the Spookhouse every few seconds, zooms fast and twisty along the roof's tracked edge. The riders laugh and shout, fake-scream around the dips, yell Fuck yeah, This ride sucks, Karen sucks dicks!

I count and recount the people ahead of Mombie while writing in my head what I'm going to say. Hello, I'll say once I have her attention. I'll say I'm your ex–Siamese twin sister's ex–best friend.

Then there'll be a long pause while she looks super hard at me and then she'll say I believe that makes us the opposite of enemies. Then she'll smile and shake my hand.

I lick my lips and bounce on my toes to get up the courage, my heart and stomach shooting free throws, slapping high-fives in my throat. I work myself up to it and finally fucking do it, go to tug at her elbow but instead pull one of her jacket feathers out!

Boom super fast she spins around like Who did that? and for the first time I see her face up close. Her eyes are wild dark blue, not green like Jeanie's. Like Jeanie's, though, they're raccoon-ringed, eyeliner like war paint over-under-out.

Hey are you Mombie? I say like no big biggie. Like I'm not wadding her jacket feather super hard in my hand.

When I say her name she smiles wide at me, her bottom teeth thick and straight like a stage. Flecks of lipstick like blood drips stick to them, a horror show waiting to play.

Are you the Quaker gutter girl who's following me? she says, her hair a mess of dark tunnels, her breath hot and drinky in the almost-winter air.

I nod my head, I'm like Yeah, that's me, then her feathered arm shoots out and I think she's going to hit me. Instead she yanks me hard up the Spookhouse ramp. Then before I know what's happening a Frankenstein points us to the empty car slamming through the black exit flaps. Mombie gets in while it's moving, pulls me so hard I'm almost sitting on her lap. She clanks down the safety bar and just like that we're riding the ride together, our black car lurching fast through the black entrance flaps.

I open my mouth to speak as our car rounds a corner and jerks fast through a hallway lined with shaking skeletons that glow. Boiled-looking devil faces jump out from fake windows and Mombie fake-shrieks every single time. Between jump scares she's laughing and laughing and this is not a good place to talk, I realize. She's laughing so hard she's got snot coming out her nose.

Finally the track goes straight and quiet and here she turns to me.

You looked like such a little asshole out there in line, she goes. You were like Mombie, Mombie, hey are you Mombie? She says it making this dorky face with buggy eyes, the light from the glow-in-the-dark skeletons shading her teeth a crazy yellow-green.

Then she puts her fingers on my face like how you touch something breakable and says something quiet I can't quite hear.

What? I say. I can't hear you, I go, so she says it again but not any louder. She's asking a question, I can tell, but the ghost moans and clangy track drown out everything. Now our car jerks all over Tilt-A-Whirl-style and she lets go of my face to hold on to the bar, leans over, and whispers right in my ear so I hear it: Do you hate her? she says. Do you hate her like I do? she goes.

And I don't know why, but I can't answer.

Our car turns a corner and starts a slow uphill climb where at the top a neon sign says BEWARE OF FALLING! The gears grind slow to give you time to think about ramming the upcoming double doors and just before we ram them, just before we smash through them into the twinkling Spookhouse night, Mombie asks me again, one more time.

Do you hate her like I hate her? she goes.

And right then we plunge through the doors, are shot fast around roof vents and chimneys, the Fair lights blinking bright on our faces like roller rink strobes. I'm screaming and yelling because I can't help it, it's fucking amazing, Yes! I scream. Yes! Yes I fucking hate her!

The track jerks fast to the right and I slide hard into her, the side that used to be Jeanie's side. Out of nowhere my brain upflings wanting bad to ride on the back of Jeanie's bike with her, how I thought hanging on to her would thrum diesel through my veins. Now I know I'd only see what was in front of me from behind her, her shoulders always there first, blocking my view.

Now my eyes are smashed in feathers and my nose curls from the smell and finally it dawns what a day it's been: I went to the library and spied on House of Friends. I got a ghostly hug and learned to raise the dead at Goth Roger's. And to top it all off, I met Mombie. I made a new friend.

SEVEN

By the time we're done at the Spookhouse the Fair's already closing. The thinning crowd gets herded out like cattle, but Mombie pulls me against the tide. When we pass the Cosmosphere I almost ask to stop so I can tell Demarcus where I've been and where I'm going, but Mombie walks so fast. Plus Demarcus would never approve.

She holds my hand past the lake all the way to the glass elevator and even inside the glass elevator she keeps holding my hand. Going down we look up to watch the stars fade above us, but even at the lake bottom you can still see them, even under green lake water they blink through the glass.

We get to her tiny dressing room where first I act like I've never been there, say Wow, I've never been in a dressing room before. Then right away I slump on her sofa. God am I so hungry, I say. God am I so starved.

I've got some licorice, Mombie says, taking off her dangly earrings. But off my couch, you're so filthy, she goes.

She's right, there's several days' layers of grossness on me, green poison boogers and blobs of mustard on my shirt.

She pulls the plastic jug of licorice down from a shelf and I get off the couch and stand at attention. Black or red, she says, her hand swirling for which to give me. Black, I say. She gives me red.

For a while then I stand in the middle of the tiny room afraid to sit down on things, eat red licorice while she does girly things in the lightbulbed mirror. First is she puts her feather coat on a hanger, then she heels off her sandals and unhooks her green slinky gown. The dress falls to the floor like a puddle of lake water you could step in, like if you looked directly over it you might see your face mirrored in the floor. Normally that's what I'd do with someone naked in front of me, I'd look at the floor or ceiling, maybe stare at the wall. But here I just can't help it, my perv eyes zoom right to the side of her, two arrows to the bull's-eye of her long flesh-ridgy scar.

I gasp. It is so much worse than Jeanie's.

It's darker, way redder, and at least twice as wide. It's a ripped-up flesh zipper made from chewed-up Jeanie and it's gaggy to look at but I'm no pussy. And this is something important I want her to know.

Your scar, I say, nodding at it.

She says I know. I am from the bad town, the bad sister, the bad mother, she goes.

Then she puts on a yellow-flowered kimono and I say Wicked kimono. She lights a gold-tipped cigarette and takes off her wig. I didn't know she'd been wearing one and for a second it frightens me, like when before the fire Sister Regina'd shove her dentures out with her tongue. I'd yell Stop it, stop it, put them back in! and it's the same thing with the wig, but with someone like Mombie no way can I yell at her, I have to stand here eating red licorice like nothing big.

Mombie's real hair's the same color as potato chips, crimped and fried like a parking lot Barbie. And the true shape of her head's roundish except for in back. In the back it's flat, like a dough ball someone pressed down on, makes my hand go right away to the back of my neck, to feel up and down where my skull meets my spine there, its atlas and axis, their bony agreement intact.

From the wig heads on the counter Mombie picks the Cleopatra and when she's got it arranged she snaps back around, her eyes super big now like I see you, I'm watching. Then at my chest she points a finger gun and shoots it, says Little girl, when was the last time you took a bath?

I HATE TAKING BATHS, I'm not Little Girl like that. Anyone who's made me take one I wanted to kick in the head. But before I can tell this to Mombie she's dragged me to Character Locker Room #3, a green-tiled cavern of toilets and showers with a shower-curtained tub in the very back. Even this late at night there are people still here: a midget lady and a normal lady, a Lady Godiva lady putting lip gloss on in the mirror. Mombie's holding my hand again and I worry we look homo, but as soon as the women see Mombie they grab their shit and leave.

Mombie points to the tub and I step in with my clothes on. I don't want her seeing me naked. I've got one weird toe and there are moles on my ass. I don't want her seeing my sides, how smooth and uncut they are. How twinless and single I am, how flat like a plain. I yank the curtain closed and pull off my Heatwaves. A weird sadness hits me when I throw them over, the one-two clunk of them when they hit the floor.

Jeanie, I'm thinking. Racing her to the carport the first day she came.

I pull off my Blood Farmers shirt and think: Jeanie. Because I stole it from her. I touch my hand where Mombie held it and think Jeanie again. It's the hand that slid her her cheese her first night at House of Friends.

I turn the tub on full hot, sit down, and let it fill until I'm almost boiling. I could sit here until I boiled my skin off, let Mombie have my scalp for a wig. On the other side of the curtain I hear her light a smoke up so I ask if I can have one.

Mombie doesn't answer, instead squirts in bubble bath through the curtain, tosses fizzy bath balls at me like tiny pink grenades. Now I'm floating and foamy but Mombie's the one sighing, her on the other side of the shower curtain all Calgon, take me away.

Somewhere a cassette player clicks and ballet music starts playing. Which makes me think of dipshit Sweetie, her pink leaps and weird tiptoe squatting across her moms' floor.

Crazy the thoughts that show up in your brain.

Crazy how thoughts change so fast to goosebumpy feelings, like someone's watching you, thinking your name.

Someone *is* watching me.

There's a hole the size of a penny in the curtain next to the faucet and on the other side of it a dark blue eye ringed in black.

Do I say Hey I see you or pretend I don't see anything or do I call her a perv or what do I do?

Here the darkest part of Mombie's eye darkens and then flashes, bigger. I See You Seeing Me is what it means. I get the message, but there's no good way to answer, so I just sit there blinking and then boom, her eye's gone.

Do you know what it's like, Mombie says, suddenly somewhere behind the bathtub now, to have your right half cut off because it decides it wants to live life on its own?

A hand plunges through the curtain, waves a lavender washcloth at me.

I say No and grab the washcloth, splash it around to sound like I'm washing but also to mask the hitch in my voice when I say I'm the only half I've ever known.

And you, says Mombie. You who are only trying to fulfill a dream, only trying to actualize your potential, your enormous talent, must take your reduced and bandaged body to the East Coast alone, must live on spit and peepshow popcorn while your other half stays behind in motherfucking Kansas? She gets the appendix and the good kidney and a mother while you get a used harp and the vestigial tail the surgeons forgot to cut off?

Wow, that must have sucked so bad, I say, and I mean it. I had not even considered that there was a Mombie-side to the story before. I can see her shadow now through the thin curtain, jabbing her fists in front of the mirrors like putting on some kind of weird boxing show.

Well I say fuck to that! she shouts.

Yeah, fuck that shit hard! I go.

Art! she screams. Art!

I think of Demarcus and scream it loud too.

Then out of nowhere Mombie yanks the shower curtain back.

She gets in my face, all creased eyeshadow, crumpled skin, whispers How hollow and full of cumrag is the heart of man. My sister stole half my body then tried to have me killed. I hate her more than life itself and now I live to make her life hell.

She straightens, backs away. I hug my knees tight to not be so naked. She stands back now like studying me, like I'm an exhibit, a specimen.

And you too, she says. You're like me. I can tell by looking at you that something's missing. Then suddenly loud she screams Get out of the tub! so I get out super fast.

My skin's hot boiled chicken, soft lobster meat, pink girl beef. She throws me a towel I wrap around myself and this is when I notice that my clothes are gone, that my Heatwaves are missing.

She sees me looking and points to a folded pile on the edge of a sink: a lavender dress, some frill-butted panties. A pair of black buckled shoes, extra shiny, white fold-over socks trimmed in lace.

Eff no, eff no, I think to myself calmly. Surely no effing way she means these for me.

Those are for you, she says, unlocking a locker next to the sink.

I do what she says and pull the dress over my head, watch as from the locker she pulls out something else black and shiny.

A gun. A fancy one, with a long skinny barrel.

Socks and shoes, shoes and socks, socks and shoes, she says, so I put on the socks and jam my feet under the buckles.

This is a Persian Luger, she says, points where on the barrel in etched letters it says Mrs. Barahari.

Who is Mrs. Barahari? I say and she says the gun, then for five minutes talks about this guy Mitch from *Microwave Massacre*. He was in Craft Services and was so so in love with her he gave her this gun, and now, ten years later, she hadn't even needed it to steal the Important Thing from Jeanie, the Thing she'd gone all the way to Cal City for.

She doesn't call it the Black Box or the Wax Arm or the Remains of My Childhood Fire. She calls it the Important Thing and I'm thinking Oh wow, she hasn't noticed it's gone yet.

Enough about me, she says. Let's talk about you. Have you given any thought to your future? she asks me. No one's ever asked me this, and I don't know, it makes me feel strange. I don't know the right thing to answer.

Right now I'm kind of on vacation, I say. Taking a break from my normal things, I go.

And have you considered show business? she asks me.

No, I have not. I don't know whether or not I'm talented, I go.

Everyone's got a talent hidden somewhere, she tells me, then for reasons I pretend not to know I say What's it like to be on screen? What's it like to be an actress? I go.

It's the ultimate mode of existence, she says fast, without thinking. Performing erases the void, the everlasting lack. If I could exist only inside movies I would, Mombie goes.

That sounds awesome, I say, because I don't know what to say to that.

You're never too young to get started, she goes. In fact, you could get your start right here. Then she does this little toss of her hands behind her, like Here, here in this very locker room here.

What do you mean? I say. It's just a locker room, I go.

Don't be stupid, I mean the Fair, she says. If you wanted I could help you win the kiddie contest, she goes, then tells me all about WGN's History Alive Live! Junior Look-Alike Talent Show Contest broadcast live from the Cosmosphere on WGN immediately following the Paul Turner Williams artist reception.

But I'd be recognized, people would see me. I'm not even close to ready to go home, I say. I don't mention how I've got serious necromancy plans for New Year's Eve, that no way can I afford an express trip to juvie.

You'd be in a costume, you could give a false name, Mombie says, circles my face with the black Twizzler she's now holding. She tilts her head to the side, makes her eyes big, says Don't you want to know what it feels like? To be rid of the emptiness? The yearning?

I'd be in a disguise? I say and she says Unrecognizable.

I think of Jeanie seeing me on TV. WGN, her favorite channel. I think of everyone seeing me for what I am: Super Fucking Gifted, a Talent Show Winner. Evelyn and Dad seeing it, Leslie and Sweetie. Le Feb and Head On The Pillow. Mangus and Jeanie.

Whatever, okay. As long as I don't have to sing, I say.

Definitely not, she goes, singing's not your talent. I ask her what she thinks my talent is.

She points down to my new shoes, the shiny black buckled ones.

Go ahead, give them a try, she says.

I'm not sure what she means so I take a step back and then a step forward, and motherfucker, wouldn't you know it, these are fucking tap shoes! Tappity-tap-tap, I'm making tap dance sounds.

EIGHT

I GET BACK TO THE COSMOSPHERE LATE, hours after closing, slink myself in shadows up the white marble steps. I'm so tired but want to tell Demarcus all about the talent show plus Mombie plus maybe also discuss our necromancy plans. I go to open the door forgetting it's locked already but before I can think Fuck, Demarcus lets me in.

You're out late, he says. And what the hell are you wearing?

It's cool in a way, I say, twirling my dress, skipping my tap-shoed feet next to him floating. You'll never guess who gave me them, I say.

Mombie? Demarcus says and I'm like How the fuck did you know that?

You're not that hard to figure out, he says.

He's taking a break from ghost-painting the cyclorama. I start eating the french fries someone left on a bench.

So how long's your art project going to take? I ask him.

Art takes as long as it takes, he says.

Something tells me not to talk about Mombie so instead I decide to talk about raising the dead.

Demarcus, what will we even say to our dead moms when we summon them? I ask him.

I don't know, he says. Maybe Where've you been?

I'm going to ask what a car accident feels like, I tell him and he says I'm going to ask if the reality narrative we shared was true.

What was she like, what do you remember about her, I ask him.

She was tall and wore a sweater even in the summer, he goes. She smelled good too, like a Pizza Hut spice packet. Probably all it was was oregano, he goes.

Yeah probably, I say.

Yeah, he goes.

One time I built a shipwreck with the Legos she bought me and I remember her stopping what she was doing and saying it was good, he says. She said I had the eye which confused me because she was painting one of her prosthetics when she said it, but eventually I understood. She told me the myth of Argus all the time, the all-seeing monster with one hundred eyes. Mercury used magic to lull Argon to sleep then as soon as his hundredth eye shut Mercury cut off his head. I remember how she used to hum in the mornings. I remember she kept her finished glass eyes in this special velvet bag.

Maybe our moms are friends wherever they are now, I tell him. Maybe they go shopping for ghost clothes and shit.

Seriously doubt my dead mom's your dead mom's sidekick, he says then brain-zaps me. On the other hand, who knows, maybe she is. Maybe God's just some dumb white lady inventing shit, he says.

Should we ask them about that? God? I go.

Ask whatever you want. It's not what I'm here for, he says.

I roll my eyes, say Whatever, Demarco. When I call him Demarco it makes him so mad.

I'm here for art first and justice second, he says.

Whatever. Like when our death portal opens and our ghost moms walk through like you're not going to freak and cry like a baby. Like you're not going to be all Mommy, Mommy, I missed you! I go.

You're a flat character, Molly. Develop yourself, he goes.

Mommy, I love you so so much! I say.

I mean it. You are in service of nothing, he goes. You've got blood flowing through your veins but what do you do with it?

He looks at me here like if he could spit on me he would.

You waste it. Every moment, he goes.

Do fucking not, I say.

The world is evil and all you do is roll in it.

Do fucking not, fuck you, Demarcus. Like what do you even do? Fucking art? I go. Like you've ever witnessed my fucking suffering. A real artist knows the heaviest things happen offstage.

Your innocence is evil, wake the fuck up, he goes.

I'm not *bad*, I say, and now fuck it, I'm crying.

You're not good, either. You're not even okay.

All this time he's staring up at the dome while speaking, no doubt thinking about his painting the whole time he's being mean to me.

I say I've had a really, really long day, you asshole.

Yeah, I suppose that's true, he says, for once turning from the dome to look at me. Finish your fries, it'll make you feel better.

Demarcus, if I asked a serious question would you answer it? Would you promise to tell me the honest fucking truth? I say.

I swear on the blood of Pontos, Lord God of the Sea.

Do you think I'm talented? Because there's a talent show, I tell him.

He goes back to staring at the domed ceiling, finger fires pulsing on and off low. I think you have the capacity to be brave, he goes.

I roll my eyes because who gives a shit about bravery. That's not even what I meant, I go.

Bravery's important, but I wouldn't get your hopes up about the portal, he tells me.

Don't worry, me and my mom will be too busy kicking ass to notice whatever dumb shit you and your mom do, I say.

No, I mean don't get your hopes up that it's going to work, he goes.

Of course it will work. It's got to, I say.

Don't get your hopes up is all I'm saying. Don't get your hopes up about ghost portals or talent shows.

We live in a world of infinite ecstatic possibility, I say.

He says I seriously doubt that, and I'm like Jeez, okay. I won't get my hopes up. I promise to never get my hopes up about anything, I go.

But mother-fucking-duh, I so get my hopes up. My hopes are a hot air balloon that's never coming down.

You need to do your invitation, I tell him. The invitation is the first step in the necromancy plan. Tell me what to write and I'll write it down.

I already wrote it, he says.

What the hell, let me see it, show me, I go, because I didn't think he could write real letters because if so why did he never write me back after he died?

It's over there, he says, pointing behind us.

I follow his finger flames to an empty spot on the cyclorama, a place in Paul Turner Williams's universe that's a swirly black void. Demarcus flicks his fingers to send sparks through the distance and when they hit the wall it's like a fuse is lit. All at once words made of fire burn high all around me: Mother, Come Home, Mother, Come Home.

NINE

To the Ghost of Sharon Louise Sibly,
Wherever You Float:

When you were last alive I was nothing but your dumb baby, but I'm much older now and the opposite of dumb. I want you to know I don't do things like shit my pants now. I cry hardly ever and am semi-badass as well. You'd know this already if you were watching over me. I don't believe you are but that's not why I'm writing, Mom.

I have learned from someone who knows this stuff how to summon spirits. Already I can see ghosts but I have never seen yours. My best friend is a ghost whose ghost mother's also missing, so we've decided to summon the two of you together, our missing dead moms. We need to see you and to know if you're there or not. Here are the details. For real, please come:

What: Your Summoning

Where: The portal of the dead I make, Submarine Palace, Chicago World's Fair

When: Midnight, New Year's Eve

I have to go now, my ghost friend needs help with his painting. Don't forget: New Year's Eve, Submarine Palace, Chicago World's Fair.

Your Daughter and Necromancer,
Molly

P.S. Also going to be in a talent show earlier that evening if you're not busy. But why would you be busy, ha ha, you're dead.

TEN

Demarcus goes all-in on his secret art project, I help him each day during Mombie's Princess shift. I help him by sitting on one of the benches in the cyclorama, keep him company telepathically, crane my head to see what he's painting but catch only the ghost paint drips.

One time this guy sits down next to me wearing chinos. A shiny watch, a navy collared shirt. You must love it too, he says and I say Love what? and he waves his hand all over. This painting, the universe, the stars, he says.

This painting sucks, I say, but it's going to get better.

Thank you, very quiet in my head Demarcus says.

Afternoons when Mombie's shifts are over I go underwater to the Submarine Palace. We eat dinner alone on her dressing room sofa then ride the elevator back to land to ride all the rides. She spit-cleans my face in line for the triple-helix coaster, finger-combs my hair under the Chevy Traumatron sign.

Each night we end up at the top of the two-story Ferris wheel. It's like the dream I had except Demarcus and Jeanie aren't there. Each night this is where all the stories Jeanie told me about Mombie return to me and I wait for her to do something terrible, shake the seat to scare me or worse, but she always sits tall and quiet, completely still. All the Fair blinking and flashing around us, her high-heeled sandals dangling in the air. She says nothing, does nothing, only looks in the direction of Kansas and stares.

Some nights after the Fair closes we break into the Gardens of Ornithological Exotica. We chase the weird birds, pluck out their weird feathers whole. Next maybe we do the hedge maze, chalk arrows going the wrong direction. Or we break into the screen print kiosk and make Barahari Death Team tees for tomorrow's workers to fold.

One night we paddleboat all around the Sea of International Waters, drag our fingers all along the top of the icy lake. We paddle a full circle around the Viking rowboat statue then write the names of our enemies in lipstick at the base. Mombie's got so many: Cynthia, Janice, Soft Rock Tony. Jules and Jeanie and Dr. Walter Peter Federmann, MD.

For me, I just write Jeanie, and after a moment, Bob Reynolds, then look up and for a second and think I see something glowing—tiny lights flashing in and out on the lap of the Viking queen. It's probably ice crystals glinting off the lake water, but in case it's Demarcus taking a break from his project, I add PAUL TURNER WILLIAMS, FUCK HIM in lipstick real big.

Later that night while Demarcus is working I watch horror movies in Mombie's dressing room. *The Rat Savior* or *Savage Weekend*, whatever she's got on tape. If it's blood and guts or jiggling tits, Mombie will watch it, bathrobed and wigless, her nightcreamed face ten inches from the screen. If I talk when the movie's on, like to ask for a pop or some licorice, she'll snap Shut the fuck up like Jeanie does except with this hurtface face. Then during the credits she'll tap the TV screen, say how this Key Grip Steve or that Gaffer Mickey had one time done her some kindness, how in a cutthroat business they'd had the balls to be sweet.

When there's nothing else to watch we watch *Can You Believe It?*, a show about freak accidents and real-life crime. Gas station holdups and cars stuck on train tracks, drunk drivers and T-bonings, the jaws of life every time. It's during the commercials when Mombie does this thing that's so awesome, she turns the channel and changes the volume using only her feet. Turns out anything done with hands she can do with her feet, eat spaghetti or open a letter, brush my hair, brush her teeth.

Your hair is so butchy, she tells me, toes curled around the brush handle. She says long is how a little girl's hair should be.

It's how my hair is, I tell her. It doesn't grow, it just stays this way. Which is true, I'm not lying, I've never had a haircut. It always just stays the one same length.

Here Mombie's quiet. I can tell she doesn't believe me. She yawns then toe-smudges the cheese dust on my cheek. Doing tricks with her feet was how she got out of peepshows. She won a contest and got a part in a movie about sex-crazed freaks.

She doesn't bother to finish the Sbarro she got herself for dinner, throws the leftovers in the trash, and pours her Diet Mountain Dew on top. *Can You Believe It?* finishes and the local news follows, anchorman Robert Jordan goes to Joanie Lum in Cal City first thing. Joanie Lum's this fancy Asian reporter who Evelyn thinks is overrated and holy fucking shit! Right now she's standing in front of House of Friends.

The home behind me, the site of last year's fatal house fire, is once again subject to heartbreak, Joanie Lum says.

She says Molly Sibly, ten years old, has been missing since Thanksgiving. Tonight we talk to her loved ones, Joanie Lum says in her best fake sad.

Then next she's inside sitting on the couch next to Dad and Evelyn. Evelyn's got a wad of tissues, a pile of fliers on her lap. Dad's got on his sunglasses and a collared shirt that looks funny.

Mombie turns to me and smiles, says Oh my god, is that your grandma? Is that your dad?

No, it's Dad and Evelyn, I say.

On TV Evelyn holds my picture and pleas for my return. She says Molly, you're not in trouble, please come home already, okay? When Joanie puts the mic in front of Dad all he does is nod, continues looking like someone just shook him out of a bag.

Then cut to Joanie Lum outside House of Friends again, on the front sidewalk where five or six people stand with candles holding hands. Here Joanie Lum says a bunch of words like Community, Prayers, Safe Return, Silent Vigil. Otherwise I'm not listening, I'm staring behind her where the people doing the Silent Vigil stand. There's Leslie and Sweetie plus two of Sweetie's rich kid friends. But also there's Debra and Rita from the gas station. They've all got on sweatshirts with my big face on them saying MOLLY IS MISSING! MOLLY COME HOME!

That night I fall asleep homesick on the floor in front of Mombie's futon. While she's busy with night terrors I dream the craziest dreams. One where I'm roller-skating with Demarcus and he's alive and not a good skater and one where I reach in my pocket and my pocket's filled with eyes.

In the last one, the worst/best one, I dream of my dead mom's dying, I dream I'm floating over her blue Pinto and watching it crash. I'm hovering over her smashed on the pavement, I'm a wad of light like Demarcus but when I roll myself out I'm a pathetic fog cloud, no fire and flash. I descend downward to the pavement until I'm not even an inch away from her, breathe fog light over her face where it's still a face and where it's not anymore I descend into the cracks. I bury myself there where her brain-blood-hair mix together, I curl up and twist around and take what I can get. I let her inside gore wash over me, it's sweet and warm and gentle, and somewhere deep there's this pulsing so I pulse myself back.

ELEVEN

THAT'S THE LAST NIGHT I SPEND in Mombie's dressing room. The maintenance closet in the Cosmosphere's where I make my nest. The floor's cold and hard, but I stole one of Mombie's kimonos for a blanket, and when late at night Demarcus balls up next to me it's kind of the best.

But Christmas morning when I wake up there's no Demarcus.

Usually his finger fires burn soft and low by morning, but today it's janitorial darkness when I stand up and stretch. Outside the maintenance closet the Cosmosphere hallways are empty. The Fair must be closed on Christmas Day. I run down the halls and galleries shouting Merry Christmas, Demarcus! and finally find him in the break room by the planetarium on the third floor.

He's watching *Hour of Power: Glory of Christmas* on this tiny TV set, his chalk eyes smudgy, his cheeks somehow wet.

This was Mom's favorite, he says, not taking his eyes off the dinky television: all these flying nightgowned angels and singing shepherd kids. Teen boys in white choir robes holding French horns and brass trumpets and fat guy wise men with hats like giant red pin cushions on their heads.

Merry Christmas, I say and look around because who knows, maybe he got me something.

Mom was never religious, she just had a soft spot for the aesthetics of camp, he says.

I find hot chocolate packets by the microwave so I make some and sit down to watch *Hour of Power*. After a while it gets boring and my mind starts to wander, I wonder what kind of Christmas is happening right now at House of Friends. Usually it's Evelyn and Dad holding hands and loud-singing "Angels from the Realms of Glory." Last year was different, it wasn't that long after the fire. Sister Regina's ghost was still chasing me into corners then. Evelyn still got weepy if anyone mentioned Bruce. So last year no stockings or Christmas tree, only things like new underwear and undershirts for presents. Only things to replace the stuff that burned. Only me on the couch, my feet up on Evelyn, her reading aloud from a seed catalog to me while in my head I chewed Santa out.

I wonder about the Christmas happening right now in Bronzeville, whether people go to K-Mart or give presents they picked from piles. I imagine Le Feb bringing Christmas donuts for Head On The Pillow, them watching TV eating them and drinking SunnyD.

What would Demarcus get me if he got me something anyway? I don't know. I can't think of anything. And what would Jeanie get Mombie, and vice versa, Mombie Jeanie?

Demarcus, I say. What do you think the deal is with the wax arm anyway? I mean, it's not even that cool. It's just okay.

Who knows? he goes, not taking his eyes off *Hour of Power*. I guess childhood things haunt you.

Except your mom, I say.

TWELVE

It's the night before New Year's Eve, it's New Year's Eve-Eve. The night before WGN's History Alive Live! Junior Look-Alike Talent Show Contest and the Paul Turner Williams reception in the Cosmosphere. The night before the Sleeping Silent Princess is supposed to get reanimated and when Demarcus and I also plan to bring back the dead. I'm under the lake in the Submarine Palace, I'm in the front pew of the Crystal Cathedral watching Mombie tap-dance in front of the Sleeping Silent Princess's crystal casket. She's shouting instructions and melting my ears.

A relaxed ankle is the key principle of tap! she's going. Syncopate! Syncopate! Swing-shuffle-cross! she says.

It's almost midnight. Above us the Sea of International Waters is frozen on top five inches meaning people can skate all the way out where the big statue is. Someone put a winter hat on the Viking lady, hilarious! But underwater in the Crystal

Cathedral there's no time for fun. Mombie won't stop talking about the awesome routine she's come up with, when to shift my weight, where to put my hands.

I really do try to focus on what she's saying but I've still got things to figure out for tomorrow's necromanteion. Also while she dances circles around the crystal casket I can't help but stare at the dark shape inside.

How does the reanimation even work? I ask Mombie. What do they do, shoot electricity through her brain?

What brain? Whose brain? What are you talking about? Mombie says, stopping her dancing, and even though I know better, I'm like Oh my god, mother-duh. Fucking *her*! I go, pointing. The Effing Sleeping Silent Princess's brain!

Mombie pauses a long time just looking at me before she starts speaking.

First what they do is fill her up with all new blood, she says. Then they electrocute her heart, *then* they electrocute her brain. She taps the casket where the Sleeping Silent Princess's brain would be, says Then they put electrodes on all her toes and fingers. They zap each one individually.

She plucks a feather from her feather jacket and sniffs it, pulls her arm all the way out of the jacket sleeve. Look, she says, showing me the white inside of her elbow. There's a circle of bruisy pinpricks, a contusion of connect-the-dots.

Where do you think they get her new blood? she asks me.

What? No! No effing way! I go, shouting. No mothereffing fucking way! I say. I leap from the pew to look up close at the needle marks.

That is so fucking cool. That is so fucking cool, I say.

She moves her elbow back a little making me have to lean in closer and as soon as I do she thwumps her arm up to smack me under my chin.

Dumbass! she goes, then starts laughing. Dumbass, I can't believe you thought it was real!

What are you even talking about? I ask her, my tongue swelling, something bleeding.

It's all fake, it's a dummy, don't you get it? she says. The Sleeping Silent Princess is *me*. Tomorrow night *I* get in the coffin and jump out after they "reanimate" me. Don't be so stupid, she says looking at me like grossed-out, disgusted. Don't be a little girl falling for every little thing.

I don't, I say.

Do too, she tells me.

I do not, I say. Besides, it's not even that big of a thing to believe. It's not like people die for real anyway, I say.

What do you mean, people don't die? she asks me.

Ghosts are real, I say. I can see some of them. And the ones I can't live in a place called the Summerland. At least some of them. The ones that don't are somewhere else. Waiting around, doing whatever.

Bullshit, she says. Ghosts aren't real. My own dead mother has never been a ghost to me.

That can change, I say and then she slaps me.

Don't you ever talk about my mother, she says. It's late, I'm tired, I'm going to get a corn dog. Stay here and practice your heel-steps until I get back, she says.

We live in a world of infinite ecstatic possibility! I shout at her leaving. I'm angry now. Maybe I'm even crying.

Do not! she shouts back over her shoulder. She's already in one of the little ride boats, already in the dark tunnel floating away.

Fuck her, no way I'm practicing stupid fucking heel-steps. I'm not her child-star, she's not my mom.

I don't know how to work the ride boats like she does so I have to wade back through the tunnel waist-deep in water. I'm bummed the New Year's reanimation won't be a real one. It would have been such a badass preshow for the necromanteion.

THIRTEEN

The registration table for WGN's History Alive Live! Junior Look-Alike Talent Show Contest is set up in the lobby of the Cosmosphere. The cheese and cracker part of the Paul Turner Williams Artist Reception is going on behind it, dressed-up grown-ups nibbling cheese and Triscuits, filling in the rows of white folding chairs. There's a stage for Paul Turner Williams to give his speech on, then after that the talent show's there. Ponytailed WGN guys unpack their cameras and boom mics and in front of me snakes the long registration line.

So I'm standing here checking out everyone's costumes thinking Shit, Molly, you got this, when the girl in front of me says Who the hell are you supposed to be? She's holding a toy rifle and wearing this cowgirl skirt-vest combo, squirrel tail fringes all over and all around.

Who the hell do you think you are, plus who the fuck are you? I say, my time living free-range emboldening me.

She says Dumbshit, duh, I'm Annie effing Oakley. She says You look like Shirley Temple in a shitty wig. She says her talent is karate then she fake shoots her gun at me. Pow pow pow, she goes then does some karate kicks.

My effing god, it's all I can do not to hit her. It's all I can do not to take off my tap shoe and smash it over this bitch's head.

I'm Neil Armstrong, out of nowhere says the astronaut suit behind me.

I don't think we were talking to you, Annie Oakley says.

Shoot him, I say and she pow pows him to pieces. See how fast I got her working for me?

Neil Armstrong just stares dead at us and to Annie Oakley I say Nice shot, I ask if the rumor's true about the talent show, about Bozo hosting.

We're not friends, Annie Oakley says then turns away from me. My face burns red, my mouth gets hot. Soon it's my turn and the man at the table asks what my name is and I say Angela Merriwether because that's what Mombie said to say. Angela Merriwether was the name she used in *Nail Gun Massacre*. *Nail Gun Massacre* was the first time she felt fully alive on screen.

For real? he goes. That's your name? he says and I say Sir, are you calling me a liar?

And what historical figure are you supposed to be, Angela? he says.

For a moment I'm stuck because I'd forgotten to think of this. Mombie only cared about tap dancing things. But I'm such a fast thinker, I'm like Anne Frank, you fucker! And he writes it down, assigns me number twenty-three. When he goes to pin it on my dress I stop him, say No, I'll do it. I don't want your hands near my boobs, I say.

They herd all the contestants around the sides of the reception and I grab some cheese cubes from the tables on the way backstage. Soon the folding chairs will be filled with people from the artist reception and Demarcus's shitbag dad will make his shitbag speech. I look up at the cyclorama—no sign of him or his fancy ghost painting. Maybe it's all too much. Maybe he decided to run away.

Behind the stage a lady with a clipboard walks back and forth in front of us, tells us in five minutes the big-shot artist goes on. Then after he's done Bozo the Clown will come out and make jokes to the audience, he'll go down our line and shake each one of our hands. When he asks us who we are we should enunciate clearly. Only speak to Bozo if he speaks to you first, she says.

Then she walks around rearranging us, cranky and finger-shushing, looks me up and down at least five times. All the contestant kids giggle and whisper about Bozo, so ultra asquirm about the stupidest things. Don't wet your pants, he's just a stupid fucking clown, I say, but I won't even lie, I too am excited to meet him. Besides Mombie I've never met anyone from TV.

Next this guy wearing a headset comes around handing strawberry pop in paper cups to us. To make our lips red to stand out on camera, Annie Oakley says.

Bozo hates know-it-all bitches, I tell her.

Bet no one comes to your birthday parties, she says.

I'm about to say back the meanest thing ever but this is when Demarcus's dad walks onstage. I move out of the contestant line to watch him, go close as I can to the side of the stage.

Paul Turner Williams is just this tall skinny Black guy. He wears a navy suit and a green striped tie. He looks like Demarcus sort of, but only a little, the shape of his nostrils, where his ears attach to his head. He's definitely not shooting fire out his eyes or fingers and his hair is cut super close to his head.

He says Good evening, everyone, thank you for coming.

He says My journey in science visualization has led me down some long, rocky roads.

He says My life's work is not only to illustrate the grandeur of the universe, but to transmit scientific understanding where scientists fail.

He says My drawings of marbled chiton, my illustrations of helium fusion in stars, he says Hell, even my technical schematics for out-of-production iron lungs.

He says Language is ambiguous but image is not, and here's when a bright flickering ball of light appears above him.

Demarcus!

His ball of light spins, bounces around three points in a triangle, then hovers still while shooting off sparks. I look around at all the other people watching and it's clear I'm the only one who sees what's going on.

Demarcus, what the hell? I thought-whisper to him and in my head he says The time's arrived for my first solo show.

His light ball spins again, triangulates above his dad's head a second time, the sparks shooting higher and this time I see a flicker of something, a flicker of a picture projected every direction around the cyclorama, but it flashes and fizzes out before the picture holds.

Thank you very much to WGN and Fair officials for making this possible, Paul Turner Williams standing at his podium says. I'm told there's a talent show starting next? he goes.

Then there's lame applause all while the light ball of Demarcus spins furiously, him trying to spark-fling his secret project into the air.

The clipboard lady hurries around with a trash bag for our strawberry pop cups, I toss mine in while on stage Demarcus begins to wail.

On stage stand up straight, do not wiggle, says the clipboard woman.

It's not working, it's not working, it's not working, Demarcus wails.

Paul Turner Williams walks off stage while Demarcus stays, spins more slowly. Me and the other contestants file up the steps and stand on the taped X's like the clipboard lady said. Music almost exactly but not quite like *Star Search* plays over the speakers while triple spotlights dance back and forth over all of our heads. Demarcus darts around with them, flings sparks around but nothing.

Why isn't it working? Why won't it work? he says in my head.

Bozo comes out and all the kids but me go wild. Wiggling and yelling and hopping up and down. Even the audience there for Paul Turner Williams sits up straighter. Their faces light up and they clap extra loud.

Bozo's way taller than I thought and also all business, right away going down the line asking each kid who they're supposed to be. When he gets to Neil Armstrong Neil Armstrong says

Ladies and gents, I'm Neil Armstrong. The audience claps like crazy, goes wild for this, like how effing cute, a little kid who says Ladies and gents!

Bozo asks him his real name and what he does for fun and the kid says I'm Derrick, future first man to walk on Mars. Again the audience goes wild and I'm thinking What the fuck, what the hell, he didn't even answer the question! What people love is Derrick's ambition, I guess.

Now Bozo turns to the giant screen that's been lowered behind us. On the left's a photo of Neil Armstrong and on the right's live footage of Bozo and Derrick, him space-helmet grinning his gap-toothed grin so hard.

And what does the audience think? Bozo says which means for them to clap for how much Derrick looks like Neil Armstrong. There's even a slit-gowned lady with a big meter for clap-measuring, a light-up board with numbers, a red arrow that somehow moves on its own. And fuck, I recognize her, she's one of the Lady Godivas! Horseless with clothes on she looks all wrong.

When people are done clapping Bozo asks Neil what his talent is and Neil says Around the World, a yo-yo trick. Then he whips out his yo-yo and does it and I won't lie, it doesn't suck, it's not bad.

Bozo moves down the line meanwhile Demarcus keeps trying to do something, flashes of ghost painting appearing around the cyclorama for a few seconds in spots. When Bozo gets to Annie Oakley she hip-cocks her tiny rifle and says Y'all, I'm Annie Oakley! Then she twirls her gun like it's a fifty-dollar baton.

Behind us the screen lights up with the real Annie Oakley, and it's true, she does kind of look like her in a way. The crowd applause this time is super fucking heavy. Bozo does some double-takes, makes a big deal, the works.

For talent she sings "Damn I Wish I Was Your Lover" by Sophie B. Hawkins while doing karate, which is so fucked up, kids aren't supposed to say Damn on TV.

By the time Bozo gets to me, I won't lie, I'm nervous. I thought this was going to be the easiest fucking thing. The kids on this stage are no-talent assholes, I know that, but that doesn't mean they can't be more talented than me.

Bozo bends down so close I can see the lines in his white makeup, the crosshatches around his mouth corners like bird prints in snow.

And who might you be, little girl? he asks me.

I say at first whispering and then again louder: Anne Frank. I'm Anne Frank, I go.

Wow, gosh, is that so, he goes, the tall, fat fucker. He raises his hand like almost to hit me, but pats me gently on the head three times instead.

Behind on the big screen they've got the real Anne Frank up and split screen next to her is me looking over my shoulder at the me on the screen. I get a few claps, but not as many as the others.

And what's your talent? Bozo asks and I say Tap dance.

A tap-dancing Anne Frank, who knew? Bozo says. He steps back, sweeps his hand out like Be my guest, sucker, and I count off from five like Mombie taught me to start the routine.

But here something happens: I can't find the steps anywhere. Like my brain's emptied all its drawers, knocked all the dumb stuff over, and the tap routine's long gone, was maybe never there. The audience stares at me, Bozo stares, Neil Armstrong and that bitch Annie Oakley rip holes through my head. My eyes glaze over, they're fish eyes, dead dog eyes. Prosthetic glass eyes from the bottom of a grocery bag.

But Demarcus, his ball of light, snaps me out of it. He's right over my head and spinning faster now, he's shouting For you, Mother over and over in my head.

In my brain this knocks something loose, but motherfucker, it's not how to tap-dance.

It's Anton Chekhov's *The Seagull*, which I do instead.

For the bliss of being a writer or an actress I could endure want and disillusionment! I say. Want and disillusionment and the hatred of my friends!

Here I lift my chin up like my dead mom does in the video of her.

But I should demand in return fame, real, resounding fame! I go.

Demarcus keeps chanting to his mom in my ear and now he's chanting as fast as he spins, so fast he's only a hum in my head, the drone building and building and Demarcus spinning and spinning and me saying Nina's speech until I get to the end. When I get to the end there's a flickering and then electricity popping, and then I look up and see it: Demarcus's massive painting in golden ghost paint overhead.

The crane-necked audience gasps. They see it too.

Over the whole round room, over every galaxy, meteor, and nebula, Demarcus's painting sparkles and wows: a ghost-painted grid with glowing bars and square cells like a prison. The cyclorama's no longer a cyclorama, it's a panopticon now.

You don't even have to look close to see each cell's got the same prisoner: Paul Turner Williams, Demarcus's dad. In some he sits on his cot, sad and crying, and in others there are cartoony word bubbles over his head: I am scum not fit to shit on! I abandon my children! I'm a Pillager, I'm a Destroyer, I'm Demarcus Nassius's dad!

But mostly there are no words, just him suffering in different ways, like in one he's on fire and in another skeletal and starving. In the next one these fat rats eat off his head.

Goddamnit, goddamnit, I am so fucking proud of him. He painted a prison over his dad's space masterpiece and then he fucking imprisoned him there!

Bravo, Demarcus, bravo! in my head I tell him. The audience is super-wowed too but also freaked out as hell, all Oh my! What the hell? Is this supposed to be happening?

So it's the perfect time to follow my heart and do what overcomes me, which is grab the mic from Bozo and make sure the WGN cameras are on me when I say: I hereby declare Molly Sibly the winner of this stupid fucking contest as she's more talented than all the other fuckers on this stage. If you want a piece of her she'll be at the Reanimation tonight, motherfuckers! She's making a portal, she's having a séance, she's bringing back the motherfucking dead!

FOURTEEN

I had to flee the WGN History Alive Live Look-Alike Talent Show Contest. Or the WGN History Alive Live Look-Alike Talent Show Contest had to be fled. The moment I said the F word the clipboard lady was climbing the stage stairs to get me so I flipped off the cameras and ran for the opposite stairs. I took one look behind me and saw the ball of light of Demarcus de-spinning, him a teetering top coming to a stop in the air. I turned and I ran, stepped on Bozo's clown feet, pushed past Neil Armstrong. I may or may not have thwacked Annie Oakley with one of my tap shoes medium-hard on the head.

Demarcus, come on! Let's go, I remember thought-shouting. But he didn't come on, he stayed there trancing out to his prison painting, unfurled and hovering high in the air.

I run down the white marble steps outside the Cosmosphere, the afternoon all icy blue air and dirt-boogered snow. With or without Demarcus I'm making a necromanteion in a few hours and I don't fucking care if I have to do it alone. And this means

I need to do a cleansing ritual to prepare my mind and body ASAP. And I still need to find some livestock to kill. Because tonight when the clock strikes midnight I'm ascending a temple of my own creation and at the altar of my oracle I'm reciting a magic fucking spell.

But for right now: livestock. I can't remember if there's a 4H building or something like that here, so I walk around looking for one of the big Fair maps to check. I pass by a ChaRa of Chicago's Cheeseburgers and buy two burgers, snarf them down wondering how many cheeseburgers a cow is. Three cheeseburgers would not be even a baby cow, I'm guessing, but maybe it still counts as one since all of the cow had to be dead.

Which gets me thinking: while I didn't personally kill the cow I'm right now eating, my eating it is the final and most important part. You might even call it a sacrifice, I'm thinking. In terms of ritual and/or ceremony, it definitely is.

Molly, holy shit! Check livestock sacrifice off your to-do list!

Fuck yeah, I say swallowing the last of the second burger. Getting shit done! I go, my stomach full for the first time in weeks.

I'm nearing Dirt Devil Raceway and wiping the crumbs off my front when I hear it: clapping and cheering and a loud buzzing sound. A sound like a chainsaw killer running after you then fading, like he's chasing you then changes his mind and runs away. It's like, Molly, what the fuck, it's just the Fair's motocross track, it's nothing. But I can't help but run hard toward the dirt bike sound.

Fairgoers line the track barrier cheering and watching, all crowded in the cold seeing what I'm too short to see. It's not until I push through them that I see her, Jeanie. She's doing wild jumps and tricks, taking sharp turns around the track.

I squeeze between two guys in thick hoodies. Aw dang, they say each time Jeanie cuts a corner tight. Oh hell no, they go like she's something so amazing.

She's my ex–best friend, I say, but the guys don't hear me. I say Everything she's doing she taught me to do too.

Now she's riding a straight line to build her speed up, her butt a black double-knuckle held high in the air. Then she figure-eights the entire track one-handed with her feet up, and I'm not going to lie, it's a breathtaking sight. It's like watching hawks swoop through power lines, Evelyn dodging potholes in her Econoline, dolphins diving through Hula-Hoops high in the air.

Finally she slows up and throws down her kickstand, the crowd cheering and hollering for more. She struts over to a tall fat white guy—Mangus! It's Mangus! I hadn't noticed him sitting over there on a cooler before.

She stands hands-on-hips all Wonder Woman in front of him and neither one of them look happy, they're definitely having a fight. Jeanie's saying something mean to him, but Mangus doesn't budge, doesn't even look at her, he looks everywhere else but her raging raccoon eyes.

I'm thinking Oh shit, oh shit, he's so going to get it, she's going to punch in his teeth or bite off his lip. Instead she kicks him in the shins what looks like just lightly, but he falls over whimpering like some dumbshit kid. Because duh: the sawed-off hammer heads in the tips of her Keds. Now he's up hopping leg to leg shouting Goddamn and Fuck it while all the Fair watchers laugh and laugh, them practically bent over with mouth-fisted giggles, them nearly spilling their Super Sips and pissing their MC Hammer pants.

Poor Mangus, the way he sat angry and scared on the cooler before Jeanie kicked him. You could just tell he was remembering their first date at Porno's Pizza when he was almost fourteen. Jeanie leaning in to French kiss him over the *Pac-Man* table then beating him at *Pac-Man* twelve to fifteen.

Whatever love they had, it's gone now for good. She kicks him another time and howls like a wolf. She grabs a beer from the cooler and gets on her bike again, loops around the lot two times then the second time clips him. This is where some feeling in me starts to make itself known.

Mangus gimp-trots after her angry until her third time around when this time she doesn't clip him, she throws down her bike. Then she throws beer in his face and then she spits on him.

I can't take it anymore, I hate her so much. I push through the crowd and shout Jeanie, Jeanie! You think you're so badass but you're not! I say.

And Jeanie hears me. She looks right at me.

You little fucker, where's my black box! she says.

And it's weird, I still hate her but her voice when she speaks somehow still soothes me, the jaggy purr of it still drops soft like a blanket over my brain.

But that's something to figure out later, I still fucking hate her, so I shout Jeanie, fuck you! I fucking hate you, Jeanie!

The crowd watches jaw-dropped, like What the fuck, even Mangus, and now Jeanie's grabbing her jean purse and pulling out something glinty, long, and black.

Time for little bitches to give Donna a kiss, she says and takes after me. At first she moves slow but now she comes fast and I'm moving through the crowd backward and probably done for, probably most likely about to be bludgeoned to death, and yet still I have time to find myself thinking What the fuck's going on? Why doesn't someone rescue me?

I imagine Demarcus poofing in from nowhere, fingertips and toetips all fiery flame, furling and unfurling and throwing himself at Jeanie. But that's story bullshit, I know it. Every girl's an island, I think. So fuck Demarcus, fuck Mombie, fuck my dad, fuck Jeanie. Fuck everyone I've ever known because they've never known me.

I turn and run hard, my heart bangs hard, my tap shoes tapping clack clack clack. And what happens next I'll never know because I don't remember—maybe Jeanie catches up to me and womps me with Donna, or maybe I hit my head tripping on the power cable from the Dippin' Dots shack—all I know is this: I get powered off, I fade to black, and the next thing is I'm having the weirdest dream ever.

In the dream I'm ordering seventeen funnel cakes and walking super careful, each one stacked on the other, divided by greasy paper plates. I put my chin on the top one to keep the pile steady, lick the powdered sugar as far as my tongue will reach. Then I'm standing by the Traumatron trying to get a better grip on the bottom ones when all the sudden Bozo the Clown is there.

I wouldn't ride this one, he says, pointing at the Traumatron.

In real life the Traumaton's an enclosed spaceship lined with forty-eight padded panels. You lean back on the panels and then the spaceship spins so fast you're stuck to the sides. It spins faster and faster until you can't even move anymore and when it reaches top speed a neon sign blinks Trauma-Tize! Trauma-Tize!

I wasn't going to, I tell Dream Bozo, because duh, all these funnel cakes?

One spun itself apart at the Missouri State Fair, Bozo says.

No way, I say. You're just saying that to scare me.

By the way, Anne, nice funnel cakes, he says.

He's wearing jeans and a blue sweater and puffing a cigarette and wearing bifocals. His brown loafers are massive. A smear of white goes across his nose.

Thank you, I say. I lit them on fire all by myself.

My cigarette's fireless, he says, waves me in close to his out-puff. It's not smoke at all but some kind of aerosol Juicy Fruit.

Watermelon flavor, he says, but I am unimpressed by this.

Everyone knows the games on your show are rigged, I go.

Dream Bozo's not surprised, it's not the first time he's heard this. He says Anne, you're right, the whole thing's fixed.

He says I'm a rich asshole who lives in a mansion. I've got a Benz and five living rooms with trampoline floors.

I thought so, I say and then he bends down close to me and whispers.

Molly, we both know that people are really awful at heart, he goes.

FIFTEEN

I COME TO NEXT TO the bleachers by the Dirt Devil Raceway with only a tiny headache and a bump on my head. The Fair goes on around me like normal, no sign of Jeanie. She's not dumb enough to publicly kidnap and murder a kid. Still, she could be watching. I need to be careful. I walk fast with my head down, pull my jacket hood over my head.

I remind myself today's the day our moms' ghosts are coming. No, fuck it. Today's the day everyone's ghost is coming who wants to come.

My plan for the cleansing ritual's to find a bathroom with a sink to wash my hair in, maybe my feet too if I can reach them that high. I'm walking around looking for a bathroom that's empty and special when I come to the big building with all the cool fish. The building with the display fish and the hall of size-descending seahorses, the room with the split whale with its guts stuck to glass.

I go inside and it's crowded so I pull my hood down tightly, crowd-sneak through the seahorses, shoulder my way into the room with the whale.

This time the room's full of people oohing and aahing and I ooh and aah again too before seeing something completely unreal: around the whale halves on both sides are three baby whales drawn in flames. But that's not quite right, they're not just drawings, they're moving! The baby whales swim all around. Their fire flippers flip-flap.

Inside the split whale each half-heart is outlined in fire and that fire heart pulses slow over the unbeating dead one.

And there, by the left tank, floating above everything is Demarcus. He's fire-painting a jellyfish surrounded by human eyes with wings.

Demarcus! I shout and people turn to look at me. No one sees him or what he's doing, only me.

I run to the left tank's corner under where he's floating, I thought-speak loud, say Oh my god, where've you been?

Starting a new project, he says. The solo show was a great success, don't you think?

I say Yeah, it was awesome, I did the livestock sacrifice by the way, you're welcome. The only thing left is to wash myself ritually, I go.

Do it here, he says, pointing. In the tank, he goes. For once in your life aim high aesthetically, Molly.

With the dead whale? I say.

In honor of dead mothers, he goes.

Wait, is this a dare? Are you daring me? I say and he says Think of it as a dare or think of it as an opportunity.

Then he shoots a finger spark to a door near the tank room's exit. The door opens just enough to see cement stairs inside, a sign next to them that says Staff Only.

Those stairs take you to the top of the tank, Demarcus says. I dare you to do it, Molly. I dare you. I double-dare you to go up those stairs and jump in.

What if I get caught?

You won't, he tells me.

You think it will help with the portal? You think it's better than my idea?

Your other idea sucks, he says, but maybe this one will get our moms here.

Then I'll do it, I say.

I bump through the crowd fast and then through the doorway, run up the stairs, take off my coat, leave on my dress. I dip my toe over the tank edge to test the water and then I do it, I jump in pinching my nose to help hold my breath.

Did I ever tell you how good a swimmer I am? I'm so fucking good, I'm practically a dolphin. I swim all around, dart through Demarcus's water art, the flame-winged eyes, the fiery whale babies aswim. A few times I bump up against the non-guts side of the whale mom, the side of her not stuck to the aquarium glass. She's crusty and gray and she feels like a tire, but I can imagine being her baby and liking it there, can imagine spending ocean nights under her fin sleep-floating.

People on the other side of the glass are pointing at me now. Some look excited, others freaked out. One guy points, says something to the lady next to him. I can't hear what he says but

I can see the shapes his mouth makes and the shapes his mouth makes is Is that Anne Frank?

I swim up to the glass where he's standing, flip him off both hands, shout You dumbfuck, I'm Molly! as loud as I can underwater. Then I swim upward fast, pull myself out of the tank, put on my coat and tap shoes and run down the stairs, check one time behind me to make sure Demarcus follows me out of the building. This dress soaking wet means I'm so fucking freezing, but I can tell I impressed Demarcus so the cold means nothing.

Wait! I shout when we pass the bathroom where I barfed on my goldfish. Wait! I need to dry my dress, wait! I'm shouting.

Demarcus wads his smallest and follows me in. It's empty and I unbutton my jacket and stand under the hand dryer.

One time I barfed on a fish in here, I tell him.

That fish? Demarcus says, only his head unwadded.

I look where he's looking which is above the stall I barfed in and where now is a goldfish ghost swimming circles in the air.

Poor guy didn't make it, I say. Which it's not a surprise but still it's a bummer.

I'm sorry, little fishy, I didn't mean to, I say.

The ghost fish ignores me, keeps circling and circling.

SIXTEEN

It's 11:00 p.m. on New Year's Eve in Chicago. There's one more hour left to 1992. In one hour I'm opening a portal, a motherfucking death oracle, because that's how you bring back the motherfucking dead. But first me and Demarcus have to stop back at the Cosmosphere. I need a necromancer wand to do the spell. The wax arm's right where I left it behind the Wet Floor sign in the maintenance closet, so I shove it under my jacket and then we run like hell.

It's 11:22 and Demarcus is worried about finding somewhere to hide before the Reanimation. He's worried if we don't hide I'll be recognized. It turns out it's all fine, it's all super easy, because when we get off the glass elevator in the Submarine Palace the normal lights are off and now it's all black light light. Fairgoers holding glow sticks crowd up and down the big hall, everyone waiting for the start of the parade before the Reanimation. The only regular light left on is the giant marquee outside the fake movie theater, it blinking above the Sleeping Silent Princess ride's velvet-roped doors. The marquee announces Now Playing: Reanimation Day Parade! and underneath two pimpled ride ushers wait to open the doors.

The plan for the reanimation is first they carry the S. S. Princess in the crystal casket out of her feature attraction, then funeral-parade her to the giant event stage constructed overnight over the food court floor.

Demarcus rolls his eyes, says something about death and Disneyfication, then an announcer comes on over every Palace speaker booming Ladies and gents!

Ladies and gents! he says, boys and girls, movie and life lovers one and all! In these the final hours of 1992, make way for a parade both educational and dramatic, a simultaneous celebration of death and life, a celebration not only of the scientific triumphs of today but also the quaintly burial practices of old.

Make way for her, our tragic iced flower! Make way so that the Sleeping Silent Princess might bloom again! Make way for our fallen movie goddess, our bright jewel of cryogenic science, our impossible beacon of eternal life! Welcome our light and shining star immortal as she travels in a living pageant of olden time funerary conveyance toward spectacular resurrection and glorious rebirth!

Then everyone cheers and throws confetti and the fake front of the movie theater opens. Spooky synth music plays over the speakers loud. Actors and trumpet players, even dancers pour out of the theater, each one dressed head to toe in gray feathers and sequined black. The men keep their heads down while lace-veiled women wail open-throated. The dancers raise their arms up and down mournfully while doing this sad griefy skip.

Finally behind them comes a horse pulling a hearse carriage: Mombie death-acting in a silver evening gown in the open-top crystal coffin inside. Her eyes are closed but her mouth is smiling. She's got a new black wig glued on tight.

People elbow and jab to throw the roses they bought for throwing while I back away, scared of her somehow knowing I'm here. I'm starting to feel sick now, I'm starting to smell ghost smells—whale piss and ocean water, burnt shingles falling. Sister Regina's ghost arms, smoky and tight.

We have to get backstage before she gets there, I say to Demarcus. He's smirking at the Disneyfication, he's blinking his finger lights.

You're the artist this time, it's your show, he tells me.

Then we go now, I say. Let's go, I tell him.

WE RUN BACK to the food court and walk up the steps to the giant stage like no biggie. Almost everyone's still at the Reanimation Parade. Still I prepare an excuse in case someone stops us: my mom said if we got separated to meet her here. That way if they ask questions I'll point in the distance, I'll say There she is, I see her! and then run away.

But no one sees us so no one stops us, we walk around like we own the place. And the stage is awesome, ice-blue velvet curtains pulled across it two stories tall like two frozen lakes. In the center there's a crystal platform with wide curved steps for dancers to dance down like in black-and-white movies how they always do. Behind the platform they've got green and silver glass columns, kryptonite icicles, Emerald City spires. I run up the steps to see everything closer and nearly fall through an open trapdoor that drops fifteen feet under the stage.

It's dark down there but I can see a rectangular glint of crystal, the pink-white sparkle of the crystal casket's stage prop twin. It's a special casket just for the reanimation. This trapdoor is how they'll bring her in.

I put my hand in the hole and give the crystal casket the finger. I say Demarcus, how the hell do we get down here?

Demarcus floats through the trapdoor and darts around in the darkness. He floats back and says There's a door in the back.

Before I leave the stage to find it I peek out between the curtains. It's twenty minutes to midnight. The parade will be over soon. People are starting to file inside the food-court-turned-auditorium, cardboard cone hats on their heads for New Year's, paper trumpets drooping dorky from the corners of their mouths.

Here I see something that catches my attention: a girl sitting near the front wearing a white T-shirt of me. Her hair's a wild mess like my hair and her shirt's my face from my Missing picture. But on top in big black letters it doesn't say MISSING, it says MOLLY BRINGS BACK THE DEAD.

I look around and see other people wearing it: grown-up ladies and dudes, but mostly kids. Mostly girls my age with their hair like my hair, unbrushed tangles how my hair is.

Holy shit, I'm a celebrity, they've already made T-shirts, I whisper to Demarcus.

Let's go or it's all for nothing, he says.

We sneak out the side curtain and around the stage's tall under-skirting until we get to an unlocked door. Inside under the stage there's bolts and bolts of more velvet curtains and in the middle sits the crystal casket on this weird platform.

It's a hydraulic lift, Demarcus tells me, pointing to the ceiling that's not really the ceiling but the stage floor.

There's no light except what comes through the open trapdoor above us and it occurs to me that any moment Mombie will be here. I throw the wax arm into the coffin like it's some sort of offering but mostly because I'll need it when I do the magic spell. Then both me and Demarcus hide in the nearest bolt of velvet, we hide until the door clicks and Mombie's quick shoesteps make all other sounds disappear.

She walks first to the casket, sees the wax arm I bet, and then real loud she's like Molly? Are you here?

Molly, I saw you on WGN! she shouts, friendly. Molly, let me help with this portal thing! she goes.

She's shouting because the band in the band shell is playing now.

Come out, Molly! Come out! I forgive you for stealing my wax arm. I also want so badly to bring back the dead! she goes.

I give Demarcus a look like Now? but he shakes his head.

Not yet, not yet, in my head he whispers. Not until the countdown begins.

Her shoesteps come closer, circle the velvet bolt we're stuffed in, and I start to worry she sees me, that maybe my tap shoes are sticking out.

The music stops suddenly and then there's a long drumroll and all at the same time everyone in the theater shouts Ten!

Now! Demarcus goes and I leap from the velvet.

Mombie smiles big, she's holding Mrs. Barahari, aims it at me all I've fucking got you now.

In the food court people shout Nine! then there's the squeak of pulleys, the sound of metal on metal.

Eight! they shout and I give Mombie the finger then jump in the crystal casket and slam down the lid.

At six the casket starts moving, the trapdoor a warm rectangle of light above me.

At five I see Demarcus float through it and by three I'm almost to it and at one I'm onstage.

It's 1993, it's New Year's, motherfuckers!

Instead of a reanimated dead movie star jumping out of the coffin it's me.

I jump out like Surprise! to the hundreds of people staring, the band super wistfully playing "Auld Lang Syne." I'm not even nervous, I feel electric, I feel like lightning. I grab the wax arm and use it to point to the glass ceiling, lean into the mic and say My name is Molly Sibly and I'm here to raise the dead!

At first there's silence except the band still playing, then the kids with my face on their shirts start to clap. Then toward the back I see Evelyn and Dad. Evelyn waves and shouts, she's like Molly, Molly! Dad's cleaning his sunglasses with his T-shirt hem. Standing behind them is Sweetie and Leslie, and holy shit, they're wearing Molly shirts. Even Leslie and Sweetie are fucking fans!

No way, Demarcus whispers so I look where he's looking. Halfway down the middle aisle, Le Feb and Head On The Pillow are here. Head On The Pillow's parked in her lung and Le Feb sits in the aisle seat next to her, he's got a portable generator he's fiddling with while in her mirror Head On The Pillow smiles.

I've got to start the ritual now before somebody grabs me, so into the mic I say Okay, I'm going to open the portal now.

There's some cheering but mostly people just sit there staring. Waiting. Part of me searches the crowd for Jeanie while the other part tries to remember the words I'm supposed to say.

Then I remember them, sort of, and say: My path is sacred and I've made an energetic contract to honor it, so blessed be my bloody scabs, my hurt feelings, my infected toes.

I say: Blessed be my grief for the Nina of Ninas, the drunken killer of drunken Bobs. I've mourned her all my life and I don't fucking cry about it. Do meteors weep? Because I am one of those.

Here it gets weird, but I have to do it. I have to say what Goth Roger told me to say.

I say I am a meteor, I am an asteroid, motherfuckers! The path of a meteor is a billion times longer than a star's. I blast through this dark universe a fucked-up white girl, but I am also a thing in the sky that burns hot!

Somewhere in the audience a girl shouts Fuck yeah at me and I raise the wax arm higher, keep saying the spell:

I burn so hot I melt through all fucking dimensions and I invite you tonight, ghost moms everywhere, ghost anyone. The portal opens now, I open the door for the dead!

Then with the wax arm I outline a big circle. Outlining a big circle with your necromancer wand is what Goth Roger's book said.

And then?

Nothing. Nothing happens. Not a flicker or bang. No smoke or spark or lightning. Nothing. Hundreds of people in the audience and not one of them speaks. Every single one of them is staring at me.

I say it again: The portal's open now! then I re-outline it.

Nothing. Nothing again. Except then there's a flicker of flame next to me and Demarcus—only Demarcus—appears.

The food court audience gasps and shouts. At first I think they're shouting and pointing at me but then I realize it's not me, it's Demarcus.

Everyone sees him. He's completely unfurled. His finger flames pulse longer, twice the fire. Brighter than I've ever seen before.

It didn't work, I say.

Something did, he goes.

And that's when I see one, over the audience in the air: a single ball of light, a white-orange orb flickering. I see the one and then there are thousands.

Then like it's coordinated they unfurl all at the same time, descend: thousands of ghosts. Ghosts everywhere. Thousands.

It did work! I shout and the band starts to play.

The ghosts are all kinds of ghosts, old ones, new ones.

Demarcus's face is like he can't fucking believe it and probably that's what mine is too right now.

Gerald! some lady screams and I look toward her screaming. An alive lady's trying to hug some dead ghost guy but she hugs through him and falls down.

The ghosts move around now among the living like searching and the living are freaked out at first, like what the fucking hell? But then there are more reunions like Gerald and the lady, people and ghosts all over laughing, in tears. I see Sweetie and Leslie running toward Helen who looks right at me like in the old times, smiling, and I see Nurse Le Feb bury his head in the shoulder of a ghosty Black lady who can only be Margaret Roberta Le Feb.

Here I search for my own mom, but I don't see her. Demarcus searches for his too, but she's not here.

What the fuck? I say.

What the fuck? Demarcus goes.

It worked for everyone but us, I say. And I won't lie about this, at this point I'm crying.

Let's keep looking, Demarcus says, and we search the crowd all over again, eye up and down all the rows of folded chairs. I scan over the center aisle super busy with phantoms and that's when a familiar face appears.

Jeanie.

Her face is one big snarl and she's shouting something at me, her arm outstretched and pointing. The wax arm. She wants it and she came here to get it, that's clear.

Well fuck her. I do a little dance, wave the arm high in the air.

Then in my head Demarcus saying Watch out behind you, the hissing beast is here!

I turn and see the upper part of Mombie pushing her lower part through the trap door. She sees all the ghosts and looks at me surprised like she can't believe what I did.

I did it, you bitch! I shout, not mentioning my mom's not there. Demarcus didn't think I could, but I fucking did! Then I do the same dance I did for Jeanie, wave the wax arm again over my head.

Jeanie gets to the lip of the stage and quickly climbs up it. It's like she doesn't know who to smack first, Mombie or me.

Mombie scrambles to her feet and Jeanie leaps at me, tries to grab the arm, but I jump back instead. Fuck you, Kittentits, you better fucking give it! Jeanie screams.

Don't you dare fucking give it to her, give it to me, Mombie says.

Now both of them are coming at me and I'm not even scared of them because side by side, moving in unison, it's too fucking interesting not to notice they're Siamese twins again, and I won't lie, it's satisfying to see.

You want it, Mombie? I say taunting, go like I'm about to toss it, then at the last second pull my arm back in.

Yeah right, I say. Here you go, Jeanie.

Jeanie puts her arms out as if I'm not also faking her out. You little bitch! she screams when of course I do.

All this time Demarcus floats back and forth behind me, excited and pulsing. Then, right as Jeanie and Mombie are both about to leap on top of me, I fling down the wax arm so hard it shatters on the floor.

And Jeanie and Mombie are so pissed! They are so very mad at me! A plume of ash covers their faces, rises from the wax shards on the floor.

Mama! they scream in unison, their hands out fast trying to catch the ashes.

Little Bitch! Jeanie yells. That was my fucking mom!

It takes a moment for it to dawn on me, what Jeanie means, the ashes. What they were stealing back and forth from each other this whole time.

Oh shit! I say. I'm sorry!

And at first it's true, I really am. Molly the dumbshit, as usual, I'm thinking. If I wasn't such a dumbass maybe Jeanie would have stayed my friend. But looking at her right now, bickering with her weirdass sister, trying in vain to rake in her mom's ashes with her steel-toed Ked, an entirely different feeling descends. It's an awesome feeling, a graduation feeling, a feeling full of Pomp and Circumstance.

Because fuck Jeanie for good. And fuck her fucked-up sister. Look what I've done! I'm just as badass as them. It's actually super delightful to see them scramble for the ashes, and it's about to get even better because here out of the ash-swirl a ghost woman appears.

Without the harsh eye makeup it takes a sec to see the resemblance, but when you do you can't unsee it, it's definitely their mom.

Jeanie and Mombie fall on their knees, start wailing. Mama, Mama, Mama! they sob.

Whoever has ears, let them hear what the Spirits say, says their ghost mom.

She looks pissed at first, ghost hands balled and scolding. But then she flickers in and out a few times and when she flickers back on she's kinder now, smiling.

I want bad to keep watching to see what happens, but get distracted by a ghost bubble floating slowly toward the stage. It's like *The Wizard of Oz*, the giant bubble of Glinda but golden. The closer it comes, the bigger it gets.

Is it her, is it her, is it her? I'm wondering. Am I finally going to get to meet my mom?

Demarcus too. He's wondering the same thing, I can tell. He unfolds completely, his finger fires burn steady, orange and purple then orange and black.

The bubble arrives on stage, hovers a few seconds before popping, and there floats in front of us a young Black woman ghost. She's got Demarcus's eyes. She's got the same nose as him. Her fingers aren't on fire like Demarcus's fingers, but if you look up close through her head her ghost brain's a sparking tangle of lights just like his.

Baby, she says. Not to me, to Demarcus.

Baby, she says, floating totally quiet and still.

I know I didn't honor you, Demarcus says, head down, slowly. I know I'm a murderer who deserves nothing, but where have you been?

When he looks up again her eyes brighten, and I'm not sure what, but something happens here. His face changes from sad to something different, then on his smeary ghost face a smile appears.

She says I'm not a ghost, she says I'm a thought form, Demarcus says to me. She's been the one thinking me this whole time, he says in my head.

Reader, it's not easy to know when the time to say goodbye is coming.

Like here, I should have guessed it, the way his mom starts to glow. The glow stretches out to him, pulses and enfolds him. But it never occurs to me that, for good, he's about to go.

Instead what I am is angry. Jealous maybe is more like it. It's not fair he gets his mom when where the fuck's mine? When I did all the work, when I did all the believing. I look around the food court at all the happy people and ghosts reuniting.

Then in a blink, Demarcus and his mom disappear.

It's not fair, I say.

It never was, Demarcus goes, the last time ever in my head.

SEVENTEEN

I SLIDE OFF THE STAGE, let sorrow engulf me. All the chairs are taken by happy ghosts and their humans, there's nowhere to sit and I'm left to pace the middle aisle. For a moment I think I see Evelyn see me like to come get me, but when I look again it's just her smiling with her head on the fat see-through shoulder of Bruce's ghost. I pace up and down twice before something like a flicker of fire bites my earlobe. Like someone was flicking a Bic lighter on and off an inch from my ear.

A swell of hope swirls high then dive-bombs my belly. It's only the ghost of that goldfish I won, on fire and trying to swim-float through my hair.

At first I swat it away, like Leave me alone, you stinky fish-fucker, then I think: Whatever, it's okay. You and me are the same. In case Evelyn or Sweetie or anyone I know remembers me and comes looking, I get out of the middle aisle, slink to the food court's edge and onto the Sbarro counter to watch the people and ghosts.

And I'm no monster, it's nice seeing people happy. It's nice this one time to be an agent of joy. I'm looking at dead little ghost kids sitting on the laps of alive mothers and fathers and it's like Molly, you little bitch, be *proud* of this. And I guess I am, but also it's like All you happy motherfuckers, what's in it for me? When the fuck do I get a turn?

But these ghosts and people don't care and I don't blame them. They're getting the one thing they've wanted every day since their dead loved ones died. Look at Sweetie over there hugging the ghost leg of Helen. Look at Helen running her ghost fingers through Sweetie's golden hair.

And if my dead mom showed up now, what would I say to her anyway? Oh, you, I've heard about you. I saw you a few times on a TV in a dark library room. I heard about your excellent career in sticker manufacturing.

When Demarcus's mom saw him, twice she called him Baby, and you could tell just by looking he remembered being called that by her. But if my own mom called me anything besides my actual name, Molly, I wouldn't even know she was talking to me.

I spot Le Feb in the crowd, him and his ghost mother chuckling.

I spot Jeanie and Mombie and their mother together, under a glass dome inside a man-made sea.

And I don't know if I'm going to cry or what, but weird how I keep getting this hot feeling. Then I remember the fish, look for the fish, and see when I find it that it's on real fire.

That the ghost fish on real fire is setting the Sbarro behind me aflame.

Fire! I shout. Fire!

But it takes a moment for the living people and ghosts to hear me. And when they hear me, the people look puzzled, distracted. Most go back to talking to their ghost loved ones right away. It doesn't matter anyway, the fire's spreading so quickly, and you can tell we're screwed from the faces of the people who don't look away.

A man and lady nearby me grab fire extinguishers but either they don't work or they can't figure out how to use them. It's too late by now anyway, the fire's burning up a beam toward the ceiling glass. Here is where it's clear to me that every one of us is about to perish. Perish or be born ghosts, depending on how you think.

Now the stage curtains are on fire and a few people start screaming, but otherwise everyone else is la-di-da, enjoying the fireworks.

Before I was trying to avoid Dad and Evelyn. I knew they'd find me by the end of things and I wanted to stretch this adventure out, run the clock down. But now that it's the end for real it's them I want to see, mostly. I run back to the stage, breathe in the burning velvet curtains, hoist myself up to the stage floor to scan the crowd. There's Evelyn, her in the back smiling. Her in the back crying, touching Bruce's transparent cheek.

Things are on fire. Things are collapsing. The overhead sprinklers sprinkle down.

And for reasons I didn't understand then and don't understand now, all I want is to find my father in the wild and burning crowd.

I scan until I spot him standing in a corner alone and when I catch his unsunglassed eyes something weird happens in a split-second. Something like what happened with Demarcus and his mom, some kind of transference, except going both ways in reverse. I cannot explain in words now what I understood looking at my father then, but it was like for the first time I saw both the whole and void of him. I saw the absence of my mother as a black, black gape, a massive empty hollow bigger than me. And I don't know what he's seeing when he looks at me but whatever it is it's the first time he's seeing it and it's definitely something he wasn't expecting to see.

Like I said, all this happens in a flash, a split second. Then right as I'm about to jump off the stage to run to him I'm struck to the ground by a falling beam.

By now everyone in the Submarine Palace is either coughing or screaming, the stage curtains on fire and the band in the band pit on fire too. People running for the glass elevator jam all the exits and there's glass shattering and a loud crash and someone's voice in my head says Molly, you know what to do.

I stand back up, but I don't run to my father.

I climb back into the crystal casket and latch the lid.

Then there's an explosion and next I might go to sleep maybe because the next thing I know I'm floating slowly through water toward the brightest white light I've ever seen. I roll circles in the casket to look out all sides of me, see the strange shapes of things in bursts of foggy light: two dead horses, one dead Lady Godiva, her long hair floating straight above her like Frankenstein's bride. I see pulsing snakes, a TV set playing one of Mombie's movies, a dead boy's face all chalky white. All this convinces me I'm either dead or about to be when suddenly I'm thrust inside the white light.

The casket's gone.

I'm on Dad's puppet stage. At first I'm cold and wet but then something makes me warm. A ball of light appears, sort of but not quite like Demarcus's mom. The light ball unfurls and motherfuck it, it's her, it's *my* mom, I know it. She's dressed as Nina from *The Seagull* and she's smiling at me.

Right now maybe you're thinking what I'm telling you is fake, all counterfeit. Or maybe that this moment's the first one, the one true thing I've said. But that's a lie, don't believe it, don't believe either one of them. The truth is that this moment is a hinge.

Mom, I say. I want to run to her but something stops me.

Mom, I say. Is it really you?

Hello, Molly, she says and when she says my name something explodes inside me. It's the feeling I felt when I saw Helen in the Summerland forever ago. This love-feeling surprises me, makes me rush forward without thinking, and I go too far, end up inside her body made of light. With Demarcus if you went through him you'd fuck up his chalk maybe, but inside my own mother it's way more strange—the amplified sounds of oceans and rivers, baseball bats cracking, a baby laughing, something that sounds like a sticker-printing machine.

I thrust myself backward out of her and she's laughing her ass off. She grabs my shoulders and pulls me back in. Her laughing from the inside is the sound of bells.

That's so fucking cool, I say when I've pulled myself out again, and still laughing she says Watch your fucking language, I don't want you talking like me.

Even her scolding me gives me a rush of the love-feeling. I don't want to get rid of it ever, I want it always inside me.

So what's the deal, am I dead? I ask her. Is my childhood eternal? I say.

No, you're not dead, but this is real, she goes.

Is this the Summerland? I ask her and she goes No, that place is only an idea. That's for people afraid to think their thoughts through to the end, she says.

That's what I figured, I say, I knew Le Feb was full of it.

He is and also he isn't, my dead mom says. It's true you've forgotten your knowing, but that's how it's supposed to be. You forget and then you remember and then you forget again.

Somehow this makes sense to me, but one big thing still doesn't.

Where have you been? After you died, why didn't you stay with me?

When you die and disappear, she says, time collapses all around you. Past, present, and future bleed together and form a loop. When that happens, at least for a little while, you have perfect fucking knowledge, Molly. I've forgotten most of it already, but I remember seeing you.

You saw me? I say, excited, so excited I hear my heart banging. What was I doing? I say, but Mom shakes her head.

That's not how this goes, she says. I can only tell you this one thing, Molly Sibly. In this world you will have trouble. And for some troubles mothers are not the needed thing. Some people are born to suffer and to suffer the suffering, Molly, and I'm not saying which you are, or whether or not there's meaning, but I need you to know: for some people a mother will only be an idea, a kind of feeling.

That fucking sucks, I say.

It's time for you to surface, she goes.

But wait, I say, wait. What do you think of me?

I think you're a twitchy fucker who bats hard, she goes. Here she reaches into her costume pocket and pulls out something yellow and small and shiny.

I do love you, she says then hands it to me. It's a sticker. A gold fucking star.

Our fingers touch when I take it and then the stage folds in on itself like to slide into a giant carrying case. And that's when everything explodes back into white lightness again. I'm afraid I've died for real this time because now in weird ways my life passes before me: dead grass poking through sidewalk cracks in clumps like old lady snatches, digging through the dark bathroom hamper for Evelyn's good towels. Black moms opening front doors to me, eating tacos with Sweetie and Helen. Stealing Bruce's Big League Chew away from him, stuffing it in my mouth.

All this happens while simultaneously I'm back in the crystal casket, launched upward through the water, explosions below. White flames float over and under me, all glowing through the casket, and I'm a white flicker too, something sad and electric to behold.

I flicker and sneeze.

I flick on and off. I float.

The casket hits the ice and I cry out for my mother. The ice cracks and buckles and I reach for the latch.

EPILOGUE

AFTER THE FIRE

IT'S ONE WEEK LATER WHEN I move into the Children's Home, the Our Sisters of Sorrow Home for Children in Wait. Before then I stayed a few days with Gas Station Rita then Goth Roger. An entire weekend with Debra, dead Jeanie's P.O. One day I even got to stay at Leslie and Sweetie's, the only other ones in this historic tragedy who didn't drown or explode. When I cracked through the ice in my crystal casket they were barricaded in the Sbarro walk-in freezer. When they found them they were doing cat dances and eating all the dough.

The day I move into the Children's Home everything's winter dreary, all these tough orphan kids following me around. All of them younger yet somehow older, all of them with awesome nicknames I've never heard before: White Tights Wilson, Dancina Trasher, a tiny boy named Butter Pat no more than four years old. His parents both got killed when the police raided their puppy mill and now he roams the Home's hallways keening for lost dogs.

A boy called Graveside Service shows me the spare pants closet, he's the one who tells me there's a girl here named Vandalisa House. The first time I meet Vandalisa I'm outside throwing rocks. She walks under a ladder and I say Isn't that bad luck, to walk under a ladder? and she says Yeah, if you're the fucking ladder. Then she says her name is Vandalisa House.

The nuns mostly leave us alone except once a month when they spank someone. It's mostly for appearances, there's even a rotation, typed-out. I'm not up for ages which makes it something each month I look forward to. Try not to shit on that, here you make small things go far.

Like I said, the nuns mostly leave us alone and let us get away with stuff. Shaving stray cats with the sisters' disposable razors, nighttime raiding their fridge to binge-eat their cheese. But the best thing is something I was not at all expecting: here my personal tragedy makes me blend in with everyone else. No one here feels sorry for me. No one notices my ghost dad following me. Everyone here's got their own fucking ghost.

Dad's is half-formed and low-floating, probably parent-guilt weighing down on him. Mornings I get off my cot and purposefully step through his ghost body, at Lice Check pretend not to hear his dumb stories about Polly the Forgiving Louse. He says I'm the center of his vision now and I definitely take advantage. I make him do whatever ghost things I need done. Sometimes it's opening the locked shed door where the nuns keep the riding mower, sometimes it's transmitting via vibration the long letters to Demarcus I continue to write.

I wasn't sure Demarcus even got them wherever he went with his mother until one day Sister Vigbor said there was a postcard for me. The postcard was from the gift shop at the Art Institute of Chicago, a Tom Thompson landscape painting called *Northern Lights*. To the left of my name and address was no message but instead a glowing drawing. A pulsing figure-eight sideways, the infinity sign.

After that I started writing my mom weekly. I tell her all about my life here but I doubt she'll write back. Sometimes, though, I find gold stars where gold stars shouldn't be. Like one time I yelled to Vandalisa Hey wait up, Vandalisa! and when Vandalisa turned around there were all these gold stars stuck to her neck.

That's it for ghosts. No Evelyn, no Mombie. Meanwhile every single night Jeanie sneaks up on me in dreams. Dream Jeanie wears glasses and a black Morbid Angel T-shirt. We're always at the mall and clipped to my belt loops are all these jangly keys.

Little Bitch, Little Bitch, your hair is so *fucked*, she always says to me. You look like a parakeet with bangs, she goes. Here I stop to check my hair in the window of B. Dalton. And she's right, my hair, it's a nest of something.

But—and this is important—No wonder Jeanie calls you Fucktard I am truly not dream-thinking. No wonder she calls you Little Orphan Dumbass, I don't go in my head. My twig and mud hair, my jingle-jangle keys, it's true, but dream Jeanie's got glasses, not X-ray eyes. She can't see inside my head where my thoughts boil to visions, to actual premonitions of future me. She can't see badass Mall Arcade Manager Molly like I can.

Sometimes at night when I put little Butter Pat to sleep I hear the reverby shimmer of pinball synths even.

Here's what Sister Bitch the Intake Nun said my first day here: You are a pilot of sorrow now, Molly. Today's but the first day of the rest of it, she said.

So far that griefy bitch has been right, but I refuse to give in. I keep my chin up like a lunch tray, a baseball mitt, a target. Days I spend kissing Vandalisa's ass under fast-moving clouds, at snack eat the body of Christ and wipe the crumbs with donated napkins. Nights I dream of Jeanie cleaning her glasses and grinning big, her T-shirt torn, her teeth spit-licked and shiny. So shiny I see the future play like a movie across them, and in the future harshness is real, it's a cat-kill-kitten world still, but for once finally I'm the fucking lion.

ACKNOWLEDGMENTS

So many people, living and dead, helped me in the years it took to write this book. I am forever indebted to Gillian Flynn and Emily Bell. Emily shaped the story with a deft and gentle hand, as did Maya Raiford Cohen, who asked all the important questions. To everyone at Zando and to Eli Mock, who designed the cover: Thank you. Your time and attention to my work means more than I can say.

Deepest thanks to Kent D. Wolf, whose endless enthusiasm, humor, and remarkable patience kept things alive. It's been a long road, Kent, but here we are. Thank you.

Thank you to my teachers at Wichita State University, especially Margaret Dawe and the late Philip Schneider, who both did their best to whip me into shape. Thank you to my teachers at Florida State University, especially Julianna Baggott and Mark Winegardner, who both read this in its earliest, ugliest draft and never once told me to put it in a drawer.

Thank you to my colleagues in the Department of Literature, Writing, and Film at the University of Wisconsin-Whitewater. Your kindness and support during the most difficult period of my life meant everything. Thank you to my students, past and present. Your devotion to your own stories gives me life.

I am so grateful for Anna Thompson Hajdik, Jessica Lauer, Katie Burgess Steenerson, Crystal Sutheimer, and Kendra Unruh for their friendship. I am grateful for my friend Nahal Suzanne Jamir, who is haunted the way I am haunted. I could never have done this without you, Suzanne. And to Daniel, whose philosophical insight, musical encouragement, and dear friendship sustained me through the final stretch: Thank you.

Thank you to my family for their longtime support, and to my parents for their years of hard work and sacrifice. To my mother, Connie Wilson, for encouraging me to be a reader despite the very real possibility that it might one day lead me to write a novel full of vulgarities.

Thank you to my late husband, Jeremy Herrmann, who is present on every page.

But most of all, thank you to my son, Theo, who pulled me through the harshest darkness and turned everything into light.

ABOUT THE AUTHOR

HOLLY WILSON's work has appeared in *Narrative* magazine, *Redivider*, *Northwest Review*, *Short Story*, *New Stories from the South*, and elsewhere. She was a Kingsbury Fellow at Florida State University, where she received a PhD in creative writing. She grew up in Kansas and currently makes her home in Fort Atkinson, Wisconsin, where she lives with her son. She's an associate professor of creative writing at the University of Wisconsin-Whitewater.